Plans for Emma

Beth Durham

*To Dimple & Family,
Enjoy the Story!
Beth Durham*

©2017 Beth Durham
All Rights Reserved.

ISBN: 978-1548275211

Cover design by Chelsie Hutchison

Chapter 1

Sunlight dripped through the overarching trees painting a golden mosaic on the hard packed dirt road. Stopping in the middle of the path, Emma England admired the beauty around her. Her imagination whizzed from thoughts of angels shining in heavenly light to fairies sliding freely down the sun's rays. The ideas made her giggle and she opened her arms and spun around as she danced with the characters in her mind's eye.

Realizing what a sight she must be, her hand flew to her mouth in a vain attempt to suppress the giggles. The effort brought tears to her eyes and she gave into the moment and skipped past her dog and flock.

Biting her lower lip she silently warned herself, *Papa would threaten to skin me if he saw this foolishness.*

Tom England had lectured many times that his sixteen year old daughter was now a woman, old enough to marry and raise her own daughters. He felt it was time to leave behind her foolish girlhood.

Emma let out a long sigh as she paused to allow the tiny herd of sheep to catch up. Her faithful dog brought up the rear. Really, he could do this job alone, but Papa always wanted someone to walk to the creek with the sheep and it was most often Emma. She didn't mind, it was a quiet time to think and to imagine.

The sounds of home surrounded her and she lifted her face, allowing the sunlight to peek under the wide brim of her straw hat. The sun was making quick work of warming the air and there was a coolness near the bubbling water which tempted her to let the hat hang from its long cotton straps and dangle against her back. Only her mother's repeated warnings stayed her hands at the knot.

In that moment, Emma felt there was no one else in the world and she basked in the woodsy quiet. Surrounded by singing birds and barking squirrels she could block out the noise of her five siblings, and all the sounds of the farm.

Suddenly her solitude was broken by a loud screeching. She jerked her head to face the noise. Someone was coming. The air was filled with the tell-tale rattle of wheels, the squeak of harness and that awful screeching as the brake was applied to slow the wagon as it started the long descent toward the creek bed.

Without a second thought, Emma stepped into the road to move her sheep out of the way with Ruff already alerting her to an unexpected visitor. As the noise drew closer, she looked over her shoulder to acknowledge the neighbor.

Yet something about this man captivated her. She never would have imagined she would be so rude, but she stared as he closed the last ten yards.

He stared too, turning his head as the wagon's momentum carried him alongside her.

The team slowed and her breath caught in her throat as she wondered, *Is he stopping?*

A flash of yellow caught Preston Langford's eye and for a second he wondered if there might be a flowering meadow at the bottom of the hill. Half standing to push his right foot onto the stiff friction brake, he allowed his eyes to focus on the moving color that was coming into view. Soon there was a girl's head adorned with a homemade straw hat and behind her wandered a dozen ragged sheep.

As she turned, he saw the profile of a beautiful young girl.

He feared he would embarrass her but he found himself unable to turn away.

As he reached the bottom of the hill, he failed to ease the pressure from the wagon's brake and the team responded to the increasing weight of the load and slowed their pace. The wheels had slowed near to stopping when he realized his error and jerked his foot from the peddle. With his head still turned to face her, Preston gave a gentle slap of the reins and the four big mules moved a bit quicker.

With the distraction gone, its noise drifting away, Ruff moved his herd on to water where they quieted their bleating and drank. Emma had not moved.

What just happened? Who was that? What's wrong with me standing here like a big ole' stone? Emma's questions rolled through her head with little hope of answers.

Above all she questioned why she had been so transfixed by the tall stranger. She had seen his face no more than a few seconds yet it seemed indelibly printed on her memory. Dark eyes set in deep sockets were clear beneath a tattered hat that had been pushed to the back of his head with a shock of dark hair spilling forward. Sharp, chiseled features in his lean face seemed to draw her. He seemed young, she thought no more than twenty. Yet that face might have endured eons of life's joys and struggles. He had not smiled and she found herself longing to see a smile on that face.

"More silliness from a silly girl. He's a teamster from The Flat Woods and he'll probably climb on that train with his logs and never think about this mountain again."

Emma looked at her sheep and patted Ruff's head, "Let's take 'em home boy." With a last look down the shady road she started up the hill toward home.

With each step, Emma's thoughts moved faster and faster, quickening her steps until she was in the middle of the sheep instead of following them as a proper shepherdess ought to. "Come on, you're awful slow today."

With the gate latched tight, Emma stepped onto the rickety porch kicking her boots to ensure she carried no mud from the creek onto the spotless kitchen floor. She hung her hat beside the door without even noticing if anyone was in the kitchen.

"Emma, you came up that hill like you'd sprouted wings but now you look a millions miles away. What have you got on your mind child?"

"Oh Mama, I didn't even see you there. I guess I was somewhere else. There was a man on the road down there..."

Jane England set the plate on the dry sink so hard Emma gave a little jerk. "Who was it? And what'd he say to you to drive you into such deep thought?"

"I don't know who it was; I'd never seen him before."

"A stranger on the Roslin road? That don't happen much."

"Well, he had a big load of logs on his wagon..."

"Oh, a logger." Jane gave a quick shake of her head as she picked up her dish towel and plate.

"I guess he must have been from the Flat Woods."

Jane turned again trying to see into her daughter's eyes, "What'd he say to you? Do we need your Papa to take the sheep down?"

Emma's eyes popped open wide, she didn't want Papa thinking he needed to straighten the fellow out for some offense caused to his daughter. "No, no. It was nothing like that; in fact, he didn't say a word to me. He turned and looked as he drove by. Only, I couldn't stop looking at him either."

Now Jane chuckled slightly, "Well it's not such an awful thing to look twice at a handsome man. I've sure seen a few boys at church taking a second look at my Em."

"Mama! What a thing to say." Emma felt her heart speed up as she cast her eyes around for something to occupy her hands. Yanking the still damp rag from its hook she began wiping the table with such fury it shook. After a long moment she took a deep breath and looked up at her mother.

"I didn't particularly notice whether he was handsome or not. It was just like I was drawn to him somehow. Oh Mama it's the strangest thing that's ever happened to me."

Jane worked in silence for a few minutes as Emma watched and waited for the wise guidance her mother always supplied.

Finally, Jane placed the last dish in its place, hung the towel on its peg and turned to Emma. "I cannot explain it. If

Plans for Emma

it was a neighbor you knew, I'd think God was giving you a special burden to pray for him. But these folks at the logging camp come and go and we never know any of them. Chances are that you'll never see him again. I'd put it all out of my mind if I's you."

Emma nodded, trusting her mother completely. She turned back to the table and finished the cleaning it did not require as Jane slipped into the front room where she always found a few minutes mid-morning to read the family Bible and pray.

Preston hunched his back and rested his forearms on his knees. He smiled, remembering his father in the same position. He often thought about the man he'd known only five years. Despite Harrison Langford's pre-mature death, his widow had kept him alive in memories so that his twelve children would know the man she had loved.

"Easy there Big Red. Keep your head up Lady." He spoke to the mules with ease. In fact, he often felt more comfortable talking to these four-legged animals than to his two-legged companions because the fellas in The Flat Woods logging camp tended to be rougher than he liked and he kept hearing his mother's voice warning him not to allow coarse talk to dominate him.

There was a child in Preston that longed to sit at his mother's knee with her hand upon his head. Yet, he'd been on his own most of his life and long ago learned an independence that belied his scant eighteen years. Still, his mother's voice often rang in his ears with the advice and warnings she'd given him.

The trip to Sunbright was familiar to him, but more importantly, it was familiar to his team. They needed little guidance through the long day's drive and he let his mind wander as the mules plodded east. In his mind's eye, he kept seeing the girl by the creek. Kept remembering that he'd first thought he was looking at a field of wild flowers. That made him smile again.

I wonder if I will always remember her like that. This time the smile became a snicker. Lil' Bess, the bay nearest his right hand, flicked an ear at his voice.

"It's okay, girl. I'm just thinking out loud I guess."

Preston had been at the lumber camp for two months now and had driven the load half a dozen times yet this was the first time he'd seen the sheep. Now he wondered why. The farms along the way were familiar and he'd begun to learn the neighborhood and its families. But this girl was a stranger and he wondered whether she had always lived in Roslin. In fact, he couldn't stop wondering for the two days it took to bring supplies back from town and as he watched for Bridge Creek miles before it would have been possible to see it he realized how much he hoped to catch another glimpse of her. There was no sign of the herd of sheep or the girl who kept them and Preston's heart sank.

Chapter 2

It was two weeks before he could get another load to Sunbright. He had asked everyday but the foreman kept sending him out to hew cross ties. Preston was good with the axe and proud that he could create the ties that would carry railroads across the country. In fact, he often wished he could know where his ties were planted and he usually occupied his mind with that question as he swung his axe again and again - but not this week. With every down swing of the heavy iron blade he thought of the girl with the sheep.

Everyday Emma trekked down the hill to water the sheep just as she'd done for the past year. This chore had been her brother's until he took to his bed with the fever and the next time he came down the hill was on the shoulders of six neighbors as they carried him to the family cemetery. Emma's active imagination made each walk an adventure and she looked forward to this time of day. However, over the last few days she found she wasn't spinning stories in her mind or imagining she was some fine lady instead of a poor daughter of a Tennessee farmer. These days she'd pictured that tall boy atop his wagon seat. She found herself drawing and re-drawing his face in her mind. She pondered the look in his dark eyes, remembered the long body folded upon itself as he loosely held his team's reins.

I wonder what his name will be. She was certain he'd tell her one day. *Would he be a Sam or a Ted? Sure, that might be it, maybe even Teddy like the paper says our president is called by his close friends.*

You silly thing, there you go again. Mama told you to put him out of your mind because I don't expect you'll ever see him again. And she's right of course. But Emma's mind kept returning to that boy with the logs; his image kept her company as she moved through the routine of her everyday life.

Preston made a second check of his harness, running calloused fingers along the underside of the leather to ensure no rough spots would rub sores on the valuable mules. As he walked around the animals, he spoke softly, calling each one by name. A memory of his father flashed through his mind as it often did when hitching a team.

"You're my sweetheart, ain't ya' Bess? That's what my pa taught me, 'Treat your team like your best girl'." He used his free hand to rub the muscled hip that reached his chest.

Satisfied with the gear, he backed the team up to the tongue of the wagon, hooked the trace chains and climbed up into his seat. He realized his heart was racing a bit. He knew the anticipation of crossing Bridge Creek was growing and he fought the urge to race the mules.

Boy, how many times you made this drive and seen her but once? What makes you think she'll be there today?

He didn't care about chances; he only cared to see that beautiful girl again. His girl. He had to admit it to himself he now thought of her as his own and he realized the foolishness of it. He didn't even know her name.

As he crested the hill above the creek he stood on the narrow footrest hoping to see to the bottom more quickly. He was so preoccupied with what he might find down there that he just about forgot to step on the brake; Lady's snort reminded him that the load threatened to push the animals down the slope and he stomped the brakes.

His ears strained to hear beyond the shrill sound of the hickory brake pressed against the four inch iron wheels. He was sure he could hear the soft bleating of sheep and his eyes darted from one patch of grass to the next bush searching for the source of the sound.

The sheep at summer's end had short stubs of wool around bodies that seemed far too skinny. In the end, it was the movement of this stubble that his eye located. They were already at the creek and he feared they'd drunk their fill judging by their restless movement. There was the dog, rising from his spot nearby, seeming to keep one eye on the herd and the other on the approaching wagon.

Where is she?

Emma and Ruff heard the rattling wagon at the same time. "Shh, you sit Ruff," her voice was soft as she spoke to the animal who lay back down in acknowledgement of her words. She turned to watch as the rig lumbered down the long hill. *It's going too fast*, she worried and took an involuntary step toward the roadway as though she could stop the team from her position on the ground.

Preston had been sure the delightful vision would always be with the animals although he didn't know why he was so certain of it and an instant of great fear flashed through his mind when he couldn't see her among the flock. At last, he watched her take one step from the deep shade and turned her face toward him.

The smile that wrapped around his face tugged every muscle. He knew he must have looked like a silly puppy but somehow in that moment he didn't care. He could not control the joy this sighting brought to him. Like the first time he'd seen her, he forgot about the pressure on the wagon's brake and the mules slowed their gait to a creep.

She reached up giving the hat a gentle push and sending it toppling behind her to reveal her face. Dark brown hair framed a full and slightly long face with a square jaw that might have been out of place except for the dimple that gave away the suppressed smile.

Preston could see that she was at home with the sheep and he admired her for it. No doubt she was following her father's direction bringing them to water. He wanted to look around for the farm house where she must live but he felt powerless to turn his head. He managed to nod a mute greeting and she let the smile bloom from her lips and creep into her cheeks with a slight blush.

Emma found she was holding her breath as the wagon's wheels seemed to grind to a halt. *He's stopping! What will I say?* In an instant she saw herself bowing to him as though he were a gentleman from the pages of a novel; she was sure he would speak the most eloquent words and she imagined she would be rendered mute.

Preston opened his mouth to speak but there were no words. He lifted his hand to tip his hat and she responded with lowered eyes.

Emma turned as the wagon crept past her. As her view of the driver became blocked by the towering load Emma watched as though in slow motion as her hand shot upward then she heard a little gasp and her hand flew to cover her mouth lest something else come out. *He couldn't have heard that above the rumble of the wagon, could he? I don't want him to think I was flagging him down.*

The mules stopped without a tug on their bits. Preston pulled his foot off the brake, *Did I stop them? What am I going to do now? She's right beside me. My girl is right there.*

Leaning forward just a bit he was able to see alongside the load and as he did his eyes met round brown eyes that reminded him of a fawn who'd scarcely outgrown her spots. There seemed to be a hint of tears glazing them. *Did I scare her?* His heart skipped in fear that he would ever do anything to hurt his girl.

Her eyes dropped to stare at the ground.

Preston gave a soft cough to clear his throat, "Mornin'. I come down that hill pretty fast today and I hope I din' scare you nor your stock."

She gave her head a slow shake and lifted her eyes as she reached to pull the hat back up. "Oh no. I'm fine and the sheep don't get very excited until you run right over 'em."

He chuckled and nodded, "Yeah, they're pretty calm creatures. I seen you here with 'em a few days ago din' I? Guess you have to bring them here to water?" Again he had the urge to look for the farmstead where she and the sheep must belong but still he couldn't draw his gaze from her face. "Yeah. We've got a good well up at the house but Papa says runnin' water is always best for stock." She pointed at the wall of squared timbers that sat not two feet from her.

Preston nodded but still didn't look toward the home she indicated. "I'm headed to Sunbright."

"Ah, to the railroad? I thought that's the direction you were headed the last time." Emma wanted to talk with him, she was trying to form the words but her breath was coming in short gasps and she found her sentences were clipped just as short. *I sure hope I don't sound mad or something.*

Preston took a deep breath and closed his eyes for a long blink as he recorded every detail of her face in his mind. "I guess I'd better get on that way. Maybe I'll see you down here with the sheep again."

"I hope so." Emma had to still her hand lest it fly up to her mouth again. She couldn't believe she'd said that.

With a loud cluck and quick flick of his wrists the team leaned into their collars and again set the big load moving.

She didn't dare even blink until it disappeared over the next hill. Then she swallowed a couple of times and took deep breaths hoping she could push her stomach back down into its place. "I sure do hope so…Teddy."

Ruff whimpered, understanding the tone of her whispered words. She took in another deep breath and took her time letting it out, "Well Ruff, his name might be Teddy." The smile came loose and brought a little giggle as she laid a hand on the dog's head. Come on, let's take 'em home."

Chapter 3

The gate slammed behind Emma as she approached the front porch; she didn't even hear it. She normally required four long strides to reach the wooden steps; today she took ten tiny steps.

"Child where is your head?" Jane England paused in her morning sweeping, watching her daughter. "I thought takin' the sheep to water in the cool of the morning would be easier on you but the way you're actin' I'm still wonderin' if you're having a spell from the heat."

Emma looked up and took the broom from her mother's hand without speaking a word. She began sweeping the spotless porch as Jane continued to stare at her. Noticing the pink cheeks and glistening perspiration on her face, she turned her daughter by the shoulder and blotted her face with a handkerchief she produced from her apron pocket.

Emma blinked, seeming to see her mother for the first time. "Mama, what are you doing?"

"You walked in here like you were in a trance. I think you need to lie down for a bit."

Emma smiled but still seemed to see something beyond the white washed house and packed-earth yard.

"Did you see a snake on the big rock? Or was it a haint in the woods?"

Finally, Emma snapped out of her daze. "Mama, what are you talking about?"

"What am I talking about? You are the one that was walkin' in a fog. Are you okay?"

Emma smiled. Mama was always concerned about her family. She watched that they were all wearing their hats for she feared the sun beating down on their heads would do them harm. She watched their plates at meals to know they were eating well. And Mama always seemed to know when one of her girls had something on her mind.

"Mama, I'm fine; not too hot. I guess I was just daydreaming."

Mama smiled, she welcomed her daughters' dreams and always wanted to hear about them. With Gustie married and gone, and Lena planning to marry when the harvest was done, she now expected Emma to begin dreaming of her own home, husband and children.

"Well tell me what started you a'dreamin' today."

Emma continued to sweep, having moved off the rough boards of the porch to whisk away any loose debris on the hard-packed dirt of the front yard. "I don't know, really. That

Plans for Emma

stranger, remember I told you about seeing him a few days ago? He came by again."

Jane busied herself pulling weeds from the herbs she grew in front of the house. "We'll be getting a hard frost pretty soon. We'll have to get these hung up before it's too late."

Minutes passed with mother and daughter working quietly. Finally, when Emma thought her mother had not believed what she saw, Jane broke her silence. "Did the stranger speak to you?"

Emma chuckled softly, "A little. He asked after the sheep and said he's going to Sunbright."

"Yeah, we knew that. They're going to ship half the mountain top out on those iron horses. I never thought you'd see that logger again; I'd clean forgot about him, hadn't you?"

Emma shook her head as she felt her mother's eyes on her.

"Well something has made him stick in your head."

The broom stopped and Emma leaned against the stick worn smooth by regular use. "I can't rightly say. I couldn't stop watching him before he was even close enough to get a good look at him."

"Was he walkin'?"

"No Mama, he was driving a big team pulling a load of railroad ties."

Jane stood slowly, "Well I'll say again, I don't think you'll see him through here anymore. There seems to always be a new logger out there."

Emma finished sweeping the yard and sat down on the bottom porch step. "What are you saying Mama?"

Jane smiled through the ragged green herbs, "Child, I'm not a'sayin' anything, just talkin' I guess. You know I've always taught you girls not to let the wrong kind of man turn your head. You want to court someone that you know a little something about him and his upbringing. You're looking for a mate and you will not want to be unequally yoked like a half crazy yearling and a big steady mare."

Emma's face fell as though her mother had crushed her every dream.

Jane saw the change in her daughter and added quickly, "If the good Lord stuck this fella in your head, he'll bring him by again. But I guess you'll want to water the sheep in the morning from now on. Now you go check on Almeta, she'd better have that crock of butter churned by now and you'll have to help her wash out the buttermilk."

None of the England girls were ever idle for long, as was their mother's example. Yet somehow they always knew that Mama cared what they were thinking and that she'd always have a minute to listen to their hearts. Today Almeta was charged with concocting three pounds of creamy butter from yesterday's milk and Emma found her in the big rocker on the back porch. She had the paddle in her hand and plunged it up and down as the chair drummed a steady rhythm swaying back and forth. However, her eyes were focused on the distant mountain and it was clear to Emma that her mind was far from their mountain farm.

"Metie, are you paying attention to that butter?" Emma's tone was sharper than she intended; this was a fault her mother often brought to her attention and Emma tried to correct it now. "Honey, the way that paddle is moving, I'll bet your butter's done. Have you scraped it down at all?"

Almeta drew her attention back so gradually that she didn't even jump at Emma's words. Her eyes looked toward the churn at her side as though she had forgotten it was there. "Oh Em, I guess I was daydreaming. Won't you help me or we'll waste half the butter in there."

Emma smiled. She knew her younger sister suffered from daydreaming just as Emma did, yet somehow Emma was always able to get through her chores while Almeta had to be snapped back to reality again and again. Emma had already taken the wooden paddle from her sister's hand as she answered, "Of course I'll help. I don't think you could lift that heavy thing by yourself anyway. Here, let's scrape it

Plans for Emma

down then you can go get a bucket of spring water while I pour out the buttermilk."

The girls giggled and chatted as they separated the soured milk, stored it and then poured cool water on the fluffy butter. Then in silence they kneaded it to get all of the liquid out lest the butter spoil before it could be used.

With three neat mounds formed in wooden bowls and covered with cheese cloth, Almeta was again dispatched to the spring to place them in the little spring house where they would be cool and ready for the next meal. Alone in the kitchen, Emma wiped down the big wooden table and looked about the rough floor for any sign of milk they may have spilled. She loved the order of her mother's kitchen and couldn't help dreaming of what her own home would look like. Many of her friends were already married and two more girls from the Jonesville church were planning to say their vows when the last of the corn was shocked and potatoes dug. A wistful thought passed as Emma thought of her friends setting up housekeeping. In the same moment, she closed her eyes and whispered thanks to God for she didn't covet those girls' lives and knew that God had a particular plan for Emma Jane England.

She could not contain the grin so she turned her head to prevent her older sister's questions as Lena bustled into the room. Eighteen year old Lena had many similarities to Emma but she did not share her sister's idea that the good Lord had a grand plan for them. She and Emma were turned alike, both gentle girls but their sharp tongue often caused people to miss the tenderness. Perhaps this similarity accounted for the closeness between these two sisters. Somehow Gustie had always been more fun-loving and little Metie was so often found daydreaming that the sisters feared she was not long for this world.

"That Metie can make a bigger mess than anybody I've ever seen. If I had a girl like her, I don't know if I'd even let her in my kitchen." Lena dipped warm water from the big reservoir on the iron stove and began wiping down the kitchen surfaces that had been splattered in the butter-making process, finding spots Emma would never have seen.

"Lena, do you ever think about the lumber camp? We never see those people, I wonder where they go to church?"

"Hmmpf, Papa says they're not much the church-goin' type. Why, didn't I tell you that Belle Peters was in Sunbright with her father when two of them boys rolled into town with a big load? She said one boy peeled off the top of the cross ties so fast he liked to broke his neck trying to get into that filthy tavern they've got there. Mr. Peters commented on it to the man at the store and he said the loggers might near tear down the town sometimes."

Emma's eyes popped open wide in surprise. "No, I never heard Belle talk about that. But do you suppose they are all like that?"

"Oh, I guess some of them are pretty much regular folk. Only, Mama has said it's never good to have a whole bunch of boys without any mothers or wives around. So I guess in short order the ones that come in from decent families are pulled down to be about the same as the coarser ones. Did Mama tell you to put the side meat on to fry for dinner?"

Emma answered with little interest in the menu for their mid-day meal, "No, she didn't say."

"I'm going to ask her if we can eat the roast from yesterday cold. I do like cold beef, don't you Em?"

Lena was gone from the kitchen before Emma could even finish processing her sister's assessment of their neighbors.

The Flat Woods was a huge tract of virgin timber that had opened for logging more than twenty years ago. However, for many years the teams entered through a road on the Emory Turnpike three miles from the England farm. In just the last few months the camp moved and began using an entrance on the Banner Road. The Englands had always known the logging was going on and would sometimes encounter the loggers when cutting through the nigh way to one destination or another. However, they had never seen the big loads of whole logs or hewn cross ties and Tom had never even considered letting his daughters interact with any of the loggers.

With the story Lena's friend Belle had related about them, Emma doubted her father would ever allow them to keep company with anyone from the camp. Somehow the thought washed sadness over Emma.

Em! You are being a silly girl again. When will you ever grow up and stop daydreaming? You will never see that fella again and I don't even know why you're worried about it. If you don't focus on what's real, you will never find a husband.

Suddenly, Emma was aware that she was no longer alone and she blushed, fearing she had ranted aloud.

"Oh Mama, when did you come in? I don't know where my mind was even at."

Jane sat at the big kitchen table, well-worn with many years of use, her hands tying herbs in bunches with such speed you didn't know where they'd reach next. "You were so beautiful with the sunlight bathing your face that I didn't want to disturb you. But you can help me now. I went out there to pull a few weeds but then I decided I'd better try to get some of this butterfly weed to dryin' or the frost is liable to catch me unaware. Lena's going to bring in another bunch so we'll have to scoot if we're gonna' get all this cleared away before your Papa's wantin' his dinner."

"With little Leonard tagging along behind him, I'm pretty surprised we haven't seen them yet."

Jane chuckled, "That tiny two year old boy does have the gruff Tom England wrapped around his little finger, doesn't he? Well, I'm just glad he's got the babies. After losing George, I feared your Papa would work himself to death. He would work and work and never rest long enough to mourn his loss."

"Well he's training a fine farmer in Leonard and it won't be any time before they've got baby-Gip out there with them too. How do you suppose he even gets the farm work done?"

"He wouldn't get everything done if he didn't have you girls. Papa wants you and Lena to marry and have your own homes but right now I think he's glad to have you grown enough to do a full day's work and still home working for him."

"Mama, do you ever think about the kind of men Metie and I might marry?"

Before Jane could answer, Lena shuffled into the kitchen with a basket overflowing with aromatic green plants. She had enlisted Almeta's help and now was encouraging the girl to assist in the next step of bunching and tying them.

It was a flurry of activity, but the four of them completed the herb project in time to set out last night's cold beef, the fresh butter to go on a pone of hot cornbread and big glasses of buttermilk before Tom and Leonard charged in with hands still dripping from the water pail on the back porch.

Preston felt he'd driven through a dream when the noise of the Sunbright railhead woke him. He spoke in gentle tones to his mules, thanking them and God for delivering the dangerous and heavy load without his full attention.

You've gotta' snap out of this Preston. You could have killed your fool self – and then you would never even know her name.

His self-chastisement spurred him to think of a way he could learn more about this mystery girl. He thought he could ask at the general store in Deer Lodge but dismissed the idea, after all, how could he ask about people when he didn't even know their name. Then he hit on the idea he could ask at the Roslin post office about the folks keeping sheep. There were few enough such herds that he might be able to mention it without raising suspicion.

Yes, that was a plan and the satisfaction of it pasted a smile on his face that seemed out of place as he entered the rail yard to check-in and off-load the cross ties he was hauling. No matter, the buyer's sole concern was the soundness of the wood and straightness of the cross ties; he wouldn't even notice the happiness of the driver.

Preston spent another sleepless night in the rented room in Sunbright. All the fellas in the woods thought it was a grand job to get to drive the big log wagon into town. He was

Plans for Emma

sure they would have spent their restless night in the noisy tavern but Preston seldom wasted his time or his money there. Every time he'd entered that smoke-filled room he was sure his beloved mother could see him from heaven and he could never get comfortable with that feeling. He kept the same schedule as they did in the woods; he went to sleep as soon as he could get to his bed and was up before the sun. The drive back to The Flat Woods was long and he was happy to leave just as soon as the list of supplies would allow.

Chapter 4

The mornings were getting cooler with the sun warming the ground until sleeves were rolled up to elbows by afternoon. Emma wrapped a thin scarf around her shoulders as she headed out the door right after breakfast the next morning.

"Where are you headed? Metie's milking for Papa." Lena questioned Emma with her arms still deep in dish water with the breakfast dishes.

"It's cool now and I'd rather take the sheep to water before it heats up."

Emma mustn't have looked as eager as she felt to get down the hill and to the creekside for Lena's questions went no further. Lena never enjoyed the sheep so she would not risk having to do this chore herself. Still, Emma tried to slow her steps for she knew Lena would be looking out the kitchen window. As she opened the wide gate to let the bleating sheep out, her eyes were already searching the road.

Emma realized she was afraid the logger would pass before she was close enough to see him, or for him to see her. She wasn't quite sure which was more important to her. Would he be watching as well? He'd said he hoped to see her again, was that just a pleasantry or had he meant it?

Wait, did he say he hoped he'd see me or that maybe he would? Em what are you doing? You're lettin' your daydreams take over your common sense, that's what. You don't even know this fella and you know you're supposed to find a husband in church. That's what the Bible teaches, ain't it?

She gave her head a quick shake and raised her eyes to take in the morning. The birds were already in the trees and their song filled the air. A big dragonfly darted around a still pool of water, the ever-present squirrel barked his protest

Plans for Emma

that the girl and the sheep were in his woods. But there was no squeaking harness or panting mules; no rattling wagon came down the hill today.

Emma dawdled more than an hour. She listened to the wind in the trees and heard mournful songs; she imagined the chirping crickets were in worried conversation. When the sheep seemed intent on returning without her, Emma began walking back home. She found it hard to believe how low she felt and she realized despite the joy she found in her time with nature today, what she'd most wanted was to see the logger passing along the road. Why was it so important to see this boy whose name she did not know?

As she walked, she wondered if she would even recognize him again for she'd seen his face for the briefest moment. But she knew those dark, piercing eyes were staring at her every time she thought of him. The wide brim of his hat had so shielded his face that he looked almost brooding. However, there had been little shade on lips that seemed destined to spread in a joyful smile.

Emma's steps quickened at the thought of him smiling and she determined she would see that happen again every time she saw him.

Generally, anytime a wagon left the logging camp, it would return loaded with a long list of supplies ranging from cornmeal to saw blades and always the mail must be picked up from the Roslin Post Office. Preston thought about that stop in Roslin for hours as he kept his team near a trot. Their load was so much lighter on the return trip that the time could be cut in half despite the heavy iron wheels and rutted dirt road.

Preston pondered how he could ask about the girl with the sheep. The postmaster knew everyone therefore if he could just describe this girl Mr. York would be able to tell him about her whole family.

I don't want to seem too eager of course. I can't very well ask about the pertiest girl in the whole world that I seen at the creek right there in Roslin.

As a smile crept into his lips, a thought crossed his mind and he asked himself, *why not seem eager?* Since he first saw her he couldn't stop thinking about her and now a very big part of him wanted people to know it.

But what if she was already promised? What if Mr. York gave him bad news? Or it could be as simple as her not wanting anything to do with him.

Preston imagined the old man peering up, for he was quite stoop shouldered and Preston stood several inches above him, with his squinting eyes telling him that this vision of beauty would be married before it snowed.

His neck warmed and he felt the hard leather of the reins when his hands clenched around them. As his jaw tightened and his teeth dug into his lower lip, he said aloud, "You fool, you're gettin' irritated by something that ain't even happened."

With a slight flick of his wrists he encouraged the team to step a little faster, "Come on girls, we'll have to get there before I get too mad at that old post man."

The low roof of the post office was tacked onto a larger building that served as sort of a trading post. Of course there were always loads going from the Flat Woods to meet the train, so the loggers had little need to do business at this post. Preston only came here to pick up the mail. Everybody in the camp wanted to hear from somebody and they welcomed the mail more than the food his wagon carried.

The porch squeaked with his weight as he made one long stride and slid the door latch open. Preston blinked and squinted as his eyes adjusted from the bright sunlight he'd been driving in for four hours.

"Howdy there. You comin' in from Sunbright today?" The little man behind the bars greeted his customer.

Preston was removing his hat as he answered, "Yes Sir. Made a delivery yesterday, guess them ties are already on their way to some new rail line. There seems to be no end to the need for a wooden bed to hold the big iron rails that move the trains."

Plans for Emma

Paul York was already pulling out a sheaf of envelopes in varying sizes. "Nope, I guess we'll chop down every tree in Tennessee before they've built all their railroads. Just glad I don't have to hear them loud whistles from my store every day. Why, I don't know how the people in Sunbright ever get a minute's rest with all that noise."

Preston smiled at the old man, "The railroad is the life of that town. Think how Roslin would grow if they built a line through here. They might, ya' know – build a spur into the logging camp. It sure would make deliveries faster, wouldn't it?"

He saw a flash of anger in the old postman's eye and he worried he wouldn't learn what he needed if the old man wanted rid of him so he looked for a chance to change the subject.

"Say, you know anybody round here that's keeping sheep? My mother got ahold of a leg of lamb once and it was the best stuff. I just wondered if Cooky would ever be able to fix one if I could get it?"

"Well now, there's a few sheep around. They're awful hard on the land so not many farmers wants to be bothered with 'em. But if you've got you a woman what can card and spin the wool, then you can sell both meat and thread and I think it'd be right profitable. What do you think?"

Preston took a deep breath. The little man was talking a lot but not saying anything that Preston wanted to hear about.

"Yeah, I think they'd be pretty good to keep. But who's got any around here?"

"The Clarks have always kept a few sheep. The old man up there on the turnpike, he liked to watch the wool grow out and he said he'd always have him a few sheep. I heard him say that once."

Preston thought he'd have to try a different approach.

"I saw a girl right down here at Bridge Creek who had a little herd with her. I don't reckon she came all the way from the Turnpike to water 'em. Wonder whose sheep they were?"-

"A girl?" The old man's grin told him he'd seen through the ruse. "Only girl that'd have any stock at Bridge Creek would be Tom England's girls. But now that Lena, she's spoken for. I heard her and Charlie Adams would be sayin' vows as quick as he could get his corn shocks hauled in. He lives over in Martha Washington, got him a farm of his own you know. A'course his folks are all over in Banner Springs but his grandpappy had a good sized place in Martha Washington. I guess he's inherited that, 'cause I heard he has a farm of his own."

Preston felt the breath leave him; he didn't know how long he stood watching the dust settle on the floor – it felt like he couldn't draw a breath.

The post master continued on with no notice to his customer's changing attitude. "He's got one girl already married, Tom has. Her name's Gustie. I think they named her right 'cause she's sort'a like a gust of wind – always laughin' and talkin'. When she walks in a room it's kind'a like she blew in. Then there's Em – Emma's her proper name but 'bout ever-body calls her Em; boy she's a perty one. I think she's the prettiest one in that whole bunch but she ain't turned like that Gustie, none of 'em are. A'course little Bessie will be a looker one day; she's got the biggest eyes I ever saw on a baby, well, not a baby now; I guess she's seven or eight by now."

Preston caught a word here and there until 'baby' snapped his attention back. "I'm sorry, I got lost. How many kids did you say he had?"

Mr. York's little eyes peered straight up at Preston and one corner of his mouth quirked upward. "You ain't a'foolin' nobody here boy. It ain't the number of kids you're wonderin' about, it's them girls. Now let me warn you, Tom England is as good a neighbor as you could ever ask for but he can be an ornery thing too. You be careful talkin' to him 'bout his girls."

Plans for Emma

The bell from the adjoining store tinkled and the old man stepped through a doorway without another word. Preston hadn't even realized he'd collected the mail, but somehow it now felt like lead in his hand.

As he drove the last few miles to the camp, his mind was torn between knowing one of the England girls was to be married and remembering there was another one of courtin' age.

Sure wish I'd understood how many kids that man has and which one is promised to marry.

As he finished his day, he moved like he was in a fog; Preston resolved that should the good Lord ever give him another chance at that beautiful girl, he would ask her name himself. No sense wasting his time hinting around to learn who she was. After all he'd seen her right there at the creek twice now, he could always water his horses there.

The very next day the foreman stood by the door as the loggers filed out of the long dining hall after their hardy breakfast. "Langford, you get the team ready. We'll send another load of whole logs to Sunbright today."

Preston's step was so light as he hurried to the barn that he smiled remembering young school-girls skipping. The thought stretched the grin on his face and he began to hum as he harnessed the team, breaking his tune to speak to the animals. "Molly, I know you're tired, but we'll take it real easy today, just got to hurry to get out on the road. You're sister Polly is a'prancin' like she's ready to pull the whole load by herself."

With a final quick check, Preston climbed atop the rough wooden seat. He clucked to the animals and they started with the hard jerk necessary to get the big load rolling. The mules seemed to sense their driver's eagerness and they pulled against the load with all their might.

They made the fastest time any load had ever made out to Bridge Creek but Preston felt it must already be noon. When he heard the soft bark of a dog not down by the creek but high on the hill he was certain he'd again missed seeing the girl with the sheep. He looked up, hoping for a glance and saw that she wasn't leaving but was just now heading down the hill behind her herd. She was east of the creek so he saw her silhouetted against the bright morning sun. He knew it was her, he was sure it could be no one else.

Preston eased the load to a full stop when he reached a level spot in the road and climbed down from his perch. He reached under the wagon's axle for the bucket that always hung there to carry water for both man and beast. He knew he'd been driving less than an hour and the mules had been well fed and watered before leaving camp. Still, he would draw water and offer it to his animals for he'd thought of no other excuse that would allow him to spend a few minutes in her company.

He tried to ignore her approach and went to the creek to fill the bucket. When he stood to lift it, all of a sudden the sheep surrounded him. He turned knowing she would be there but was still shocked to find her so near.

He stared. He wanted to speak; he meant to speak. In fact, he'd rehearsed the words he would say to her when they would stand face to face. Yet all words escaped him now and he felt his cheeks growing warmer and warmer as he faced this girl he'd been seeing in his dreams.

Emma tilted her head to see beyond the wide brim of her ever-present straw hat and looked up at the tall man. In an instant she filled in the details her mind had tried to imagine after her last two glimpses. The dark eyes were set deep beneath heavy brows. There was a thick mustache – she had not realized he wore a mustache. But his face was clean shaven and she knew many of the loggers were bearded.

Preston gave a soft cough to clear his throat as he tried to find his voice. "Uh, I was going to get some water for the mules. They drink a lot when it's hot."

Emma smiled and nodded, tugging the scarf about her shoulders. Preston noticed the scarf and ducked his head remembering the cool morning air. He tore his gaze away from her and stepped toward his team.

Plans for Emma

"My name's Preston Langford. I'm workin' at The Flat Woods Camp – well now, you could guess that from this big load, couldn't you?"

She smiled with a quick nod. Ruff barked at a ewe that had moved too far down the creek to suit the dog and Emma turned at the sound.

Preston stepped to the next mule when Polly had drunk a few sips. He looked at the milling sheep, looked up at the chattering squirrel. He kept trying to keep his eyes off the girl but found the effort futile.

"How long you been keeping sheep?"

Emma looked at the sheep seeming to only then remember that they were her purpose for coming to the creek. "Oh, umm, Papa brought home the first few lambs I guess it was four years ago."

The sound of her voice again halted all his thoughts. Even standing a few feet from her, she had still seemed nothing but a fantasy. Now hearing her speak made her somehow more real. And it was the voice of an angel – soft and melodic. Preston shook his head again –*Mercy, she's gonna' think you've got the palsy if you don't quit waggin' that head*, he scolded himself.

He found his voice and asked, "Have you always looked after them?"

"No, my brother George cared for them the first couple of years but he died from the fever almost two years ago."

Preston knew the pain of losing loved ones. He was so young when the neighbor man carried home his father's broken body that Mother had pulled his head into her skirts trying to shield him from the awful sight but it was too late and the memory was burned in his mind's eye.

"I'm sorry for the loss. How old was he?"

"George was sixteen. There was an awful fever, even Papa was down with it. It was spring of the year and all kinds of work to be done. But the neighbors helped and we got the corn in the ground before too late in the year and now Papa's as strong as he ever was. But he's sad sometimes."

"It's good of you to step in and help with the farm work."

Emma faced him straight on now, "Oh, we all work. Mama says that's the best way. There's nothing good will come of being do-less."

Preston smiled at her frank assessment. "Don't guess I can argue with that."

The smile crept out of Emma's eyes then spread to her lips.

It emboldened him. "I don't believe I caught your name? You're one of the Englands ain't you?"

"Yes, I'm Emma. Em. They all call me Em." She felt her face warm and lowered her eyes, maybe she shouldn't have shared the family's pet name for her with this stranger. *Stranger?* she thought. He seemed more familiar to her than neighbors she'd known all her life.

"Em. I like that." His heart leapt as he remembered it was Lena who was promised to marry in the fall.

He realized he still held a half-full bucket and smiled up at her, "I guess they aren't as thirsty as I thought."

"I'm glad you stopped. It's nice to pass the time with you."

He emptied the bucket and shrugged, "I guess that's what I was hopin' for."

"Are you taking the logs to the rail road?"

"I'm taking them to Sunbright. The hewn ties we carry to the rail head there but sometimes we take whole logs to a sawmill they've got on the edge of town. Do you get to Sunbright much? Do you know the town?"

"Oh no, we don't much get out of Roslin. Fact, I've never been to Sunbright that I can remember." This boy seemed polite enough, nothing like the ones Belle Peters had described. She was sure he wasn't one of the troublemakers Belle had talked about. "Do you like taking the trips into town? Do you make the trip very often?" She bit her lips as she realized that must sound awfully forward.

She felt a sudden urge to get back home – what if Papa saw them talking? He would think it looked bad to talk to a logger at the creek. What if someone from church happened along the road? Even in her near-panic, she had to admit there wouldn't be two more wagons cross this creek all day. Still, in case one of those wagon drivers was to see them, she wouldn't want her neighbors talking about her.

Preston was answering the question and she had to remind herself what she'd asked.

"...We have a load of ties 'bout twice a week. I don't always get the load though, sometimes I have to hew. They say I'm good at it, been swingin' an axe since I was ten on account of chopping wood for my mother."

Em smiled, how much evil could be in a man who chopped wood for his mother? She couldn't imagine who Belle Peters had described to her sister, but it could not have been this boy.

"We go to church down at Jonesville, but I don't believe I've seen you there. I suppose you've been visitin' at Roslin Baptist?"

Oh my, that was the worst thing yet. What if he isn't the church-goin' type like everybody says about the loggers? How's he gonna' answer that question?"

Preston's neck did redden a bit and he turned to inspect a bridle on the nearest mule. "Not many of the boys in camp come out for services and I guess I've been too lazy."

He jerked his head back to face her, he would not let her think he was raised to be a heathen. He couldn't dishonor his mother like that. "But now, I'm used to goin' to church. Mother, she insisted we attend ever time there was a preacher come through. Even when I lived away from Mother, I still knew I had to be in church regular. I've just been lazy without someone to set me a good example." He finished with his eyes studying the dusty toe of his boot.

As he raised his eyes, Emma smiled at him and he felt he could confess anything to this girl, yet he wanted nothing more than to never, ever disappoint her.

"I do have to get the sheep back up, Papa will be wondering about me and there's always more work waiting. I hope you get to drive the next load, I'll be watchin' for you."

She'd said she would be watching for him; Preston couldn't imagine anything more wonderful to hear. He slung the water out of his bucket with such zeal he nearly splashed her; he ran to the side of the load and had to try twice to hang the bucket back on its hook. He realized he was going to have to pull himself together before he climbed up on this big load.

With a deep breath, he smiled at her, "Thank you Em. I'll be watching for you too."

Chapter 5

Emma had to force herself to look up the hill despite the groaning of the heavy wagon as it crept up the far side of the hollow. As the sound told her he was nearing the top, she allowed a quick peek over her right shoulder. The dark felt hat was soon dwarfed by the stack of logs and as Emma tried to focus on the man she felt the slightest disappointment that he wasn't watching her.

You silly thing, he'd break his neck if he tried to look over that load and then where'd you be? You'd have a beau with a broken neck.

Beau? The name had seemed as natural as any name could be but it was a little embarrassing to think of him that way. In her youth, anytime she imagined having a beau he was dressed in something like velvet and often carrying a long sword at his side. A giggle escaped as she thought, *That must have come from an old fairy tale of some sort.*

Now, when she thought the word *beau*, Preston's face was in her mind and instead of velvet she was thrilled to remember the tattered pants and thick, plaid shirt. Well he had no sword clanking against his boots with every step but the noisy brakes of the wagon were the music that announced his presence to her.

She wondered if she could now consider him a beau? With a slight shake of her head, she conceded she should be content to see him again at the creek, or better yet at church. Mama always told them to pick a husband from the church and she knew that Papa expected it. But now that she thought about it, she couldn't remember reading it in the Bible just that way. Maybe God could choose a husband for her that didn't sit in a pew at the Jonesville church.

There were lots of boys in the little congregation but none had ever seemed right for Emma. Papa mentioned a name here or there and she understood his hint. For years she'd clung to the belief that God had a very special man chosen for her and all she needed to do was wait for him to reveal his plan.

This fella sure seems right. Would God send you a man from among the heathen? That's what Papa would no doubt call the loggers — heathen. But Preston said he was used to going to church; that wasn't a very strong testimony but it's a place to start.

Her steps were slow as she mulled over the possibility that God would choose a husband for her that wasn't a church-going man. Certain that was not a possibility, yet believing Preston had been sent to her straight from God, she decided, *I'm sure he'll be at preaching Sunday mornin' and then there won't be a thing to worry about.* Then she worried, *Did I even make it clear I was invitin' him to preachin'? He'd know he was welcome at church without an invitation, wouldn't he?*

Sure that she'd see him soon, she picked up her pace and bounced up the hill faster than her sheep were interested in walking and she kept trying to urge them to move a little faster. Finally, she reached the gate well ahead of the lead ewe and stood waiting for them with her mind a million miles away. It was no wonder she didn't hear Papa as he ambled up to the fence.

Papa enjoyed watching his stock. He said they grew better if someone was watching them grow. Yet he wasted little time at the side of a corral or pasture. Today, Emma couldn't be sure whether he was watching the sheep or his daughter. Now she wondered if he'd seen her talking to the boy from the logging camp and whether he would be angry about it. She didn't want to feel like she was keeping anything from him, dishonesty was not to be tolerated in the England home.

"You got ahead of 'em today din' you?" Papa asked without looking at Emma.

"Sometimes they move slower than molasses in winter. I get to thinking about everything that needs doing on top of this hill and I get to wantin' to push them up it."

Plans for Emma

Papa just nodded and spit out the straw he'd been chewing on. "Has your Mama got everything caught up in the house? Do you want to go load up wood on the sled?"

Emma was glad for another chore that would give her time alone to think about the morning – to think about Preston Langford.

"Let me run check. Even if I need to help her a little, I'll get down to the wood line before dinnertime." With that, Emma was off at her characteristic fast walk and in the back door of the house even before Papa had the sheep pen closed.

As she entered the spotless kitchen she was taking inventory. There were two buckets filled with spring water on the dry sink, the floors had been swept and there even appeared to be a kettle of cabbage already simmering for the noon meal. Mama had laid out sweet potatoes and carrots to scrub and peel but that could be done much later so Emma felt free to head down to the woods without even finding her mother.

Jane had trained her children from their earliest days to do what needed doing and she never questioned her older girls now. Somehow the house ran like a well-oiled machine.

Emma looked down at her dress wondering if she should change before loading the firewood. She loved the bright yellow gingham but it wasn't as strong as the nut-brown homespun and there were often briars pulling at her hem as she picked up the wood Papa had sawn into stove-sized chunks.

She caught a glimpse of her scuffed boot and smiled, thankful she had not been barefoot at the creek this morning. The dew was heavy and the morning air held a chill so she'd slipped on the heavy-leather boots she and Lena shared for their farm chores. Dropping her hem to the full floor-length she wondered if Preston would have appreciated how rough the shoes were. Emma smiled as she realized she had no idea what his shoes looked like.

After she changed into her heavier skirt, Emma walked out to the loafing shed where Papa had already harnessed his big mare Bay. Emma's experienced hand hooked the trace chains to the waiting sled and walked with a loose hold of Bay's bridle. The horse's long legs could lengthen a stride for even a tall man but Emma had no trouble keeping up without any pressure on the bit.

The short pieces of wood lay scattered in thick grass and Emma had to fight against saw briars that sought to hold them in place. Her stomach was growling by the time the sled was filled with its low sideboards straining against the wood. Emma smiled, enjoying the energy and the cool breeze that licked at her sweaty brow. She slipped the strap from her chin and fanned her face with her hat as Bay pawed at the ground, impatient from standing too long.

"We'll head home now girl. You've been very tolerant of me. I know I'm not as fast as Papa, but it sure helps him if I can do this kind of chore. I don't think Lena much likes being out in the woods and we'd never get Metie home if we sent her out here alone. Come on now Bay, get that sled movin' and you'll be free of this harness in a minute."

The big horse leaned into the harness for only a second before the bent-sapling sled runners began gliding along the thick grass. Emma didn't even touch the horse as they walked back toward the house. The animals would always find their way home.

Emma took in the sights of the farm that had been home her entire life. Grandpa England came from North Carolina and bought this land when it was covered in timber and rocks. Papa always told that he spent his last penny to buy it so he had to get right to work or he would've starved to death on his own land. He'd left three boys on the other side of the big Smoky Mountains and Emma had never even seen those uncles. But Uncle Kernel came with his Pa and helped him and Tom begin the clearing work. By the time the farm was handed to Tom England, they'd cut enough logs to build a small house and cleared a hog lot and a big garden patch as

Plans for Emma

well as a couple of fields along the creek for corn. Now, Tom had enlarged the house with milled boards on three sides so those logs showed on the back porch wall but nowhere else. He'd also cut trees and cleared stumps for the pasture where the sheep now grazed, and now he was working on this back pasture where he'd left the firewood. Emma smiled with pride in her father. He worked hard and she knew he was proud of what he'd accomplished here. She felt rooted in this hillside and wondered how she could ever leave.

Makes me wonder where Preston Langford will end up settling. Surely he don't plan to live in that logging camp forever.

Again she chastised herself, why did every thought today include this strange man?

Chapter 6

The sun crept higher in the sky heating Preston's dark hat and drawing flies to swarm around the mules' ears. The animals snorted, the harness squeaked and the logs groaned. Yet Preston felt as though he was fanned by angels' wings and serenaded by the heavenly chorus. He could think of nothing but the girl with the sheep.

"Emma." He said her name aloud and liked the feel of it on his lips. Molly turned an ear at the sound of his voice.

"Emma. Emma. Emma, Emma, Emma." He grew louder and louder with each repetition. It made him smile just to say her name.

Then it was a whisper, "Em."

It felt like a gift that she'd shared the nickname with him."I think she is a gift," he told his team.

As the miles passed and the picture of this girl etched itself into the deepest recesses of his mind, Preston thoughts grew serious. He remembered his fear when the postman told him one of the England girls was promised to marry. He remembered the hours spent swinging the axe wondering when he could again catch a glimpse of this girl.

She is the one. She is the girl I'm gonna' marry.

It was a vow to himself. It was a goal that he would reach one way or the other.

Should I tell her?

He spent several more miles reasoning out when he ought to inform Miss Emma England that she would one day be his wife. Maybe he could see her on the trip back to the camp, he could skip the stop at the post office this once, couldn't he? Would she be happy to hear this?

Something stopped him.

Plans for Emma

How he wished he could talk to his mother, could take Em to meet his mother. But she was gone now, 'home to her Lord' as she would have said it. There was a comfort in the faith she had always shown but still he missed her. Right now Preston missed the woman who had always known the answers. He remembered his sisters sitting by the fire talking with her about a beau or working on pretty things for their hope chests. Before he went to live on the doctor's farm, he had been too young to pay attention to the advice his mother gave. But even then he was sure she always had the right answers. As he entered his teenage years, Mother managed to pack a great deal of teaching into their few precious hours on Sunday afternoon. Yet, he never felt like she lectured him.

"Well Preston, she ain't here to help you now so you're going to have to figure this one out on your own. It will work out though. It just has to."

He wondered if he should seek out one of his sisters. Mary Jane had married even before Papa passed away and Preston knew little of her. Some of the boys had thought of sending little Merita to live with her after Mother passed, but James' wife offered to keep her and it was better for her to stay in Glades which had been her home since her earliest memories.

I need to get back over there and see my family. Mother wouldn't want us to get scattered; she always said kin was important – one of the most important things you can have. I wonder what Emma would think about all of them? Is she used to so much family? I don't even know how many brothers and sisters she has.

Preston resolved that while he wanted to learn more about the Englands it was also important that he share his own family with Emma. He spent the next few miles imagining how it might have gone if he had taken Emma to meet his mother.

It was the practice on the England farm to save water in the wooden barrels that had come filled with everything from special sheep feed to flour. Papa paid close attention to these aging vessels patching them when necessary and keeping them positioned under the drip of the barn and house. In that way, the stock could often be watered without the trip down to the creek. However, Emma found herself making excuses why she shouldn't waste that precious water and how she must always take the sheep for their regular drink.

As Preston slowed the team down the long hill, he beamed at Emma who surprised him by waving to him from the protection of the low-hanging oak branches. "I's afraid you wouldn't come today since it's been raining. Din' figure the sheep would be needin' water."

"Oh, we always catch our water of course. I've never known a farmer to draw water for their stock you know. But you know I'll be down here at the creek if there's any way possible." She lowered her eyes but Preston could see the grin that split her face.

"I sure am glad of it. Em, you know this little stop is the brightest spot in my days."

Emma couldn't lift her face as she could feel the blood filling her cheeks. She nodded hoping Preston understood how she treasured their few minutes together.

"I been thinking about my family; haven't seen them in months you know. I drive this big wagon pretty close to Glades on every trip but without Mother there to hold us together, it seems hard to get back."

She faced him squarely, her look serious as she stared into his eyes. "Preston, family is the most important thing we have other than the Lord. You mustn't let them down. I know they need you."

"Nah, they've got kids of their own. Nobody would need my help but Ben and little Merita and they're okay with James. A'course my brother Ben's two years older than me so I guess he'd be married by now anyway. He could have left home when Mother passed away but since James was takin' Merita in he thought he'd stay on to kind'a earn their keep."

Emma clung to every word for she had many questions about his childhood and her heart seemed to break every time she heard any of his childhood stories. "Why did you not stay with them Preston?"

Plans for Emma

"Well, I's used to be'in off you know. And I'd heard about the loggin' camp over here so I thought the best thing for everybody would be me getting work that paid some cash. I guess at the time I thought I'd be going back and passin' some of the money along to them. I been saving about everything I make you know."

She nodded acknowledging she followed his reasoning.

He turned to smooth the mane of the nearest mule, somehow he couldn't look at her as he added, "Now I wonder if the good Lord didn't send me over here for his own purposes. And I reckon that money I been savin' will go for other uses."

Emma cocked her head hoping that she understood what he was saying. She held her breath a moment wondering if he planned to add more. Was this confirmation that he was feeling drawn to her the way she felt? Her palms moistened with sweat and she dabbed them against her waist as she steadied her hand there.

"Hhmm," Preston cleared his throat and turned to climb back on the wagon. "Miss Em, it's a pleasure talkin' to you. I guess I'd better be on my way."

"Oh, okay." Emma had so many questions she wanted to ask. She wanted to know all about his family, his brothers and sisters. Yet she held the questions for fear her emotion would overtake her.

As soon as he returned to the camp he began asking the other drivers if there were loads ready to go out tomorrow. A joke had already grown up in the Flat Woods that Preston Langford would do two men's work just to get the chance to drive the ties to the railhead. And he didn't argue with them.

Preston began bargaining with the other drivers, offering anything he could and the foreman was happy to let him hew ties until dark in order to get to drive tomorrow's load.

The loads, and therefore the visits by the creek, became more regular and both Preston and Emma grew accustomed to visiting at least once each week. The length of the visits grew too, even as the hours of sunlight lessened with the shorter autumn days and Preston now had to work hard to get into Sunbright before it was too dark to navigate the muddy roads.

He didn't mind the harder driving, it was worth it to spend the time with Emma.

"Have you always lived here in Roslin?" he asked one day.

"Oh yes. My grandfather first bought this farm."

Preston glanced up the hill where the homestead overlooked the Jonesville Road and Bridge Creek. He'd never seen any other view of the home but he was beginning to feel like he knew it. "I can't imagine having such a place. But I've got it on my mind."

Emma shuffled her feet and searched for a new subject. *I don't want him to feel like we would look down on him.*

After a silent moment she asked, "You moved here from Glades, right? Was your family always there?"

Preston turned to watch the cold water bubble around a tree branch caught against a rock. "My Pa had a place in White Oak but he died when I was but five years old. So, Mother moved back to Glades with her people. I guess she couldn't manage without any help 'cept us kids."

"I've never been to Glades, but we don't get out of Roslin much," Emma answered softly. There seemed to be something troubling Preston about his home. "Did you enjoy it there? Did you live with your mother's family?"

"No, Mother had a little house that had been her folks' but they were already gone. Her brothers helped her some and my brother Elec, he was sixteen when Pa died so he stayed close and helped Mother. But I was sent to live and work on a doctor's farm."

A quick gasp escaped before Emma could compose herself. "Oh Preston, how old were you?"

He heard the concern in her voice and rushed to erase it, "Oh, I was a feisty eight-year-old. Slept in the loft of the barn and just as quick as anything, I could climb up a skinned pole they had set in the center of the back wall. Spent all my time in that barn and they had a whole passle of cats out there. I'd

Plans for Emma

get to watchin' them chase the mice and jump at bits of straw I'd toss in the air. It was a show every day."

"How long were you with the doctor?"

"Oh about six years. You know I got to see Mother about every Sunday. She would have skinned me if I hadn't been at church. And most Sunday's I'd go home with her and eat dinner. It wasn't too much having an extra mouth for one meal a week. Anyway, she took sick and all the boys except Wilburn had already moved off with their own families so I thought I could help her. But she was growing weaker by then and she passed on about two years ago."

Emma didn't know what to say. It was obvious to her that he was still hurting but she didn't know how to comfort him. Her hand lifted toward his arm but she stopped, reminding herself that it wasn't even appropriate for her to be talking to this man here at the creek alone and she knew for sure she couldn't touch him.

Preston took a deep breath and turned to smile at her. "Too much talk about yesterday. There is so much of tomorrow that I want to think about. Mr. England has a fine spread of land up on that hill. Does it flatten out up top or is it steep in the back too?"

Emma looked up at her home and described the lay of the land she had known her whole life.

"I'm going to have me a farm like that one day," Preston declared as he moved to climb up to his seat among the cross ties. "And I'll see you next week Miss Em and we can maybe talk about that farm I'm gonna' have."

He tipped his hat with a playful wink and clucked to his mules to resume their long walk.

"Preston, I'll be happy to hear about your dream," Emma said softly, knowing he could not hear her. "But I have some dreams to talk about too. We're going to have to figure out where you are with the Lord before we start farmin' together."

41

Chapter 7

Emma had been in the vegetable garden since dinner and with the combination of warm afternoon sun and stooping to reach the weeds she was feeling very tired. Her mind moved as fast as her hands, perhaps that was as tiring as the work. Preston was on her mind. *My Preston*, as she'd begun to call him, at least in her own thoughts. He was on her mind more than anything else these days and she wasn't altogether happy with that.

Lord, is it even decent for me to think of him all the time? Do I need to repent for this?

She even took a quick look at the sky to see if God might have stepped out on a cloud to send an angry answer to that question.

Shaking her head she chastised her own foolishness. *He is faithful and just to forgive even your foolishness Em.*

Even without an audible word from heaven, Emma knew she must be praying for this man. *Could God have sent him to me to pray over him? There must be a reason I can't get him out of my head and Lord if it's evil trying to root itself in my mind, please create in me a clean heart.*

Mama had often warned about allowing evil into your heart and mind. And that was a familiar subject in the preaching services at church so Emma was always cautious to guard against it.

She paused and sat back on her heels for a split second as she considered the question.

Okay. It's never wrong to pray for someone. Lord, please keep Mr. Langford in your will, keep him safe while he's in dangerous work. And Lord if he ain't saved, show me that for I'm afraid I'm losing my heart to him and that can't happen with someone that doesn't believe in you.

Despite her confession she imagined him as her husband, drawing mental images of their life together. She wondered

Plans for Emma

whether their children would have his jet black hair instead of her softer brown. She smiled as she imagined sitting beside the tall straight figure on the bench at church.

With a deep sigh she grabbed a final handful of the pesky morning glory vines that were trying to wrap up the tomato plants and tossed them toward the split rail enclosure. *Em you spend too much time daydreaming. Mama would tell you to go memorize the Proverb detailing the ideal woman or the fruit of the spirit from Galatians.*

Ready for a break she walked to the house. She untied her long cotton chin straps as she stepped onto the back porch and tossed the hat over the chair that always sat next to the door. After an afternoon in the garden she was hoping for a moment's rest before her mother asked for help with supper. Her right hand moved to smooth the loose rolls of hair. She tucked in the sprigs that had pulled free from the high bun and dabbed at her damp brow. She heard her mother's voice in her mind reminding her, "It only takes a minute to keep yourself neat. You can always spare a minute."

Emma smiled at the memory and wondered how many times she'd heard those words.

Mama also taught her girls to never let the devil catch them with idle hands and Emma looked up the dark stairwell wondering if she should spend this quiet moment working on her hope chest, those pillow cases would be beautiful when she finished the embroidery. Instead, she headed through to the front porch, grabbing the family's Bible from its regular spot in the parlor with one hand. She always wanted to read the Bible but she had to admit an ulterior motive today. Neither Mama nor Papa would interrupt her rest if she was spending it with God's holy word.

Settling herself in a hickory rocker she breathed a prayer, *Lord please forgive me for using you as an excuse not to work. Can you use this time to speak to my heart anyway?*

As though His Spirit whispered peace to her heart, she smiled as she opened the big book and smoothed the worn pages. Her eye was drawn to the movement of a hummingbird visiting the big flowers of Mama's Columbine where it wrapped around the corner porch post. She smiled as she thought, *You are always drawn to the flowers with the brightest colors – I don't think you can help yourself.*

Her eyes popped wider as the thought struck her, *She can't help herself anymore than you can help your attraction to this young logger.*

But why?

Sure, she realized that he watched for her at the creek and she never had anyone wanting to see her that much. He was kind to her, but Emma was surrounded by kindness. Still, this was special somehow.

How well do you even know him?

She cocked her head to the side as though trying to see a new angle on the problem. The movement spooked her tiny visitor and a sigh escaped Em's lips.

He is a bit of a mystery, isn't he? The realization brought a smile to her lips. *It's not like all the boys at the church that you've known your whole life. There is an awful lot you don't know about him.*

She took a deep breath and returned her eyes and her mind to the big book in her lap. Papa always encouraged the family to read the whole Bible from the beginning, and each night he read a full chapter to them working his way through the book time after time. Today, Emma found herself flipping through the book allowing her eyes to scan familiar verses. The book of Proverbs caught her attention warning her to "lean not unto thine own understanding," and "enter not into the path of the wicked." And then in the sixteenth chapter she read, "A man's heart deviseth his way; but the Lord directeth his steps." She stopped with the verse resounding in her head. She read it again, maybe she'd misunderstood.

The verse planted itself in her mind and understanding began to sprout from it.

The screen door squeaked and Emma squinched her eyes tight, hoping for just another minute alone to work this out. Before she could open them, she heard the squeak of a

Plans for Emma

nearby chair and opened her eyes to see who her company was.

Jane had a tin cup of water in one hand and a scarf in the other. When she saw her daughter's eyes opened she smiled."I took Bessie and Leonard down to the big rock for a few minutes and Leonard fell asleep. He is sure a wad if you have to carry him up the hill."

Emma smiled, "I'm sorry Mama, I didn't see you coming up or I would have tried to help."

"No, I wouldn't have wanted to interrupt your time with the Lord. How's the weeding coming?"

Emma knew her mother was doing nothing but making conversation and not prodding her to get back to the garden."The morning glories are trying to take over the tomatoes but I've fought them back for the time being."

"It's an ongoing battle. What are you reading?"

Emma looked at the book in her lap. "Proverbs."

Jane nodded and smiled. Her toe set the rocker in motion and she seemed to study the distant horizon.

Emma had spent many hours like this with her mother. Jane was happy spending time with her children and didn't need to always be talking or questioning them. But Emma knew that her mother was very wise and that she could help with most problems Emma encountered in life so she decided to share her thoughts.

"Mama, why do you think it is that the Bible talks so much about not relying on our understanding? Do you think that there are things in this world we can't ever figure out?"

Jane leaned her head against the back of the rocker and blinked slowly. "There are many mysteries in the world. Who can say why the big winds come and destroy our crops or homes? Why do good boys get the fever and die when rowdy boys all around are strong and healthy? What makes the snow fall or the grass grow? Some things are for God alone to know."

Emma nodded as she let the words sink in. "Does everyone question those kinds of things?"

Depends on what's happenin' in your life I guess."

Emma ran her finger down the tiny print on the page before her, "Why do you suppose it says 'A man's heart deviseth his way...' it makes it sound like that's a bad thing."

"It's not a bad thing necessarily, not to make a plan. Where it goes wrong is when the plan is yours and not God's."

"Uh huh."

"I better be makin' a plan to get some supper or the good Lord is gonna' get after me for not caring for my family. I'm always a'quotin' the Proverbs' woman to you girls so I've gotta be sure I'm giving 'meat to my household'."

They shared a laugh and Emma closed the Bible, "I'll come help you."

Jane's gentle hand pushed her back into the chair, "Not yet. You stay here with the Lord. He's feeding your soul right now."

Emma closed her eyes and the prayer seemed to spill from her heart, *Lord, I've been daydreaming about being wife to this man I met by the creek. Then you send my godly mother to me and by her presence alone you've reminded me that I have to honor her and Papa. In all of my planning about catching this man for a husband, I've never once thought that Papa has to bless it. You've reminded me that I can make the plans but you're directing the path so please help me remember that.*

I know that if Preston Langford is the man you've got in mind for me then you'll lead him to speak to Papa. Only, if you could lead him quickly, I'd sure appreciate it.

With a smile at her own audacity before the sovereign Lord, she pushed herself out of the rocker and headed in to help with the evening's chores.

Chapter 8

Emma looked for opportunities to ask Preston about his faith in God. There were quiet times in their visits. A part of Emma wanted to talk every second she was with him, wanted to hear his deep rich voice and to learn his heart. But it felt so good just to be near him that she couldn't find the strength to break those silent moments unless something important occurred to her. As they watched the water in the creek one day she had such a thought, "Have I told you that I was baptized in this very creek?"

His eyes shot up from staring at the water and turned to smile at her, "No, you haven't told me that. Right here?"

She giggled, "Nah, this creek forks and part of it runs down by the Jonesville Church. There's a wide, deep hole not far from the road so that's our baptizin' hole – and a favorite swimmin' hole too."

He looked off to the south as though he could see the very spot despite the steep hill in front of him. "How old were you?"

"Hmm, I guess I was eleven."

Nodding he closed his eyes, "I's baptized about that same time. Course I don't guess anybody recorded the date, but I was about eleven, maybe already twelve." He shivered and folded his arms up as though he needed to rub warmth into them. "It was the coldest dip I've ever had. These creeks that keep runnin' all year long don't ever warm up much. And I was a skinny fella' anyway so it was a cold thing. Mama stood on the sandy creekside and beamed like I'd accomplished the greatest thing she could imagine."

She nodded and smiled at the creek, "It must have felt like that. Mama always says she can't hope for anything more for her kids than faith and obedience to the Lord. Was the baptizin' right after you accepted the Lord?"

She didn't look at him and said a silent prayer that she wasn't being too pushy.

"Yeah, we'd had revival meetin's all week and I walked that aisle just as sure as anything I'd burn if I didn't."

A chuckle escaped, "I know those preachers. I've often wondered if you get to heaven any faster if you're running scared to get there."

They laughed together as each remembered fiery sermons and enthusiastic preachers they'd heard over the years. Emma thrilled to hear Preston talking about church in such familiar terms. She breathed thanksgiving to God that he continued to reassure her that this man she'd found at the creekside was a faithful child of God.

The minutes sped past and the pair parted smiling, promising to see each other at the same spot in a few days.

As they continued to find times to discuss their faith, Emma discovered he had learned Bible verses that he could still repeat to her. When she heard the holy scripture roll off his tongue she wondered if he might one day preach.

"Preston, you have such a deep, rich voice you could hold a congregation spellbound."

Preston shook his head as his neck reddened despite the joy her compliment gave him. "Nah, preachers have to do more than just memorize a few verses like any Sunday School kid would do. I can't read much and my sermons would dry up mighty fast on the verses I already know."

Papa had insisted each of his children learn to read for he said they must all be able to read God's word for themselves. Now Emma appreciated that lesson more than ever. "With your Pa gone, I guess you weren't able to get much schoolin' were you?"

"That's right. Fact is, the doc he din' have no boys to do the farm work and what with his time spent lookin' after sick folk I had my hands full seein' to all the work around the place. Weren't much time for school and the old man wasn't payin' for my learnin', just my workin'."

"But he was a doctor? Surely he valued education."

"Uh huh. His girls all went right through Glades School."

Emma couldn't help but wonder what kind of educated man would have not seen to an education for this boy that grew up under his roof. Without asking another question, she was sure he'd had very poor treatment from that man and Emma had an instant dislike for the doctor.

She couldn't shake the thoughts about that man even as she said her good-byes to Preston.

In heavy rain Emma dared not attempt the walk down the hill and she prayed that Preston would not be sitting behind the team in such weather. But when the skies cleared and the rainbow appeared reminding them of God's promises, she made her way to the creek as soon as she could manage to excuse herself.

She was rewarded by the creaking of wagon wheels that could be heard several minutes before she spotted the big load.

Before he could even climb down from his seat, she was questioning him, "Preston, I feared you were on top of this load in that driving rain. Do you have to take the loads even when the weather is bad?"

He grinned and tipped his hat, "Howdy Miss Em. What a surprise to find you here in all of this dampness."

"Preston Langford, don't act so foolish. I'm not kidding that I's worried about you."

With a slow nod of his head, the grin softened into a genuine smile, "I know you were and I thank you for it. It means an awful lot to a feller to have someone carin' about him."

He gestured toward the square ties, "We keep cuttin' and hewin' if the weather will let us at all. But we don't take the load if it's too dangerous. Don't think they care much for my hide, but the mules are valuable and ties that are dumped over the hillside don't bring 'em any money."

"Humpf, well that's a fine thing, to care more about a stack of wood or an animal than the men that hew out their fortunes for them."

"I'd rather have you carin' than the straw boss at the yard." His cheeks pinkened but he couldn't stop the emotion pouring from his heart. "I don't want to think anymore about logs and loggin' companies. Tell me about the Englands. What have y'uns done on these rainy days?"

Emma took a deep breath to quiet her thoughts, "We did what little we had to in order to keep the farm runnin'. I milked each day and couldn't get the bucket to the house quick enough to keep the water out. Mama said we'd never make butter out of that weak stuff, but it didn't taste any different."

"Mothers like to fuss like that I think. Do you always attend to the milkin'?"

"Do you think I'll be a fussy mother?" She blushed despite the teasing nature of her question and tried to change the subject. "Mama says she never could get the hang of milkin' so Papa always did it until us kids started getting old enough to help out. Lena can milk as well as anyone but she don't like it either. I don't mind. I like being out with the stock."

Preston smiled at her, enjoying the image of her with her animals. But he chose to answer her first question, "Em I think you'll be the finest mother a child could hope for."

"Ah, Preston. You praise me too much and it embarrasses me."

"I'm sorry Em. I din' mean to; just sayin' what I feel."

The answer came out as a tiny whisper, "Thank you Preston."

Both Preston and Emma seemed to dance around the prospect of a life together, but neither ever dared speak of it.

Preston talked about dreams of his own place.

Emma talked about living a godly life.

While Emma never said it outright, Preston realized that Emma was expecting him to be in church. And his own heart

Plans for Emma

convicted him the same way. Finally, he resolved he must begin to attend the little Jonesville Baptist Church

Fall had gained firm footing over the weather when Preston dragged himself out of his cot and pulled on boots so cold the leather felt like stone. Several gruff voices asked why there was so much noise on a Sunday morning as he stirred up coals in the squat little Franklin stove but he ignored them as he began heating water. Today he would shave off this clump of a mustache. He wouldn't be looking unkempt when Mr. Tom England met his future son-in-law.

Stepping out of the bunk house, the wind slammed against his back and threatened to carry away his hat as he turned down a worn path. Soon there was enough scrub timber left to block the wind from him and he became more comfortable in his walk.

His mind moved from one thought to another as he dreaded the cold winter in the logging camp, remembered Sunday dinner with his mother and thought about Emma. Always his thoughts turned to Emma. This led him to think about her parents.

It felt like he'd known her for a long time and that they'd spent a lot of time together. But when he thought about it awhile, he realized he'd spoken to her about five or six times at the creek and the first time it was only for a few minutes. Still, he felt he should have spoken with her father before now.

Preston wondered just how he should approach Mr. England. He'd tried to ask around Roslin about the man and he heard mixed responses. Many people seemed to think he was a little gruff and very miserly. But others thought he was the salt of the earth that would help a neighbor in any crisis. Preston hoped it was the salt he would get to talk to today.

That turnpike will be right around the big bend in this path. Why have you put off coming to church this long? You're about wild to get a chance to see Emma and you've known for a month where she goes to church.

As the thought passed through his mind, Preston had to admit to himself – or to God – that his sole purpose in coming to church today was to see Emma and to speak to her father.

There's nothing wrong with doing a little business at church.

"Whoa." Preston stopped as though an invisible bridle rein had jerked him out of a flatfoot walk.

He looked around, half expecting to see someone who had physically halted him.

Then he looked up.

The cold wind set bare tree branches waving above his head and clouds scooted around the sky in varying shades of gray. He tried to peer between the clouds as though he could see God among them. The noises of the forest reached out to him as though they spoke a language he'd known from childhood.

The message was clear and he hung his head at the realization.

He had been too long out of church. It had been far too long since he'd prayed and even without his mother's prodding, he should be looking at her Bible and making out whatever words he could.

He dropped to his knees in silent, wordless prayer. The cold earth soaked into the heavy canvass of his pants but he paid it no mind. At some point his hat came off his head whether from the wind or holy urging to respect the God he now communed with, he did not know.

As Preston raised his lanky body, the cold had melted away. He no longer noticed the heavy clouds above and his path seemed clear despite the broken treetops and stumps that surrounded him.

Thank you Lord, he said one more time as he dusted off his old hat and secured it on his head. He couldn't help one last longing look down the path that would have taken him to see Emma today but he chose to turn back toward camp.

Plans for Emma

Guess I got a better sermon than the circuit preacher gave the folks at Jonesville anyway. Mama would be proud to know I was listenin' to the original preacher this morning.

Preston still wore the warm smile as he walked back into the camp. The bunkhouse that had been so quiet a couple of hours ago was now buzzing with voices as the men drank coffee and gossiped among themselves. Preston spoke to a few of his buddies as he made his way to his bunk but he didn't want to get drawn into the chatter today. Without a word to anyone he retrieved the little black Bible, its cover frayed and the lettering faded beyond recognition. Holding this book, Preston felt as though he would see his mother at his side.

He made his way to the cook camp where he knew there would be a fire and not much noise as the men had finished their breakfast and scattered through the camp except a few who would have stayed there to play cards or whittle in front of the fire. Sure enough, he found a table in a corner with enough light that he thought he could work through some verses.

As he opened his mother's Bible, another wave of emotion washed over him and he sat for a moment remembering her. She had read the great stories from this book as Preston and his brothers and sisters sat around her feet. The memory was fuzzy for this recollection was one of the earliest ones he had. Someone held him, whether to make him quiet or comfortable, he couldn't be sure nor could he quite remember who it was. Maybe Mary Jane, although she married by the time he was three so maybe it was Lexie. Eleven years older than Preston, Alexandra had always seemed important to him just as he thought her name sounded important. Of course the family all called her Lexie and she was a steady presence beside her mother ensuring the younger children had all of the care they needed. Preston remembered Lexie crying when she learned he was living at Dr. Cherry's. But she had been married only a couple of years and he supposed her husband was not interested in taking in a young boy nor were they any better able to feed him than his mother had been.

A deep breath cleared his mind of the past and Preston focused his eyes on the words before him. He'd opened to the center of the book and found himself in Psalms. One at a time he worked out the words and realized that his reading was suffering from lack of practice. *I cried unto God...*he turned the page thinking he had already done his crying for the day. *O clap your hands, all ye people; shout unto God with the voice of triu...* he didn't know that word so he turned back a few more pages.

The Lord is my shep-...I shall not want. Preston smiled, he knew this one by heart and he recited it from memory rather than struggle with the printed words. *The Lord is my shepherd; I shall not want. He maketh me to lie down in green pastures: he leadeth me beside the still waters. He restoreth my soul; he leadeth me in the paths of righteousness for his name's sake. Yea though I walk through the valley of the shadow of death, I will fear no evil: for thou art with me; thy rod and thy staff they comfort me. Thou preparest a table before me in the presence of mine enemies: thou anointest my head with oil; my cup runneth over. Surely goodness and mercy shall follow me all the days of my life; and I will dwell in the house of the Lord forever.*

With a finger marking his place, Preston closed the little book over his hand and sat with his eyes closed meditating over the words and remembering sermons from this text. He couldn't help but think of Emma beside the bubbling water of the creek with the green hillside behind her and the bleating sheep.

Father God, I know I need to be focusing on you but this girl invades my every thought. I don't know whether to thank you for that or ask forgiveness. But I know you've given her to me. So maybe I just need to ask you to make me worthy of her.

He spent a while longer schooling himself in reading by looking over the printed Psalm and comparing it to the words he knew by heart.

The noise level rose as the men's stomachs drew them to the dining room even before the big triangle jingled notice

Plans for Emma

that food was ready. Preston rose to return Mother's Bible to his bunk when the foreman approached him. "Preston, have you ever known a more miserable kind of weather?"

"Well Sir, I reckon it could be worse. It's damp but there's not much rain fallin'. And it's muddy but the roads are still passable."

The gruff man began packing tobacco into a beat up pipe, "Well if you're likin' it so much, I'll let you drive in it tomorrow. There's a wagon load of ties ready to go to Sunbright so you be ready as soon as you can eat a bite in the morning."

The two men nodded, Preston in acceptance of his assignment and the foreman in farewell as he walked toward the little log building that served as both his sleeping quarters and office. Preston felt light as a feather as he made his way back to the bunk house to store his Bible before the meal.

With the final "Amen" said, Emma stepped onto the church's porch and the wind tore at her skin. Papa stood inside the doorway talking with other men while Mama and Lena made their way to the wagon to tuck Gip, Leonard and Bessie into the waiting blankets. After the warmth of the crowd and the roaring fire at the back of the room, Emma had forgotten about the wind. Somehow she hadn't noticed the weather as they approached the church earlier for she was certain this would be the day she would see Preston walk into the service. Even now, her eyes darted over the parting crowd hoping that somehow she had missed him.

"Emma, are you going to stand in the cold or come home for dinner?" Papa had finished his chat with the men and was heading toward the waiting wagon.

Well I don't know why I'm waiting. Silly girl. As she stepped from the porch, she thought the words she was sure her parents would have said if they could read her mind. No one wanted to talk on the ride home and she tried to use the time to sort her feelings.

I'm sure he believes as I do and he's been raised to be in church. Why isn't he here? He seems as eager to see me as I am when he comes to the creek. Is he not an honorable man? Does he not want to ask Papa to call on me?

The questions churned in her mind and she could find no answers for them. No one cared that her eyes were closed against the cold and she had no need to announce her prayers to the rest of the family.

She thought of the stories he'd told her about how he'd spent his youth and she wondered how much of those days affected his life now. Would they always impact him?

It broke her heart to realize what a hard life this man had known. Yet, he didn't seem angry with God that things had been so much easier for Emma or other people. He seemed to take his state in stride and he didn't dwell on the past but kept his eyes focused on the horizon. And Emma admired that. She found she admired everything about this Preston Langford.

Lord, you know that I've been dreaming about the husband you have planned for me. Am I still being silly in believing you've now shown me who that man is? Why does my heart keep turning to him if it isn't from you?

The words of Proverbs chapter three popped into her head, *Trust in the Lord with all thine heart; and lean not unto thine own understanding.*

She nodded her head with a new understanding of words she'd heard her entire life. *I'm not having much trouble obeying that one 'cause I don't understand any of this. I've spent a lot of time dreaming is it now time for me to be more serious? That always seems so easy for Lena...,"* she looked toward her sister who sat with little Leonard snuggled beneath her arm. Emma smiled thinking that soon Lena would begin her own home and children would be blessed to have such a mother.

Lord, will anyone ever think the same of me? I don't think Papa believes I'll make much of a wife and mother. Please help me Lord to become the woman I need to be to make Preston a good wife. And if Preston is not the one, please show me that – soon.

Chapter 9

The long, log bunk house had but one clock and Preston felt he heard the soft click of every passing minute through that night. Yet, when the big iron triangle was clanged to awaken the workmen at five o'clock he jumped from the bed with no fatigue. He was in his boots and heading toward the door before he had his suspenders pulled onto his shoulders.

"Eh, Langford, you're a'gonna kill us all openin' that door a'fore the fire's even blazing," he heard as he stepped onto the rock doorstep. He paid no heed to the complaints the same way he'd ignored the teasing that sprang up over the last weeks as it became clear to the loggers that there was a girl at the root of Preston's new interest in driving the big loads and working ever-harder.

The mules had not been fed yet so Preston had to attend to the needs of his team before he could even consider rolling out toward Bridge Creek. As he scooped oats into a wooden bucket, he peered through the gaped boards of the hastily built shelter and gauged the time. He wanted to be at the creek before Emma so he didn't miss a single minute with her. Yet he knew he couldn't wait too long both for the sake of his mules on this cold morning and for fear Mr. England might happen to notice the loaded wagon sitting at the bottom of the hill.

I wonder if he knows by now that Emma has a friend at the creek? Preston pondered as he listened to the soft sounds of the barn. He passed the time by feeding the rest of the animals which would be used to skid out logs through the day and pull out the wagon that would be loaded with hewn crossties by day's end.

The watering troughs were filled from the drizzling rain that had plagued the camp for about a week now. Preston led his team two at a time for a long drink at the trough before hooking the trace chains onto the single trees that would make animal and wagon into one machine. He made a quick visit to the kitchen for a lunch bag and left without taking time for breakfast.

Despite heavy clouds, Preston thought he could see the brightness of the sun well above the horizon as he started down the rutted path that would lead him out of the logging zone and onto Beaty Road.

As he stood on the brake approaching the creek, his eyes made an automatic scan of the hillside and were rewarded by the mottled white movement he knew were Emma's sheep. His heart seemed to leap in his chest and Preston had to remind himself to breathe. Finally, he was close enough to pick the straw hat out of the herd and he watched that spot until her face came into focus. The smile that lit up her whole face was the most glorious sight Preston could imagine and right then every cloud seemed to disappear from the sky.

The big load of neatly stacked ties sat in its now familiar spot as Preston tore his hat from his head to greet Emma when she was swept off the slope by the mass of wool. Words threatened to gush from him but as he opened his mouth, they seemed to get all jumbled together into something that he could not speak.

"Mornin' Em," he managed, using the family's nickname for her, as he always did now. "It's so damp and bad this morning that I was fearful you wouldn't come down."

"Well, Papa did say that he thought there was water enough in the trough today but I made excuses and, well, I knew those ties would have to get to the railroad no matter the weather." She first looked right in his eyes, trying to read his intentions. Finding no answers to the questions that plagued her, she looked everywhere but at him.

"I've got something real important to talk to you about today. 'Cept there's never enough time to say it all, is there?"

Emma gave a slight shake to her head as her pulse quickened. What serious subject could he have on his mind?

Plans for Emma

How could she make him understand that there would be plenty of time in front of the fire at the England house? He needed only ask Papa's permission to call.

"I started to Jonesville yesterday." His hand moved to smooth the now missing mustache. "Even shaved; thought your Papa might think better of a neater fella'."

Emma jerked her head and drew a quick breath. "You did? Yes, you did shave it. I was thinking something was different about you. Papa wears a mustache too you know so he couldn't think bad of you for it, could he? Still, it was good of you to try to think what would please him."

She flashed that dimpled grin that was etched in Preston's mind. "I've been looking for you at church. Thought for sure I'd see you yesterday."

Oh my, she thought. The words had slipped out before she gave them much thought, *What's he gonna' think about you looking for him?* Trying to collect her thoughts she continued, "You know that most of the young folks in Roslin meet there about every week. And there's a singin' on Saturday that's mostly for the young'uns."

"A singin'? Oh that would be fun. I guess you've got you a beau to take you to it?"

Emma waved her hand at him as though dismissing the very idea. She was pleased the mood had lightened. "Why would you say a thing like that?"

"Because Em you are just about the prettiest thing I've ever laid eyes on and if I can see it then I know good and well that every half-grown boy in Roslin can see it too." It was the longest sentence he had ever managed to get out in her presence and it was the biggest compliment he could've paid her. He felt desperate to know whether she was feeling as devoted to him as he felt. And he needed to know what kind of competition he had too.

Emma lowered her head and smiled at the worn toes of her boots as she tried to calm herself with deep breaths. Ah, this was *her Preston* again. Gone were any misgivings that he might have no honorable intentions to court her properly.

Her sharp tongue surfaced despite the dimple that accompanied, "Preston Langford, do you think I'm going with every half-grown boy in Roslin? What do you think I'm doin' trotting down to this creek bright and early every morning?"

Preston grinned, now it was a game to him. "Thought you were comin' down here to water your sheep."

Again, she flicked her hand dismissing the teasing. She was now willing to be more serious and asked, "Well what was it you were wantin' to talk to me about? You said it was something serious."

Preston took a deep breath. He was no longer teasing and wanted her to understand the depth of his heart and the importance of the time he'd spent with the Lord yesterday. He knew that Emma had a deep faith and strong belief in God and he knew that she would not soon join herself to any man that did not share those things. And Preston was determined that she would be joined to him.

"Em, I did start to church yesterday but I think the Lord stopped me."

She cocked her head and looked up at him as she often did, "Now Preston, I don't believe God would ever stop a fella from going to church."

"No, no, I'm not makin' any sense. Let me try again. I was comin' to church and thinkin' about you of course – and thinking about talking to your Papa so that maybe I could start calling on you regular. And I was struck that I ought to get myself straight with God before I went into His house for courtin' purposes."

Em smiled at him with a little dip of her head. Again her heart pounded, thrilled to hear aloud his plan to court her properly. Her mind seemed to spin and she fought the urge to dance around like a little girl. Just hearing him say the words 'courtin' purposes' and 'talking to your Papa' seemed to validate her own feelings. She breathed a silent prayer of thanks to God that she had not been completely errant in allowing her heart to love this man.

Plans for Emma

Preston was still talking, seeming to need to empty his heart to her and she tried hard to refocus on his words. "...I tell you it was like one of them Old Testament men, I just fell on my knees right there on the loggin' road. Now that sounds foolish, don't it?"

Emma felt an overwhelming compassion for this man. Even knowing he'd walked an aisle and been baptized, she had wondered about his relationship with the Lord and had prayed if he wasn't already a true believer in Jesus Christ that he would come to believe soon. Both Papa and Mama's teaching was very clear, and they'd shown each of their children where the Bible taught that you should never form close relationships with anyone who did not share your faith. Now she breathed a one word prayer of thanks to know that Preston had the kind of relationship with the Lord that could cripple his spirit with conviction.

"Preston every Sunday since we started talkin' here at the creek, I watch the door at our little church and think I'll see you Langfordin' through it. And when I don't see you, I'm awfully disappointed. But to hear of you humblin' yourself before God – that's a far greater gift than gettin' to see you for an hour or two on a Sunday morning."

Preston realized he'd been twisting his hat round and round and forced it down on his head. He took a deep breath to clear the emotion that fogged his thoughts. "Thank you Em."

"Well, did you get things worked out with the Lord? Do you expect you'll be able to sit through preachin' now?"

The slight smile that tugged at the corner of her pink lips told him this was her turn to do the teasing. Yet somehow he knew that there was no mockery in her spirit.

With a grin he started to retort but thought again. Instead, he answered from the humility he'd learned against the cold earth yesterday. "I don't rightly know Em. I do know that I've got to keep talkin' to him and learnin' about his commandments."

"How will you ever learn if you don't hear? The Bible says something like that, don't it?"

"Yeah, I reckon it does, but I think that's for people that don't believe yet. And Em, I do believe. Like I've told you, I asked Jesus Christ to forgive me of my sins years ago, and I know that he answered that prayer. I've about let myself get side-tracked. But what I learned yesterday was that God's not gone anywhere. He's still right there waitin' for me to come back."

"You better be careful Preston Langford, you get to preaching like that and we're liable to have a shoutin' right here at the creek."

Preston smiled and wondered if this girl would always be able to bring laughter to his heart even in the face of the most serious subjects. There was no question that touching her was forbidden, but right now his arms ached to hug her. Shaking his head to clear that thought away, he tipped his hat and bowed ever so slightly. "Have yourself a good day Miss Em. I'll be gettin' on toward Sunbright now."

Emma watched the wagon disappear over the next hill, the same way she so often did lately. She felt a tugging at her heart and an urge to run after the heavy load. *Lord, I was just talkin' to you yesterday about bein' a little more serious and now Preston's come with this very serious subject. I know you were prodding me yesterday even as you were dealing with his heart, weren't you? And I was sad that I hadn't seen Preston at church. Turns out you knew what you were doin' again. When will my faith ever be strong enough?*

She turned toward the farm, "Come on Ruff, bring the sheep."

Chapter 10

Saturday was one of those perfect autumn days. After some strong winds, the hardwoods were almost bare now but today the sky was the brightest blue and the sun reached down into every crevice of the woods. The mules seemed to have more energy than they'd shown in months and the slightest cluck would set them trotting out with their loads. Preston's days were no different on Saturday than any other day of the week except for a little earlier quittin' time. The triangle clinked to start the morning at five then he sat at the rough board table and shoveled in a mountain of sausage gravy, eggs and biscuits. Some of the men climbed aboard the empty wagons to ride out to the cutting areas while others positioned themselves to hew out the square crossties. The tall trees swayed in the light wind with a few stubborn leaves rustling at the top. The mood was quiet and some of the men seemed to move a little slower in the cooler weather yet Preston swung his broad axe with great vigor for despite the sameness of the day, tonight would be different. Emma's invitation to the singing was unmistakable, even though he'd never gotten around to the part that he asked if he was supposed to be taking her there.

She'll be there. And I'll be there. Maybe I can even manage to sit with her. It won't be like a Sunday morning preaching, all the young folks will sit together.

As he knelt onto one knee to smooth the side of the tie he was working on, he purposely tried to redirect his thoughts back toward prayer. He'd prayed all week and rehearsed verses he'd memorized through the years for there was neither time nor coal oil provided for a logger to read at night. As with most of his days lately, the beautiful Saturday passed in no time with prayer and planning.

Several of the boys cleaned themselves up and headed out after the animals were put away and supper eaten. Preston looked around, wondering if he would be sharing the road to the Jonesville church with any of his logging buddies. But he didn't ask them. He didn't want to answer their questions about who was drawing this almost surly, quiet boy out on a Saturday night. Early in his time in The Flat Woods, Preston had been invited to drink with some of the men or play cards in the cook camp where there was a big fireplace that would offer both warmth and light. After he said no a few times, they stopped asking and came to think of him as a loner who didn't want their company. Preston cared little because somehow he'd found no attraction to their activities and now he realized that he was far more interested in the church singing than playing cards.

The sun hung low as Preston made his way back down the logging road he'd walked out of just a couple of hours before. When he reached the wide dirt road, there were already groups of people walking toward the church and an occasional wagon carrying a family. Preston fell in with the traffic and listened to their conversations hoping to learn a little about the people of the Jonesville Baptist Church. He was surprised by how full the road was and asked someone along the way if everyone was going to the singing.

"Oh yes," answered a fair-skinned girl wrapped up snug in a blue cape and walking with two boys he learned were her brothers. "Everyone in Jonesville and Roslin will be here tonight. It will be great fun and there'll be cider and sandwiches afterward. I saw Mr. Ashburn pass with his wagon loaded down with food. Mrs. Ashburn is the best cook in the church."

It turned out the pale girl knew what she was talking about. As Preston approached the church house he could see little hope to even get inside the doors. Makeshift tables had been setup on wooden trestles and food was piled on them from one end to the other. A big fire was roaring in the

Plans for Emma

corner of the yard and it seemed a very popular place as people cooled down after their long walks.

Preston had a flash of fear that he would never even find Emma among all these people. However, that was soon laid to rest when the England wagon pulled in and he saw Emma hopping off with her sisters to unload their contribution to the evening's refreshments. He smiled when he saw that she too was searching the crowd for a particular face. Their eyes met and they nodded an acknowledgment. Emma turned to her chore and Preston tried to make small talk with boys around him.

Emma's face heated the moment she spotted Preston in the crowd. She ducked her head, knowing the smile she could not contain would betray the secret she carried. *Lord, how will I get through this night without the whole community knowing what I'm thinking?* She tried to busy her hands hoping her mind would follow suit but she dared not speak anyone's name for fear she would say "Preston" instead.

The little sanctuary bulged with bodies as the pianist struck a chord to begin the first songs. Preston managed to get inside but he had less than twelve inches of board underfoot, and there was no chance of a seat on the bench near Emma. Although some of the music was new to him, Preston joined his rich bass voice in the old songs he'd heard his whole life and the joy of the evening was unmistakable. He focused his eyes on the song leader but kept noticing Emma's profile. *Is she looking this way?* His heart thrilled to hope that she was as eager as he was to catch a glimpse of her.

After an hour of lively music, the group spilled outside and found cookies and hot cider, sandwiches and coffee waiting. Emma and her younger sister found him with a group near the big fire. Everyone in the group seemed to know one another and no one bothered to make introductions so it took a few minutes for Preston to figure out the sister was Almeta. He then placed her by the stories Emma had told him about her. They called her Metie and she

65

was a bright spot on the darkest days. She was a dreamer and could spin a story from her dreams that would mesmerize you. Preston hoped to hear the little girl talk but found she was pretty shy among all the older kids. Still, she stood by Emma wearing a sweet smile as tales of hard work in the harvest and longing for new dresses swirled around her.

"Mr. Langford, I'm glad to see you here tonight," Emma addressed him for the first time in the group. "Did you bring any other boys from the logging camp with you?"

Despite her racing heart, Emma managed to tease him again and he made a mock-angry face at her for just an instant. "No Ma'am, came alone tonight."

Sarah and Mary Nichols stood beside Emma and giggled as they looked over the newcomer. "Emma, we didn't know you had friends in the logging camp," Sarah whispered.

Emma restrained herself from rolling her eyes. All through school she'd felt these twins were some of the silliest girls she'd ever met. In the mountain jargon they were called "Surry and Murry" and were seldom seen alone. She'd never known them to be unkind, but they were quite adept at making Emma feel uncomfortable.

Finally she managed a response, "Surry, I've met Mister Langford a few times. I wouldn't say I have friends in the camp."

Mary planted an elbow in her sister's side causing new giggles to erupt and Preston's face to blush deep crimson.

He smiled at the silly girls and wished he could talk to Emma alone.

The sisters seemed intent on drawing him into their evening fun. "Did she say your name's Preston? I like that, it sounds strong somehow, don't you think so Murry?"

Mary wagged her head in agreement while flashing a toothy smile. "Surry, I ain't seen him in church, have you?"

Emma drew a quick breath and looked hard at Mary.

"No Murry, I guess he's been attendin' somewheres else. Maybe you're considerin' a change now Preston. What do you think?"

Plans for Emma

"Huh-hmm." Preston cleared his throat trying to find the right answer. "Well everybody is sure friendly here. You've all welcomed me like a regular tonight. That does make a feller think." He was well aware that Emma watched him as much as Sarah and Mary and he looked straight into her eyes as he smiled.

A million thoughts raced through Emma's mind, there were so many things she wanted to say to him. She forced herself to take a deep breath as she said, "Well we'd sure like to see you in service tomorrow; the church would love to have more people coming out of The Flat Woods to services. You're all welcome here you know." A chorus of voices echoed the invitation with 'oh yeah,' and 'we sure would. '

Mary and Sarah moved away from the group and Emma heard them giggling with other friends. Emma's eyes cut toward them and she bit back the jealousy that boiled up in her stomach. She couldn't help but wonder if Preston would be coming to services tomorrow to see Mary and Sarah. They were more fun than her and of course Preston wouldn't know they were never seen apart. Maybe he was thinking about which one of the girls he might marry.

Emma's eyes locked with Preston for a second before she had to turn to answer a question from another part of the crowd. The friends and neighbors kept her talking and every time she glanced back toward Preston, someone else called on her. Singings were no place for long, private talks and Emma realized how spoiled she was to their time at the creek when no one interrupted and when there were no other girls vying for his attention. Finally, Jane called her girls to help at the food table and Metie started off ahead of her sister.

Before she stepped from the group, she did manage a quiet invitation. "I hope we'll see some of you loggers in preaching service tomorrow."

Preston watched as Emma walked toward the food table. She went straight to a somewhat heavy woman with bits of gray at her temples. He was struck by the familiar and pleasant look this older woman carried and knew right away that she must be Em's mother. *Is that what she will look like when we are old?*

Short snips of chatter were all the time he got from Emma all evening. He was disappointed but not surprised, nor was he angry with her for he had no permission to visit with her particularly. Still he felt much closer to his Em as he walked back through the narrow trail and thought over the events of the evening. Only as he headed back up the road and was joined by two other boys from the camp did he realize he would have company on the walk home. He preferred to be alone with his thoughts and dropped a pace behind them as he thought over the evening. The loggers didn't seem to miss him as they talked of one girl and then another that they'd visited with tonight. Preston kept one ear open lest they mention Emma for he knew he'd leap to defend her if anything amiss was said.

The next day, the Sunday morning crowd was much smaller and Preston couldn't stop the sigh of relief when he saw it. The Englands were already seated as he stood shaking the preacher's hand beside the door.

"Good morning, and welcome to you. I'm Bill Franklin, I'll be preaching today."

Preston gave the proffered hand a firm shake, "Morning, I'm glad to be here. Name's Preston Langford."

"Well Preston, where are you from?"

"I was raised most of my life in Glades. I'm working in The Flat Woods now, live at the camp there."

"Fine, that's just fine. Glad you could make it in."

He stepped out of the doorway to allow others into the warm building and surveyed the seating. Choosing a bench near the back, he sat along the wall making sure there was still room for a family to fill the rest of the space. Several men made their way over to shake his hand and a couple of the boys he'd met at the singing thumped his shoulder or waved from across the aisle. Preston already felt welcome in the little church and regretted he'd taken so long to attend.

Plans for Emma

Emma had been watching the doorway for a quarter of an hour which felt like a week when she caught a glimpse of the dark head as he bowed to speak to the shorter preacher. Her breath caught in her throat and Jane turned to ensure she wasn't choking. Emma brought her handkerchief to her mouth and closed her eyes with a little cough in an attempt to cover her excitement. *You mustn't look Mama in the eye, she can read you like a book.*

Jane smiled at her daughter and darted a quick glance to the doorway.

Emma watched as her Papa approached Preston. *There's no time for him to ask now, is there? But surely I'll know before dinner whether Papa will allow him to call on me. Lord, please give him the words and open Papa's heart to this man that you've put in my path.*

"Mornin' son, I'm Tom England. Wanted to welcome you to the church. Preacher said you're one of the loggers?"

Preston took a deep breath when he heard the name. Last night he'd asked one boy to point out Emma's father to him, but in the dim light and crowded space he hadn't been able to make out much about him. He looked into eyes that seemed to bore straight into his soul. All of a sudden Preston Langford felt like a lying criminal. He was so overwhelmed by guilt at having met Em at the creek without her father's knowledge that he almost choked as he tried to utter a polite greeting. With a firm shake of his hand Mister England was gone.

As he watched the straight back of this man he'd so longed to meet slip into the pew beside his family, Preston resolved to speak to him as soon as possible.

Do I tell him we've been talkin' regular at the creek? No! He'd never let me court her if he thought we'd been sneaking around. How will I ever make him believe me to be an honorable man? But would it be dishonest not to tell him? Oh Lord, I need you to give me the words.

The congregation stood around Preston and jolted him back to the present. He mechanically went through the songs then sat and tried to give his full attention to Preacher

Franklin. However, as he stepped out of the church house, he was already trying to remember the subject of the sermon.

Several people spoke to him, one man invited him home for dinner and Preston was trying to give a polite refusal when he saw a blushing teenaged girl watching along with the woman he assumed was the man's wife. He headed out of the yard stopping to glance back toward Emma from the road's edge. She was watching him from the porch and her gloved hand came up in a tentative wave as he turned back toward the road.

Lord, why didn't I ask the man today? Surely he wouldn't refuse us. Maybe he doesn't even know we've been talking. Lord, I feel so ashamed, like I've dishonored this angel that I believe you've sent me for a wife. How can I redeem myself to you and to her father?

By the time Preston arrived back at the bunkhouse he could scarcely drag himself to his bunk. He tumbled in still wearing his coat and prayed himself to sleep.

Emma felt a little dazed, like the time she'd fallen from the hay loft and had to lie still on the hard ground until her breathe came back to her. She looked around, as though the man she'd just seen walk away was some stranger. She felt sure Preston was still in the yard somewhere, maybe talking with Papa right now. No, she looked again at the straight back and tattered hat that she'd memorized as she watched it driving away from the creek time after time. She knew this side of him better than any other and there was no mistake that it was Preston Langford walking away from her. *Lord, did he change his mind? Oh, he doesn't want to court me after all. Is he not the honorable man I believed him to be?* She shook away the thought and excused herself from the porch to sit in the family's wagon. She'd go to the creek tomorrow and she was sure he would explain everything – or if he didn't meet her there then she'd know he simply changed his mind about her.

The tinkling triangle announced supper as Preston opened his eyes. He felt like he'd taken a beating and he wanted nothing more than to lie still, but his rumbling stomach urged him to make his way toward the grub line. No one spoke to

Plans for Emma

him; something in his look warned away the teasing voices that ordinarily would have haunted him. After supper he returned to his bunk and, removing his best coat and shirt that he intended to save for church meetings, he went to bed and slept fitfully till the five o'clock alarm.

It was raining regularly and the weather was cooler each day. It was getting hard to explain daily trips to the creek but Emma managed to make it there everyday. However, she did not find Preston there. By the third day, she'd dedicated the time she spent walking down the hill to prayer and she found she truly enjoyed it. *Lord, maybe it's better to talk to you here at the creek than to Preston anyway. I guess he won't be back; like Lena said, he was just passing through. Can you help me to understand why I was so convinced that you had sent him to me? Tomorrow I won't even bring the sheep down.*

There were no ties for Preston to haul until Thursday and he came close to asking to be excused from the load. In the end, he found he couldn't resist the opportunity to at least see Emma from a distance, maybe he would only see their farmstead sitting high on the hill.

There was no sign of the wooly sheep at the creek and while he slowed his team for the crossing and looked longingly at the creekside that now held so many fond memories, he allowed the mules to continue walking and he idled his way to the railhead. Everything seemed to be lackadaisical in Preston's head right now. He was so overwhelmed with guilt that he wasn't even praying.

As he veered onto the turnpike a ray of sunshine broke through the heavy autumn clouds. It rested on Preston's hands and began to warm them through his thick leather gloves. Somehow Preston felt comforted by this warmth and slipped the glove from his right hand. His eyes traveled up to the cloud cover somehow trying to peer through to heaven. Then he remembered that God had not abandoned him when he refused to read his Bible or attend preaching or fellowship with God's people. And he knew that God had not abandoned him now. He opened his heart to pray and as he prayed God spoke to his heart.

He didn't realize how far he'd driven until he heard the train's loud whistle. Preston straightened himself from the hunched position he always assumed when driving. "Girls did I give you water on this whole trip? I don't remember it."

Reaching for his bag lunch, he found it practically empty and said aloud to the team, "Reckon when I ate that? Don't remember that either. Well girls you are looking pretty pert so I guess I didn't mistreat you too bad. Still, it's late, I guess that whistle is the train that should have taken this load. Nothing to do about it now, is there? No use in running you to death to catch a speeding freight train. But I feel like I've had a whole revival preached in my head while we've been driving so I guess it was reasonably good time spent."

Things did look brighter for him and now he felt he had a plan. He resolved not to be beaten down by feelings of guilt and shame. He would confess his feelings to Mr. England and would beg for an opportunity to properly court his daughter as they looked toward marriage.

He checked in with the freight master, unhooked the team from their heavy load and walked them a few hundred yards down the dirt road to the livery stable. It felt good to stretch legs that had been folded up in the cramped wagon seat all day. His mules clearly felt the same way about their own freedom from the wagon and they stomped and rattled the harness with every step. Preston paid them no heed and spoke little with the stable boy. He picked up the key to his room and went directly to bed without even waiting for a meal. Sleep came quickly and he rested better than he had in days for a peace returned to his heart during today's drive. He'd committed to God that he would talk with Tom England right away and he felt certain God would bless his obedience. There was no longer a sense of shame or guilt in his heart.

By Saturday Jane had noticed Emma growing quieter. "Em, what have you got on your mind?"

Plans for Emma

"Hmm?" Emma stood at the tall kitchen work table chopping cabbage and seemed engrossed in the work. "Child, that vegetable don't take half your mind. Where is the rest of it?"

"Oh, Mama, I'm sorry I didn't catch what you were sayin' to me."

Jane chuckled as she took her daughter by the shoulder and turned her so she could look into her eyes. "That's what I was saying, that you aren't really here. You haven't been down the hill all week and I think those walks were doin' you good. Why don't you let me finish that choppin' and you walk down to the big rock. Some air will clear your head. When you get back maybe we can talk."

Emma smiled, "Mama how do you always know just what we need?"

"I don't really know but I do love each of you and I guess the good Lord gives a mama a little help."

"Thank you, I will take that walk."

"Get your shawl, it's pretty nippy out there."

Emma grabbed the knitted wool wrap with one hand as she hurried out the back door.

She meandered down the hill but instead of going all the way to the road and the creek she veered onto a well-worn path that led to a big rock partially over-hanging the roadway. This was a favorite spot for the family affording a great view of the distant mountains on one side and the bubbling creek on the other. Emma sank down with her heavy skirts billowing around her and found herself staring down at the creek.

Her mind conjured memories and images of her friend. She smiled as she remembered Preston's teasing and the funny way his eyes squinted when he laughed with her. Taking a deep breath she reached out to God.

Lord, I'm trying to trust in you but it really hurts right now. Is he gone from me? It seemed so clear when he expressed a need to be in church and that he had really humbled himself before you. Why didn't he ask Papa? When he finally got to church with us, why would he just leave?

She looked down the road, her eyes searching for the loaded wagon but finding only a gray horizon. She stared at that road until the cold seeped up from the familiar rock and stiffened her legs. Pushing herself up with her hands, she dusted off her skirt and turned toward home with no more answers than she'd come with but still resolved to trust in God despite the ache in her heart.

Chapter 11

Sunday morning was so cold there was a thin sheet of ice on the top of the water bucket. There were only a handful of the men moving about as Preston stirred up the fire and set the copper wash-pan on the iron stove to warm the icy water. He thought to himself, *The good thing about cold mornings is they make a fella' get to movin' faster.*

The brisk wind smacked at skin sensitive from this morning's shave as his long stride covered the few paces to the kitchen's back door. He knew he could get a cup of coffee to fortify him against the walk to Jonesville. The homey smell that greeted him at the door brought a smile and the threat of a tear as he remembered his mother as well as the dreams he now had of his own household with Emma at home in the kitchen.

"Mornin' Mrs. Goodell, any chance a cold fella could get a hot cup of coffee?"

She was always a little sharp of tongue but Preston was kind to the old cook and she generally helped him out if she could.

"I reckon you can have a cup if you can he'p yourself. I ain't got time to be waitin' on nobody."

Preston smiled as he lifted the heavy coffee pot from the back of the stove. It was strong and this morning he was glad of it.

"What're you about this morning Preston?" Mrs. Goodell didn't look at him as she continued her work. She already had a row of pans filled with dough and sitting near the iron stove to rise. Her hands were still covered in flour as she patted out dozens of biscuits to feed the loggers. "Perty early for a young man to be up on a Sunday mornin' and I don't reckon you gotta feed the stock, do ya'?"

"No Ma'am, I'm a'goin' to church. Gonna walk to Jonesville so it takes me a little bit to get there."

"Jonesville? Well I reckon there's a girl at the root of this. That's the one reason a boy like you'd walk that fur on a mornin' like this."

Preston hung his head for a minute as he pondered how to explain it to her. He was certain that he must explain. "Well now, that's how it started but then the good Lord got ahold of me and made me to understand that I had to be in his house on account of him or else nothing good would come with that girl."

Mrs. Goodell paused in her biscuit-making and looked him straight in the eye. "I hope that girl knows what she's got."

He took a last sip of the coffee in such a big gulp he got a bite of grounds in his mouth. He set the cup in the deep wash tub and pulled his hat down on his head. "Thank you Mrs. Goodell."

She shoved a handful of bacon toward him and winked as he stepped out the door.

Emma pulled from her hair the thick woolen rags Mama had wound through it the night before. After she returned from her walk Mama spent most of the evening talking with her but never asked a single serious question. She'd helped Emma wash her hair in rainwater they'd caught in the big wooden barrels and warmed on the kitchen stove. Then brushing the long brown tresses just like Emma was a little girl, she parted out thick sections and wound them with the rags. Now they revealed volumes of loose curls and Emma couldn't help smiling as she remembered how beautiful the curls had made her feel when she was younger. She drew them up into a loose bun at the crown of her head. She was finishing pinning a few free strands when Lena stepped into the doorway.

"Are you still working on your hair? My goodness, me and Mama have breakfast on the table and we're waitin' on you."

Plans for Emma

"Oh Lena, I didn't realize it had gotten so late. Mama pampered me so last night that I'm still bein' lazy this morning. I'll have to get the milking done so I will skip breakfast I guess."

"Metie's done the milkin'. Took her twice as long as it does you, but there's fresh milk on the table and that's all that matters."

"Oh, thank you – or I guess I'll have to thank Metie. There was a mud stain on the hem of my Sunday dress and it took forever to get out. Here, will you pin these last bits behind?"

Lena obliged with a deep sigh, "There's mud everywhere Em, why did you waste your time on that stain?"

"Mama always says God deserves our best."

"I'm thinking it ain't God your doin' this for."

Emma smiled as she stood to follow Lena downstairs.

She chastised herself as they went, *Lord, I guess she's right. Am I tryin' to win this man with my looks now? Please forgive my vanity.*

The children were already seated with Papa at the head of the table when the girls made it into the kitchen. Jane looked directly into Emma's eyes fearing she was not well.

"Em, you had me worried. Are you feeling well?"

"Oh yes, Mama, I'm fine. Just lost track of the time, that's all."

"Well you are dressed for church so I guess you're feeling well enough to go?"

"Yes, of course I'm going to church. Metie, thank you for taking care of the milkin' for me."

Almeta was already reaching for the gravy, "Well it's perty cold out there but we have to help each other out, don't we?"

The whole family smiled at her echoing the lesson Jane had taught them again and again.

Tom hadn't slowed his eating when Emma and Lena joined them. "We've already returned thanks so you'll need to pray for your food yourselves."

Emma nodded her head and bowed it to say a silent prayer over the food, and the day. *Lord God, thank you for these blessings and please bless Preston Langford this morning. Lead him to the preaching service I pray. Amen.*

Preston arrived at the little whitewashed church along with a few other folks on foot and one wagon loaded with a family. The stove was already heating the small space and despite the overcast day the oil lamp on the lectern cast a golden glow around the room. The lamps along the wall were still dark to conserve the precious coal oil until they just had to be lit.

Preston greeted the men who milled around the warm stove but took his seat straight away and listened to the talk about the community.

This week there would be no preacher as he was elsewhere on his circuit. Benjamin Nichols would be leading the prayer meeting. Preston didn't mind these "off" weeks when a layman led the service. Others could deliver God's word besides the men who spent their time riding a horse from one community to another to preach, marry and bury folks. Often the humility and sincerity of these laymen allowed them to deliver the very best sermons.

Each time the swollen door was yanked open Preston looked hoping to see the Englands coming in. When he saw little Bessie toddle through the door holding Almeta's hand, he moved to take a spot around the stove in order to talk with Mr. England.

He had been watching Tom England every chance he got and he'd come to understand that he always looked a little gruff. However, the congregation seemed to care a great deal about the whole England family so Preston was sure Emma's father had a good heart. He was banking on a deep kindness as he prepared to ask the man if he could court his daughter.

He nodded along with the other men as Tom reached his calloused hands over the stove's heat. There seemed to be little chance to get a conversation with him as everyone asked

Plans for Emma

about the sheep, whether he'd butchered a hog yet and if he thought it was going to be a bitter cold winter.

Tom recognized the young logger and offered his hand to him, "Name was Langford, right?"

"Yes sir, Preston Langford."

"How's the loggin' business? Blades sharp and trees straight?"

Preston smiled, thankful that Mr. England sought to speak to him on a comfortable subject. "Yes'sir, but it shore is gettin' cold when I have to drive."

"Drive? You have to take the loads to the railroad? You take 'em to Sunbright or Monterey?"

"Most of 'em go to Sunbright. In fact, I've never been to Monterey. That railroad is newer, ain't it?"

"Yeah, I reckon it is. Guess it came through there a little over ten years ago."

Preston shook his head acknowledging the fact while his mind looked for a way to talk about Emma instead of logging and railroads.

Tom continued, "Guess drivin' the team is a pretty good job."

"Well, everybody wants to drive in the spring and the fall but nobody wants to climb up on that big load when it's hot, raining or freezin' cold. This time of year can go either way. November's got sunshine and rain, don't it?"

Tom took a deep breath as he wagged his head, "Yep, you can count on any kind of weather this month. Did you learn to drive a team from your Pa?"

Preston studied the ragged hat he was rotating round and round in his hands. "No sir, lost my pa when I was real young. My growin' up years were spent working on another man's farm. He only kept a pair of buggy horses and I never got to drive them. But you learn pretty fast when you've got to wrestle four-up pulling the big loads of cross ties."

"I reckon you do. I bet your pa would be proud if he could see that you've learned so much."

Preston beamed and hoped that Tom England might be proud of him too. Encouraged by the compassionate words, he opened his mouth to make his request. But he'd waited too long and Brother Nichols began calling the congregation to order. He returned to his seat on the end of the wooden pew and forced himself to watch the music leader instead of Emma.

Emma refused to turn her head to see the handsome logger sitting behind her. She chewed her bottom lip and bounced her knee. Gip thought the bouncing was for his benefit and giggled aloud with joy. "Shhh, Gip you must be quiet during preaching," Emma cautioned him and tried to stop her leg's movement. Her heart pounded and her palms sweated and it all served to anger her greatly.

With the final 'Amens' Preston again looked for a chance to talk with Mr. England. However, a rosy faced lady positioned herself between Preston and Tom as she questioned Preston about his family and his future. Preston was trying hard to be kind to her but he saw right away that the Englands were wasting little time visiting on the cold day. They were already out of the church yard by the time he reached the porch.

As he walked home he couldn't help but ask the Lord, why he was never able to speak to Tom England about Emma. He was desperate to talk with her; it had now been several days since he'd even been able to say hello to her at the creek.

Lord, is this just me being fearful or are you making me wait?

Somehow Preston knew the answer even as he formed the question in his head. Yes, God was restraining him and God didn't do anything without a purpose.

Okay, your timing is always right. I guess I'm not ready to marry anyway, am I? I've been a'savin' everything I could from logging and I'm getting a pretty good nest egg. Guess I'll need to think about a place for me and Em to live, probably need to work on buying a farm but where will I ever get enough money together for that?

Plans for Emma

He stopped. Once again, standing among scrub timber left by the logging crew he spoke aloud to himself, "Preston you're talking foolishness. Here you are planning on buying a farm and you've not even got the right to call on her yet."

As he started walking again, he tried to silence his thoughts, *And you might be a little crazy too – talking to yourself in the empty woods.*

The winter of 1903 started out bitter cold and so wet nothing could dry out between rains. It snowed then warmed, melting the snow into a muddy mess that the loggers had to wade through in order to continue their work. Preston laid the logs he was hewing up on three cross pieces for support and as he chipped away the round sides of the log, it sank deeper and deeper in the mud and the gritty water splashed up dulling his blade. All around him the other hewers cursed and complained. Then they marveled as Preston went again and again to the grinding wheel to sharpen his blade without uttering a word of complaint.

He heard the chatter around him, "Somethin's happened to Langford. He never was one to make much of a fuss but now nothing seems to rattle him."

Still there were loads to drive to Sunbright but Emma was never at the creek now. Preston understood there was no excuse to take the sheep down the hill when it rained about every day and every trough, gulley and mudhole was filled with water. Each time he passed the England farm, he watched the house passing by him. He tried to imagine what she was doing each day. Winter was hard on a farm and he knew that with no older brothers Emma's days would be even harder. He also knew from his own sisters that she would fill idle hours with needle work and reading. He was sure she was a good reader, although he wasn't quite sure why he thought that.

He passed the long hours on the road in prayer and with each trip he felt even closer to the Lord. He had no doubt at all that God was working out a plan for him and Emma.

For weeks he walked every Sunday to the little Jonesville church. Despite Preston's quiet disposition, everyone soon knew his name as well as critical facts about him. Most of the mothers of older girls thought the most important fact was that he was unattached. The lady with the rosy round cheeks always made a point to speak to him and he learned that her daughter Treva was a fine cook and kind soul despite her bucked teeth. He was invited to enjoy roasted deer that Treva cooked just for him. Preston figured out the woman was working to make a match between him and her daughter but he could find no way to excuse himself without being impolite. As he climbed up on the back of their wagon beside Treva, he could feel Emma's eyes glued to his back. *Lord, please don't let her see this and give up on me.*

Emma did see Preston driving away in the Hall wagon, seated beside Treva. Hot tears stung her eyes and she bit her lip to hold them back. *Lord, I don't understand.* It was her most common prayer these days.

The venison roast was very good and Preston appreciated a meal around a family table. The Halls had only the one daughter who was still at home and she sat across from Preston saying very little and refusing to look him in the eye. Mister Hall did not hesitate in making his wife's plan clear. Preston gulped down the food on his plate and refused any more. "I'll have to head on back to the camp or I'll be walkin' after dark. Mighty cold when the sun goes down these days, ain't it?"

He tried to be as kind as possible when he praised the meal and said his good-byes. He warned himself as he walked away, *You'll be findin' a way to say "no" the next time won't you Preston?*

Preston always talked with Mr. England as all the men huddled around the church's pot-bellied stove talked among themselves. Then at long last he found both the right time and the courage to speak to him about Emma. It was the end of the Sunday service when the preacher had been present. A cold wind crept into every crack in the church and people

Plans for Emma

drew their coats up and buttoned them tight. As the congregation stepped out the front door, Preston discovered he was walking out of the door beside Tom while the rest of the Englands hurried ahead and climbed onto the wagon to pull heavy blankets around them.

"Mr. England, I've been a'wantin' to talk to you about your daughter."

Tom England's eyebrows dipped low over his eyes and his ever-present frown deepened. "Which one?"

"Emma."

"Emma's a fine girl."

"Yes sir, I recognize that. Fact is, I admire her a great deal and would like to ask your permission to call on her."

Tom looked him straight in the eye, then his eyes travelled over the young man seeming to assess him from head to toe and Preston felt a little like a piece of livestock for sale.

"Word is you've been callin' on Treva Hall. How many girls you wantin' to court?"

Preston took a quick breath, "Oh no sir. I'm not callin' on Miss Hall. No, no. Mrs. Hall insisted I eat dinner with them one Sunday and I couldn't find a good way not to. Oh no, I'm sure not courtin' anybody else."

A quick smile flickered across Tom's lips before he resumed his scowl. He knew Bertha Hall and wasn't surprised she was at the center of both the talk and the visit.

It was a long moment before he looked straight into Prestons eyes and said, "Langford, you're a good boy and I'm tickled to have you at church with us. But I don't believe you can court my girl."

Tom stepped away from Preston indicating the finality of his answer. Preston's lungs screamed for air and he realized he'd been holding his breath. He watched the lanky frame climb onto the wagon as though it were inches from the ground, grabbing the waiting reins in a single smooth movement. "Gy'up", Tom called to his faithful horses that were ready to move after waiting in the cold.

As the wagon pulled away, his eyes met Emma's as she sat in the bed of the wagon, now facing him. He knew she could read the disappointment on his face and he was sure she would know he had at last talked to her father. Emma's face fell then she tore her eyes from his gaze and closed them. Preston wasn't sure if she'd turned to prayer or if she was crying. He wondered if she would ever look at him again, much less grant him the beautiful, infectious smile he'd enjoyed by the creekside.

He stood immobilized until the wagon disappeared, then with his head down and shoulders slumped he began walking down the turnpike kicking at every rock and stick in his path. Saddness turned to anger and hot breath spewed from his nostrils. *What right has he got to judge me not good enough for his daughter?*

The icy wind reached down his collar and he jerked his head up to face his attacker. Alone in the woods he calmed. "He has every right you fool. And why shouldn't he refuse you? What have you got to offer a girl like Emma England? Look at the fine farm they have up on that hill. They've got sheep and cattle and horses and you've got nothing but calluses and a dull axe."

He felt like a snake slithering over the frosty ground as he made his way back to the camp.

Jane England had the eyes of a hunting falcon and she missed little that happened with her family. "That looked like a serious talk young Preston Langford was having with you Tom," she asked as they stood right inside the back door of their house, peeling off layers of scarves, wraps and sweaters. Emma had volunteered to unhitch the team while Almeta and Bessie took little Leonard upstairs for a much needed nap. Emma stepped onto the back porch and caught the end of her mother's question. She would never want to eavesdrop on her parents but she couldn't make herself move away.

"Yeah, he asked about courting Emma," Tom answered.

"Well that couldn't have been much of a shock to you. They can't keep their eyes off each other in church. I've been

Plans for Emma

pretty surprised we didn't see him about more during the molassy stir offs and singin's and such.

"I don't reckon he knew about all that fellowshippin' since he ain't a real part of the Roslin community. He just works in that logging camp you know. Besides, I b'lieve he came to one of the singin's."

Jane stepped into the kitchen and stirred the fire in the cookstove. "I guess you're right, but that makes me realize we need to do a better job including the folks at the camp in the community."

Tom growled, "Why would you want to do that. Riff-raff. That's what the most of 'em are."

"What? Riff-raff? Why in this world would you say that."

"Well they wander from one camp to another, they drink and play cards and who knows what else."

"But I don't think Preston's like that. Why, he's been real faithful to church; he even comes when he knows the preacher won't be there. Course he's quiet but I imagine he'd talk more if you got to know him."

"Yeah but you know he's an orphan and he told me himself that he spent most of his growin' up years in another man's house. He was sent away from home to work on a farm."

"Oh that poor little boy."

"Little boy? He's a full grown man and stout as an ox. I hear that no one can match him splittin' ties."

"Well that's now. It sounds like he was just a little boy when he was sent away from his home. Lots of families have to do that in order to survive but I can't even imagine having one of my children away from home before they were full-grown."

Tom ignored her compassionate thoughts and went on with his own assessment of Preston Langford. "He's had little or no schoolin' either. Ben Nichols told me he asked Preston if he would read a few verses one day and Preston said he couldn't much read."

Jane dropped the spoon onto the waiting saucer and turned to her husband with a spark of fire in her eye; with one hand on her hip and the other laying out her points in the air she said, "Tom England, this is sounding to me like you are lookin' for a reason to reject this boy. Now who in this room has got much schoolin'? It's by the grace of God that me and you can read enough to get through the Bible and can cipher enough to keep account of the farm. And that's a blessing that none of our parents enjoyed. Why, your Grandpa Tom could barely count the chickens in the coup yet he bought this very farm and built the cabin that is the center of the very house we live in. Now, our life is not so bad and we've come from uneducated folk."

Tom crept toward the door hoping he could escape his wife's chastisement. Jane didn't often take to a subject with such passion but he knew from long experience that he would win no fight when she had that fire in her eyes.

"Tom, where are you going?"

"Don't know but I'm betting you make me ride over to that logging camp and bring the poor boy home with me."

Jane smiled, he always seemed to say something that quieted her tirades. "Well, I'm much more concerned with his spirit than his pocketbook or his education.

Tom nodded as he pushed open the back door where Emma dodged to keep from being hit.

"Oh Papa, I was coming in right now."

Tom took in the red eyes and nose, "You'd better get yourself in there, looks like the cold's about got you."

Emma walked straight to the big fireplace, still wrapped in her heavy woolen shawl. She couldn't believe what she'd heard and she was devastated that Papa was so against Preston Langford. But Mama had defended him and that warmed her heart.

Father in heaven, I've been so convinced that Preston Langford was the man you had prepared for me that it never occurred to me you wouldn't also be preparing my Papa to accept him. Now I need to ask for your intervention. I know that you would never want me to disobey

Plans for Emma

him so if Papa says 'no' then that's the end of Preston and me. It's the end of my dreams. Will there be someone else or will I end up an old maid?"

She could no longer hold back the wall of tears; her eyes darted from one corner to another searching for a private place to shed them. Seeing no good options she eased out the front door and off the porch. The front gate groaned its usual protest to moving in the cold as she swung it open and started down the hill.

Jane heard the squeaking gate and stepped into her front room to see if someone might be calling to share their Sunday dinner but saw only her daughter's back. She'd left her bonnet by the fireside and the bun of hair was fraying in the wind. Jane held herself back from chasing after the girl, realizing she must have discerned at least a part of her father's decision.

At the bottom of the hill lay the big flat rock they often visited. The children loved playing on it from the time they took their first steps. Now, as it overlooked the creek where Emma had built so many happy memories with Preston, she sought whatever comfort could be had in this familiar spot. The wind stung her face as it licked at the tears streaming down her cheeks. The creek's rushing water stopped her and she sank onto the rock as nature's melody calmed her.

Lord why? She asked the question again and again.

Why would you send this man into my life only to have Papa refuse him? Why Lord?

Did I misunderstand? Did you never intend us to marry?

She sniffed and waited. No answer came and while the tears stopped her heart still churned.

As she watched the turbulent waters below she took a deep breath and attempted to slow her racing heart.

Well one thing is for sure Emma Jane England. You are not doing anybody any good sneaking down to that creek. If Papa says 'no' then no more meetin's down there.

Her resolve was strong but somehow she felt her heart breaking anew.

Well it's not like you've even seen your beau down there for weeks and winter is comin' on fast.

A snapping stick broke her reverie and she jerked her head and saw her mama ambling down the hill. "Dinner's ready Em."

She nodded.

"I guess you know that Mr. Langford talked to your Papa this morning?"

Emma nodded again, her eyes fixed on the frothy water below.

"Were you expecting him to talk to your Papa? I guess I'm surprised this has upset you so badly."

She nodded.

Jane stood beside her seated daughter now and they stared down the hill together.

"I've talked to him, at the singin's and you know I first saw him down there at the creek."

Both women stared down the hill as though the young man might appear at the creekside even now.

"So you were expecting him to court you?"

Emma nodded. "Mama, I guess I had come to believe he was the one that God has for me. I never dreamed Papa would refuse to let him call. I guess God didn't send him to me after all."

Jane lifted her daughter to stand and face her, "Em, you keep listening to God. Just because he doesn't work things out exactly the way you expected doesn't mean he ain't workin' on them."

Emma cocked her head as she tried to understand the words.

Jane smiled and pulled her daughter close enough to wrap a bit of her own shawl around the shaking shoulders. "Keep praying Emma. You don't have to understand everything today. Me and Papa are always praying for you."

"Do you think Papa is hearing a different calling from the Lord?"

Plans for Emma

"I can't say. But I know for sure that God will work it all out in his perfect will." Jane started walking up the steep hill toward the house pulling Emma along with her.

All of a sudden Emma was exhausted and leaned against her mother. Her mind was still not at peace though she knew Mama had tried hard to calm her thoughts. Even as she complied with Mama's gentle urging to move, she struggled with her Lord.

Lord, how can two calls from you be in conflict? How can I honor my father when I can't see that he's honoring your will Lord? Am I misunderstanding – letting my heart pull me away from your will? Do I follow my heart or my Papa? I can't believe you'd call me to disobey him when your word has clearly taught me to honor him? Yet why do I feel so drawn to this man that Papa won't accept? Please show me the way.

Chapter 12

With the corn shocked, hay piled in the high barn lofts and hogs fat enough to slaughter, everyone knew that Charlie would soon be calling for his bride. The Englands watched their practical and serious Lena transform into a giddy bride-to-be. With every degree the temperature fell, she smiled more broadly. As she sat pulling ears from corn stalks with the rest of her family, she laughed and joked with them more than they'd ever seen.

"Lena, I sure hate to see you leave home, but it's a blessing to see you enjoying the fall so much," Jane said as her hands kept pulling and reaching for the next stalk.

Lena giggled. "Mama, I can't seem to help myself."

Tom was not enjoying either the work or the anticipation as much. "Hmmph, we'll see how giddy you are after a winter alone in Martha Washington. Next fall you'll be shuckin' your own corn, just you and Charlie."

Lena's happiness could not be marred by her father's mood, "I'm sure we'll be fine Papa."

She bit her lip to try to contain the smile as her eyes caught Emma's.

As expected, Sunday morning Charlie arrived while Tom was still milking and he entered the house with the steaming bucket in one hand and a new felt hat in the other.

Jane found she was not quite prepared for the sight. "Land sakes, Charlie Adams, you'll spill milk on your weddin' suit. Set it down here on the table real easy."

"Yes ma'am," Charlie grinned at Lena's mother while his eyes surveyed the room.

Jane knew what he was looking for, "She's expectin' you so it's taking her longer than usual to come downstairs. I don't suppose you want me to rush her, do you?"

Plans for Emma

Charlie ducked his head and began inspecting the band of his hat, "Oh no ma'am. She'll be along when she's ready, I'm sure."

Jane smiled at him and gave Metie a little push toward the stairs hoping she'd get the hint and run tell her older sister who was waiting.

While Jane got the breakfast meal on the table, Emma made quick work of plucking a chicken for the special wedding dinner they'd enjoy after church. With all of the excitement and extra kitchen work, they had to rush to get the younger children dressed before Tom had called them more than two or three times. Lena was permitted to ride ahead to church with Charlie, with Metie joining them for appearance sake.

Emma held Leonard close both for warmth and to try to contain his constant movements. As she sat with her back to the seat of the wagon, she watched the England farm grow smaller with each turn of the wagon's wheels. She couldn't help but wonder what thoughts were in Lena's mind. *Is she so consumed with thoughts of Charlie that she doesn't feel sad to leave our family and her home?*

However, no sooner had the thought entered her mind than she was thinking of Preston. She had to admit that if she ever had an opportunity even to ride on the wagon seat beside him that she would not be able to think of anything else - not even the home, parents and siblings she loved so much.

It would be hard not to see Leonard and Gip everyday. I'm so used to playing with them and trying to teach them little things like, say "bird", or stay out from under the cows feet that I just don't know what I would do with my time if it was me and Preston in our own home?

She felt her cheeks warm at the thought of keeping house with this man. *What does he eat? Could I ever cook to suit him? Could I make a home that he'd want to be in?*

She let out a soft sigh, *Foolish girl, you go from one kind of silliness to another. Papa has not blessed a courtship with Preston Langford so you have to stop your dreamin'.*

91

Shaking her head, Emma tried to turn her attention to the square blocks Leonard and Bessie were grasping and shaking at each other. "Block, Leonard, can you say that?"

When the Englands pulled into the church yard, a small crowd had formed around Lena and Charlie. All of the girls recognized that Lena had a new dress. Emma smiled, remembering that she and Lena had stripped every dogwood tree on the Eastern slope to dye the homespun fabric to what Lena considered the perfect blue. With her sharp tongue and dry humor, it wasn't often that Lena was the center of attention like this and it pleased Emma to watch.

Charlie too was obviously proud of his bride. He stood with a boy Emma did not recognize; shorter by a head than Charlie, he had a bright smile and light brown hair. However, the resemblance to the man who would be her brother-in-law was remarkable.

Jane also noticed the stranger and raised the question Emma wouldn't have dared to mention. "Tom, do you know the boy with Charlie there?"

Tom gave a nonchalant nod as he pulled the reins to stop his team. "Charlie said his brother would meet us at church. Name's Austin, that's what I think he said. Stout-lookin' boy, ain't he?"

Jane nodded and turned her attention to her little children. "Emma can you manage both of them if I keep hold of Gip?"

"Yes Mama, I'll be fine. Bessie, you sit still 'til I get Leonard down."

Tom looked to his wife, as though he was unaware that Emma was still sitting behind him. "Charlie says his brother's got a little place. It's just about five acres but it's all cleared. And you remember Charlie a'tellin' us that their Daddy was set on all his kids being able to read the word of God so this boy's bound to have some education. Might be a good one for our Em."

Plans for Emma

Emma's eyes popped open wide when she realized the direction of her father's thoughts. She jerked her head toward Mama hoping she would dissuade him.

Has Papa completely forgotten about my Preston? Does he think I could have forgotten him?

Jane looked long at Austin Adams before she responded to Tom, "Well, I'm sure he's a fine boy and I guess Emma will meet him today along with everyone else. Will he come home with us for dinner?"

Tom was wrapping the reins around the brake handle, "I don't know. Charlie didn't mention it. I think he may have stayed with his folks in Banner Springs last night. He turned up awful early at our place to have come all the way from Martha Washington, don't you think? Anyway, guess I'll ask the brother if he wants to eat with us. It'd be a good chance to get to know him and see if he'd be what we're looking for in a man for Em."

As the family unloaded the wagon, Emma's breath came in short gasps.

"Come here Leonard, take my hands." She held up her arms but her eyes watched Tom as he made his way slowly through the gathering crowd. She could hear his voice greeting first one and then another of their neighbors and church family. It was clear his path was pointed toward the newcomer who stood on the edge of the group alone but for the occasional welcoming handshake.

"I can't reach. Em can't reach you." Leonard's whine jerked Emma's head back to the wagon and she realized she stood two feet further from the wagon than her brother's stubby little arms could ever reach.

"Oh baby, Em's sorry. Here you go, I've got you now." Bessie thudded to the ground beside them.

"Bessie, you must be careful. That's a long drop for you."

"It din' look like you were gonna' get me down. What're you lookin' at? Is it Charlie's brother?"

93

Emma felt her cheeks warm and she dropped her head lower than necessary to answer Bessie. "I was just wonderin' where Papa was headed."

"How come? Din' you hear him tellin' Mama that he's gonna invite Charlie's brother to dinner?"

Emma's eyes darted from right to left hoping no one could hear Bessie's prattle. "Shh, we're goin' in church now so you've got to be quiet."

"Not till we get set down surely." Bessie continued to complain and Emma tried not to squeeze her little hand despite the band that constricted her own heart.

Her eyes scanned the group but there was no sign of Preston. *Well thank you Lord that Preston neither heard Bessie nor saw Papa making a bee-line for that boy. Would it hurt him as bad as it's hurtin' me thinking Papa's going to find me a different man?*

Emma seated her charges one on each side of her in the hard wooden pew. Then she closed her eyes and tried to pray – tried to will away the tears that threatened to spill. Finally the amens were said and Emma let out a relieved sigh hoping the family would quickly be home.

Everyone smiled as Brother Franklin stepped toward the family. He reached Tom with an outstretched hand and a light in his eyes. "Tom, that boy over there says he's got your blessin' to marry Lena. He ain't regular here so I can't say how honest he might be."

Both men grinned as Tom nodded to his would-be son-in-law. "Well, he showed up at one of the molassy stir-offs last fall and he's been comin' around ever since. So, I reckon I'm gonna' let 'em marry, if you're willing."

The preacher nodded. "Well my wife usually stands as witness, but you know she can't ride the circuit with me very often. Would you and Miz' Jane stand with 'em?"

Tom was reaching for Jane's arm as he answered, "Yep, we can do that."

The little church house was very quiet as the last folks left the yard and rattling wagons faded into the distance. Emma had her hands full when Mama handed baby Gip to her to

Plans for Emma

hold, and she still had Leonard and Bessie sitting on either side. She tried to peek out the nearest window, wondering if Preston had known what was happening and left already. She'd caught a quick glimpse of him when he arrived and took a seat right in front and across the aisle from her. She both loved and hated when he sat in front of her – she wanted to watch his every move but when she did, she usually couldn't remember much of what the preacher had said.

There was no sign of Preston in the little bit of yard she could see and she reminded herself there was no reason for him to stay and wait on her. Looking back at her sister, Emma had to take deep breaths to stay the tears welling in her eyes.

Emma watched as Lena and Charlie said the words that vowed they would love, honor and cherish each other for all of their days. She smiled with joy that her beloved sister had found someone to share her life with. Emma had never watched this ceremony as weddings of her church friends were usually held with just the preacher and his wife.

A tiny pang of jealousy bit at Emma's heart and it angered her that she could begrudge Lena any happiness or blessing. *Lord, please don't let me forget that you still have a plan for me.*

The preacher waved from the little porch as Charlie lifted Lena up on his short buckboard wagon and the Englands assembled themselves for the ride back home.

Emma glanced around but saw no sign of Austin. *Well of course not. He'd have no reason to stay. But maybe that means he's refused Papa's offer of dinner. Who ever heard of a groom takin' his brother with him – wedding dinners are meant for bride's families after all.*

Emma so completely convinced herself that they were rid of Austin and that Papa would soon enough be happy to have one daughter married into the Adams clan that he'd forget trying to match her up with Charlie's brother that when they pulled into the yard she nearly missed the saddled horse that stood by the watering trough.

"Well I see Austin has come on ahead," Tom announced as he leaned back on the brake stopping the wagon just beside the back porch.

"Where do you reckon he's got to," Jane looked all around the yard.

"I told him to go on in and get warm. It's sunny today but that wind will bite at you. Y'uns go on in there and I'll get the horses put away."

Emma stood up on her knees in the wagon's bed, "Papa I'll take care of the team if you like."

"No child, your Mama needs your hands in the kitchen. I don't reckon we can count on any help from Lena today."

"Nor should we Tom. A girl only gets married one day in her life. She needs to spend that one day out of the kitchen for she'll be in it for the rest of her life." Jane swung around with Gip still in her arms and stomped onto the porch.

Tom looked at Emma, "Din' mean to upset your Mama. What do you reckon I said?" Emma smiled and shook her head. She slid to the back of the wagon and unloaded Leonard and Bessie. "Let's go see if we can help Mama get our dinner on the table."

Each child wagged his head and Leonard even rubbed his round little tummy in anticipation of the good food he'd soon place there.

Bessie barreled into the kitchen and stopped short when she saw Austin standing with Mama.

"Austin, these are my children." She turned and placing her hand gently on Emma's waist she drew her into the room. "This is Emma, and Leonard with muddy shoes again. And Bessie will stop staring at you as soon as she realizes your just an ordinary fella'."

Austin chuckled at Bessie then slowly raised his eyes to Emma's. Emma dropped her gaze and pulled Leanord into her skirts feeling like a young cow for sale.

"Hhhmm, Guess I ought to help Mr. England with his team. Charlie will be along shortly so I'll put his horse up too." Austin swung his hat onto his head and took two long strides to the door that still stood ajar.

Jane didn't even turn as she answered him, "Thank you Austin. That's very thoughtful." She began to hum softly.

Chapter 13

"Hoo-ey, this place sure does smell good." Charlie sang out before he'd even gotten the door closed.

Voices mingled as scarves were unwrapped and cold fingers reached for the warmth above the cook stove.

"Y'uns get on in there by the fireplace till we finish up here. Won't be but a minute," Jane chided.

Tom led the way, "Come on in here boys. Charlie I guess we'll have to bring Lena's boxes down. She never done any travelin' so she don't have a proper trunk. Still, I reckon she's got a hope chest to rival any girl on the mountain what with all the fancy stitchin' she and her sister have been doin' for years now.

I guess a man can't appreciate the pretty stuff they make but now both Lena and Em can cook and can and grow a fine garden. My Jane, she's taught 'em well."

Emma heard her father through the wide doorway and blushed despite her solitary work at the table. *What's he doin' talking about me? Is he trying to sell me to that Austin?*

Tom's voice droned on talking about the farm and all of the help his girls gave him. He turned to face Austin and looked down on the shorter man. "Austin, you got your own place don't ya'?"

Austin nodded, "Yes Sir."

Picking up the poker Tom absently poked at the wood, "You keep a hired man on? Don't know how you'd manage without one not havin' any women folk on your place."

Both men stared into the fire as Austin answered, "Nah, I'm only working about five acres and I manage just fine on my own. I do have five milk cows and I regularly trade the milk for cheese and bread that I can't much make myself."

"Well it's good you've found a way to manage but..."

Plans for Emma

Jane's voice echoed from the kitchen, "Come on and eat now. It's good and hot but it won't stay that a'way."

As the men made their way around the table, Emma couldn't help but look at Austin as she wondered whether he realized Tom was trying to get them together. His eyes seemed wider than when she'd first seen him in the kitchen and his face a bit flushed.

Tom took his chair at the head of the table and pointed out places for the others, "Charlie, you've married her right and honorable so you can sit beside Lena today. Austin why don't you sit beside Charlie there. Emma I guess you'll sit along the wall and help Bessie. Metie can take care of Leonard I think."

Emma was firmly on the bench before she raised her eyes to find Austin watching her from his seat directly across the table. With a weak smile she nodded a silent acknowledgment of his attention.

The meal was delicious and the mood jovial while Tom alternated between praising Emma for everything from the cornbread to the clean table cloth. He lamented Austin's difficulties running a farm and keeping his own house. By the time they'd finished eating Emma feared her father would pack her off with the man this very day.

Charlie slurped his last sip of coffee and plunked the pewter mug on the table with a thud. "Miz England that was the best meal I've eaten since Christmas. I sure thank you for it, I know it was a'plenty of work for you and Emma too."

He flashed a grin at his new sister-in-law and winked.

Anger sparked in Emma's heart but it fled with the smile that threatened to burst from tightly pressed lips. *If Charlie is wise to Papa's purpose it can't possibly be hidden from his brother.*

Still, the absurdity of the whole afternoon tickled her. *So long as Papa forgets this crazy plan pretty soon.*

Charlie continued, "Mister England, I reckon we'd better get the boxes loaded and head toward Martha Washington. The days have sure gotten shorter so we may be dark gettin' there."

Tom nodded even as he popped a final bite of apple cake into his mouth. He rose without another word and reappeared dragging a long wooden crate by the leather handle attached to the end. Lena and Emma had painstakingly packed this homemade trunk with treasures collected for years and a few given by Mama.

"Charlie's house will be all furnished since he's gotten it from his grandparents. But I still want you to have some things from home and things that belonged to your people over the years," Jane said as she wrapped pewter and wooden bowls in the socks and dish towels already packed in the box.

Once the crates were loaded and Lena was wrapped in one of the patchwork quilts she'd made for her new home, Charlie clucked to his horses and started down the rutted road that led to the creek. Emma waved with mixed emotions as she began already to miss her sister while looking beyond the newlyweds to the creek and allowing sweet memories to flood her mind.

She still had the picture of Preston in her mind when Austin Adams's voice broke in, "Martha Washington must seem a long way off to you Emma. Have you ever been there?"

"Hmm, me? Oh no, I've never seen Martha Washington. Lena hasn't either you know." She turned the corner to the back door.

"Do you ever think about where you'll live?"

Emma stopped, still facing the closed door. She could see from the corner of her eye that Austin had followed her to return to the house. *Why is he still here?* She wondered.

Austin cocked his head slightly, "Have you ever thought about leaving Roslin?"

"No Austin, Roslin is my home. I can't imagine living anywhere else."

"Even if you lived somewhere in the nearby area? I don't think your father would mind you moving to Banner Springs.

She rolled her eyes to get a better view and one side of his mouth tilted upward in a mischevious smile. Without another

Plans for Emma

word she pushed open the door and began helping Metie carry leftover food and dirty dishes from the table.

Austin stepped through the kitchen and took a chair beside the fire. Tom sat next to him but neither man looked up.

"Would you let me call on Miss Emma?"

Tom nodded as he poked at an ember-laden log. "Uh huh."

A long, quiet moment passed before Austin shifted to the front of his hard chair, "Reckon I'd better head out. I don't have to go all the way to Martha Washington but the cows will no doubt be ready to milk when I get there."

Chapter 14

Most families on the mountain stayed close to home during the harshest part of the winter, and this one was looking like it would be colder than average. For weeks the family was confined to the farm as one snow storm followed another. Finally, temperatures warmed enough to allow a trip to the Roslin post office. Tom was sure to return with more than the mail.

"What's the news in Roslin?" Jane asked. She was stirring apple butter while Emma rolled out paper thin dough for fried pies. Christmastime was fast approaching and Jane always determined to feed her family special treats during this time of year.

Tom looked both eager and troubled as he went through the list of neighbors suffering sickness and babies born on the coldest nights. One barn burned with everything lost so he had made plans with some neighbors to go help rebuild on the first fit day.

Amid the news and with no explanation Tom pulled a crumpled envelope from the bib of his overalls and laid it on the edge of the table where Emma worked.

"You look troubled Tom, what else is there?" Jane prodded.

Emma stole a quick glance at the letter before watching for her father's response. It was addressed to her and she fought the urge to leave the pie dough immediately and read it.

Tom seemed to have forgotten the mail as he looked at his wife. "Had an offer to buy the farm."

His tone was so matter-of-fact that the magnitude of the statement did not register with Emma at first.

Plans for Emma

Jane chuckled and continued stirring the bubbling pie filling. A moment later she realized Tom wasn't laughing. Scooting the heavy pan off the hot front of the stove, she turned to him, "Are you considering it?"

"Well, it's a good offer. A great one in fact. And Charlie Adams has offered me a piece of his land in Martha Washington at a very reasonable price. Wouldn't you like to be nearer Lena? And we need to think of our Emma – living near Charlie might get her to know his brother. I've kind of got my eye on him for her."

Already shocked by the idea of selling the farm, Emma felt herself swaying at the mention of Austin Adams, as though her father had thrown a blow at her. She looked again at the envelope he'd given her. *Who would have written me? It's not Lena's hand and Preston wouldn't dare send something when Papa has refused us courting.*

Jane ignored Tom's matchmaking; her eyes roamed over the floor as though she might find an answer to this question in a corner of her kitchen. "Well I thought I'd die right here and be buried at the foot of the hill beside your parents and your grandparents."

"I'm not a'plannin' on dyin' anytime soon. And there's other land near Charlie that I might buy and be able to set up our children. Wouldn't you love to give them a place the same way we got this place from my Pa?"

Jane smiled. She always knew the depth of Tom's kindness but he didn't often speak aloud of such generous plans. "I can't argue with that, now can I?"

His response was so soft she strained to hear him say, "Shouldn't argue with me anytime."

Emma pulled her hands from the shallow dough bowl and wiped the remaining flour on her apron. Tom and Jane continued talking as Jane inquired about first one neighbor then another and their voices faded as Emma dropped into a chair by the window as she tugged as the wax seal.

Dear Miss England,

Please don't think me too forward writing to you. Mr. England gave me his blessing to call on you when I was there in the fall but the early and hard winter has kept me away. So I thought I would put pen to paper in order to tell you I've had you on my mind.

Your father had so many good things to tell me about you that I can't help but recount them and the more I do so the more I believe I would very much like to spend more time in your company.

I am but a half hour's ride from Roslin and when the roads clear I will certainly pay that call.

Until then I am minding my farm. As you well know there is plenty of hard work in the winter months even without crops to tend. I've had some bad luck and lost one of my milking cows but she left a strong calf that took to another mother and will make a fine replacement in time.

I guess these days when everyone is so shut in are the times that make me long for a wife.

Until we can see each other again, I remain

Your Friend,

Austin Adams

Emma dropped her hand as the letter suddenly felt hot and dangerous. For a long moment she stared into the weak light filtering through the window.

"Maaamaaa!" she finally shrieked.

Jane ran into the room for her Em never shrieked nor demanded attention. "Em child whatever's happened to you?"

Jane spotted the letter on the floor and reached for it, "Did Papa bring this home today? Whatever is the news?"

Her eyes scanned the page and every muscle froze as she read the signature. "Austin. Austin Adams wrote to you?"

Tom stood in the doorway scraping the bowl of his pipe. "Took him long enough. What's it been? Two months since he was here when Lena and Charlie married? I told him then he could call on her. I 'spected we'd see him before cold weather. A'course it got cold mighty quick."

Plans for Emma

He turned back to the kitchen more concerned with reloading the pipe than hearing his daughter's reaction to the letter.

Emma sat frozen, "Mama he... well I think...Mama he's looking for a wife. Why would he say that to me when he's never even written before?"

"Well Emma he's been in our home, talked to your father. I suppose he feels he has a right to think you'd be willing to marry him. Do you dislike the idea so very much?"

Emma's breath came in short gasps and Jane reached a comforting arm around her gently stroking her back.

"Mama... Preston... Mama I couldn't... I don't...I never thought."

"Shhh, child you need to calm down. It's just a shock to you, you weren't expecting to hear from this boy. And what of Preston? We don't hear anything from him."

"What! He can't write or call, Papa has refused him."

"Now you know your Papa is looking for the very best fellow for you. And Austin has that five acres. Tom told me it's cleared land you know. And he's got cows. It might be a good life for you. We all want a good life for you. He comes from a good family."

Emma's shoulders slumped but she said no more. A sizzling sound sent Jane rushing back to the kitchen and her cooking apples.

Emma swung her legs around the side of the chair and turned her eyes toward the window and the creek. *Honor thy father and thy mother that thy days may be long upon the land which the Lord thy God giveth thee.*

The verse came unbidden from deep in her memory, *Lord is it you that whispers your word to me when I'm not looking for it? I will honor you by honoring Papa. I can't help but notice that you promise long life but you didn't say it'd be easy.*

She sat there until she knew the sun had set despite the heavy clouds for the light faded to nothing and she had to turn to the blazing fire to see her way into the kitchen. The children sat around the table as Metie placed bowls filled with a hearty stew of deer meat, potatoes and carrots.

"Oh Mama, I must have fallen asleep. You should have called me."

Jane smiled and nodded toward the cornbread waiting to be turned from its skillet. "Your eyes were open when I fixed the fire. I thought you might have been praying. And that's time well spent."

"I guess I was praying."

Chapter 15

Between shorter hours and heavy clouds, daylight was scarce in the Flat Woods and a general malaise descended on everyone there. Preston first felt buoyed by prayer and assurance that God was in control of his life, then deflated by fears that crept into every hope and plan his mind created.

As he stood near the open stove door in the dining hall he thought back to his mother's little house in Glades. Christmas Day was much the same as any other day in the Langford house. There were no extra provisions for a feast nor were there gifts like he'd seen Doc Cherry's daughters playing with in the days after Christmas. His mind recalled the years spent with the Cherrys. Missus Cherry never wanted him at her table or spendin' much time with her girls. But every meal, she'd always hand him a heaping plate onto the back porch. If the weather was wet or cold he would carry it back to his room in the barn, sometimes sharing a few crumbs with the cats that always kept him company. He remember thinking that Christmas dinner must be something special in that house because there were hams hangin' in the spring house and the doctor was often driving into Sunbright and returning with his buggy laden down with packages. However, Mother insisted he spend Christmas with the family even if the meal was nothing special for them but she never failed to read aloud from the Bible the story of Joseph and Mary and the baby Jesus. Preston remembered her fretting over Mary Jane, Wes and Elec who she'd left near White Oak when she moved back to Glades. She never got to see them and it seemed she always thought most about them around Christmastime. "Preston," she'd say, "Don't you ever lose sight of your kin. Family is the most important thing you've got besides the Lord."

He slowly shook his head as he remembered these words; he counted the months since he'd seen any of them. It was a hard walk back to Glades and he didn't want to miss any time working. Of course they would neither cut trees nor hew ties on Christmas Day but Preston shook off the idea of walking the twenty miles round trip on that day. Sure, there were lots of the men that would leave for a while this time of year, some wouldn't be back until spring. But Preston was intent on saving the money he'd need for a home with Emma. *I think Mother would understand it.*

He had to remind himself that Mother was no longer in Glades but gone home to be with her Lord.

On Christmas morning Preston decided to walk down to the Bridge Creek. Of course Emma would be snug in the little farmhouse atop the hill. The sheep had plenty of water and she would have work today at her mother's side. As he walked down the rutted log road to reach the Jonesville Road, Preston made a special point to pray blessings down on the Englands for he knew if he didn't ask God to bless them today he'd be tempted to curse Tom. *One day we'll spend our Christmases side by side Emma.*

Looking up the steep hill, smoke curled out the chimney and Ruff gave a single bark to some unknown disturbance. He could make out the top of the barn near the house and knew that Mister England would have his stock there for the day. He smiled as he imagined the family preparing a special meal and settling themselves around an overloaded table. He wondered if Miz Jane made presents for her children; maybe there'd be a new rattle for the fat baby that always sat on her lap, Preston had forgotten his name. Little Leonard would be thrilled with any toy Mister England could carve out for him and Bessie would want to dress and wrap up a baby doll. He hoped she had a doll with a painted porcelain face.

"Preston you're a'makin' yourself sad and cold standin' here. Git on back home now." He turned back toward the Flat Woods but shook his head, *I don't guess anywhere will be home until I have a home with Em.*

Plans for Emma

The day after Christmas saw Tom headed out at the crack of dawn despite low hanging clouds. He had promised to meet the farm's buyer at the post office then he would ride across The Clear Fork creek and over into Martha Washington where he would spend at least one night with Lena and Charlie.

Jane brought out first one thing then another that she wanted to send to Lena. "Woman, where do you think I'm a'gonna' carry all that plunder? I'm on horseback and I'd need a second pack horse for everything you're handin' me. You'll see Lena soon enough I expect."

The children were all still in bed when Tom left but Emma crept down the stairs and stood shivering with bare feet sticking out of her nightdress as the cold air blew in the open door. She wasn't sure what took her breath away, the frigid temperature or the realization that Papa was actually going to sell their home.

Three months had passed since Preston spoke to her father. The Englands had attempted the drive to church a handful of times over those weeks and each time, Emma saw the longing in Preston's eyes as she passed him in the aisle. Emma thought she had her emotions well in hand, having resolved to obey her father's wishes. Then came the announcement that they were moving to Martha Washington and Emma felt a great weight fall on her chest. She realized she had held onto a hope that Papa would change his mind if Preston kept working on the nearby lumber tract while he proved himself faithful to attend church.

Sure she'd missed her sister in the months since Lena married but living near her was small consolation to losing Preston.

"Em whatever are you doing down here without so much as stockings on your feet. You'll catch your death."

"I'm not sure I care Mama. Papa seems to wish me dead anyway."

Jane opened her own shawl and wrapped Emma in both the wool's scratchy warmth as well as her mother's arms." What a silly thing to say. Why your Papa is going right now to work toward setting you and your sisters all up with a little land. Won't that be a blessing?"

"What does a spinster need with land?"

"Spinster? You? Emma you are the prettiest thing from Jonesville to Banner Springs. You would never have been a spinster. And now you've got Austin Adams promising to court you in the springtime. A'course moving across the holler may complicate that a bit but living next to his brother will balance it all out. I'm sure that we'll make a good life in Martha Washington."

"Who wants to be in Martha Washington?" Emma grumbled.

Jane led her into the front room where Tom had stoked up the fire before he left. She settled them on the little bench she kept there in the warmest spot in the house. "Your sister Lena is in Martha Washington and her letters sure sound happy enough."

"But she has Charlie so of course she's happy there."

"You'll soon have your own home and family Em, just you wait and see."

"Mama don't you see? I've been waiting – waiting on Preston Langford then Papa refused him and practically promised me to Austin. Now we're abandoning Preston altogether." Emma stood and started to pace the width of the fireplace repeatedly. "I don't know what to do but I think I'll go completely mad if I don't do something. I've prayed and prayed and now God answers by moving us all the way to Martha Washington."

Emma turned her mouth down in an exaggerated frown and repeated, "Martha Washington."

Jane smiled at her daughter's exaggeration. "Em dear we are not abandoning anyone. If the Lord wills you and Mr. Langford together, six miles and a deep holler won't keep you apart. What you must do is pray and trust. And be open to the possibility that God has actually sent Austin into your life for a purpose."

Plans for Emma

Emma sniffed and nodded her head. She wouldn't argue with Mama even if she could, but she knew there was no arguing with that point. If God willed it, she knew she could count on it. Still she kept thinking about girls she'd heard of running off with their beaus. She and Preston could go to Jamestown and be married before Papa could even get there.

If the good Lord has sent Preston to me he means for me to be with him. I'm going to write him and tell him my plan. He will come for me, I know it.

Her eyes darted to the stairs in the dim light. She started from the room without another word to her mother.

"Em, where are you off to? Are you going back to bed?"

With one foot already resting on the bottom stair, Emma turned toward her mother and pasted a smile onto her face. "Yes Mama, I believe I will."

With each step she climbed, Emma felt heavier as though she were pulling a great weight up with her. Her own voice seemed to whisper to her, *I think that's the first time you've ever lied to Mama. Oh my, where is this going? Will you always have to lie to her?*

She tightened her fist until the nails dug into her palm but she welcomed the pain for it diverted her thoughts from Preston and the ache in her heart.

She stopped on the top step. She opened her palm and looked down at it despite the darkness that she knew would prevent an inspection of her injury. *I wonder if it will bleed on the letter to Preston?*

She rubbed her hands together as she settled herself at the little table in the girls' shared room and turned up the lamp. Shuffling the books and papers stored there she found a piece of writing paper and a bit of pencil. As she absently dabbed the lead against her tongue the torrent of words in her head tried to assemble into sentences.

Dear Preston...

Nothing more would come. Emma squinted her eyes tight and turned her thoughts to God instead.
Lord, why can't I even write the letter. Seems like I can't do anything right now.

Turning her head she looked out the room's solitary window into the grey sky. The house would begin to wake soon for they were all accustomed to the early mornings farm life demanded.

If I don't get this written quickly, it will be evening before I'll have another chance cause I'm going to have to milk and feed with Papa gone already.

She read what she'd written so far, Dear Preston, and began a new sentence.

I hope this letter finds you well. It is now Friday morning, very early. My Papa has left before daylight on an errand I can't believe even as I write this letter. He's gone to sell our farm. We will move all the way to Martha Washington by springtime for he intends to put in a crop over there. I overheard Mama and Papa talking and I know he's refused to let you call here and for that I am sorry.

Emma Jane England, you are dancin' round the subject here. Get to the point while you've got the chance.

The pencil pressed a deep point into the paper.
The thing is Preston that I would be happy to go away with you instead of going to Martha Washington if you would just come for me.

Metie turned over in the bed with a soft sigh and Emma jerked her head around as though responding to the loudest of noises. Turning back to the paper she read her last sentence, ...*happy to go away with you...* She pushed away from the table aghast at even allowing such a thought into her head. The movement woke Bessie who began to whimper.

Plans for Emma

Instead of going to her sister, Emma grabbed the offending letter and dashed from the room. She tripped down the stairs so fast Jane dashed from her seat in the kitchen fearing one of her children was ill.

"Em, whatever is the matter? Are the girls…"

"Fine Mama, everything is fine." She didn't even look at her mother as she tore past her, holding the letter she'd written in a death grip. Almost frantically, she looked around for a means to rid herself of it. She heard her mother climb the stairs to check on the other children and she grabbed the stove door, swinging it open without a pot holder and singeing her hand in the process. The pain meant nothing to her for the words she'd written seemed to burn all the worse.

For a second she watched the paper bursting into flames then she slammed the door, finally noticing the pain in her fingertips.

Jane stepped into the kitchen, with Bessie in her arms as Emma rushed toward the back door. "Em wherever are you going now?"

"I've got to get to the stock. It's getting late to be milking."

Jane grabbed her by her sleeve, "Em, you're still in your night clothes and bare footed. You'd catch your death out there. I don't know what's in your head right now but you need to sit down by the stove and calm down. Let me get you some mint leaf tea, that might settle you some."

"Thank you Mama."

Jane didn't question her, nor did she make any demands of her daughter. Instead, she brought the steaming mug of tea and without saying a word she began preparing breakfast.

As she held the warm tea, Emma realized she'd been shaking and she wasn't quite sure whether it was her rebellion that caused it or the draft of the cold house. Once she was warmer, and calmer, she slipped from the kitchen to dress for the day upstairs. The bedroom was empty now with her sisters downstairs in the kitchen. The room was brighter and she caught a glimpse of herself in the small wall mirror. There was still a frightened look in her face and it froze her.

Emma you've scarcely ever had a thought of rebelling against Papa much less God. What ever came over you this morning writing such a letter?

She stared a long moment as though she expected the pale lips in the mirror to move in answer. With a shake of her head she turned from the mirror, yet somehow the answer crept into her heart.

No one paid her any attention as she passed through the kitchen on her way to the barn. Leaning into the side of the old brown milk cow, she searched her heart for answers and realized that she had been willing to do anything for Preston Langford, even something contrary to everything she'd ever been taught, or ever believed.

Did honoring your father and mother mean you never disagreed with them? That was a question that would require more than one milking to answer, but by the time she'd finished in the barn, she'd decided that in at least this one situation she could not trust her own heart and she'd have to trust her papa to be following God.

Chapter 16

It was four days before Tom returned home. No one was worried because it was hard to travel in winter and they knew he had a good place to stay while in Martha Washington.

Still everyone was overjoyed to see him riding up the hill to their house. Emma stepped outside to help him with the horse.

"Let me unsaddle him Papa, I'm sure you're about froze through."

"Thank you Em, I am pretty cold right now."

Emma unsaddled, brushed and fed the tall gelding with as much speed and skill as anyone could have. She was eager to hear the news Papa brought despite lingering mixed feelings about the possibility of a move.

"...Lena's the best little wife. You know she can make cornbread 'bout as good as yours," Tom was detailing his time in Lena and Charlie's home when Emma came into the warm kitchen. "And she's got good soft straw ticks, I slept as well there as I ever do here. They put me right in front of the fireplace – well in fact, they offered me their bed but I said I could still sleep on a pallet on the floor 'cept I didn't have to sleep on the floor 'cause she had that straw tick so I was just fine."

Emma was glad things were going so well for her older sister. Gustie, the eldest surviving child had been married for three years and it seemed like an eternity to Emma. In that time she and Lena had grown close enough that it often felt like they were the only children in the England family; Metie, Bessie and Leonard were so much younger that they seemed like Lena and Emma's own children instead of siblings. Yet jealousy stirred somewhere deep within Emma to hear of Lena's happy home. Despite much prayer she still felt that she would never find anyone after Preston, and it was clear Papa was not going to let that relationship prosper.

Over the last few days she'd prayed again and again, *Lord I'm trusting you with this and I'm trusting you to send me the husband of your choosing even if it ain't Preston Langford.*

Still, as she heard Papa talking about Lena's married life she had to ask again, *Lord is it not in your will for me to have a home like that too?*

Finally, Jane could wait no longer and she changed the subject from her daughter to the land. "What happened with the farm? Since you went on over to Martha Washington I reckon I know but you've got to tell me for sure. Are we movin'?"

Tom just nodded his head. He said little about the sale of the only home he'd ever known, where the Englands had labored for three generations to carve out a flourishing farm.

"I've bought fifty acres on the north side of Charlie's farm. On farther to the North and East are tracts that I believe can be had and we'll have the money once we get moved so I'll start working that deal right away. But fifty acres is more than me and little Leonard can till and plant and it will keep us very well I think."

"Is there a house on it?"

"There is. It's not in much shape but I think we can make it livable. Charlie said he'd help me get a field turned for corn and a good sized garden for you. Lena will plant extra onions and peas since I don't expect we'll get moved before they need to be in the ground. We'll have to plant our taters late but I b'lieve they'll make."

"Well Tom, it seems like we are pretty old to be startin' over but I reckon I can do it if you can. It sure sounds like you and the kids were busy plannin' everything."

Tom smiled and reached for his wife's hand. "You ain't so old."

Over the next weeks, Jane, Emma and Metie worked steadily to prepare for the coming move. Despite sadness to leave their home and fear of what might lie ahead of them, a

Plans for Emma

nervous anticipation grew among the family while a malaise settled over Emma that worried Jane.

"Our Em's lookin' awful pale Tom," Jane commented as they sat before the fire after the children went upstairs.

"Just wintertime. She'll be lookin' pert again come spring. And Charlie said he'd send for Austin soon as we get ourselves settled on the new place."

"Tom! What do you mean? You've been talkin' about this to Charlie?"

"Well it din' do no harm. He'd love to have his brother married to Lena's sister."

"Well maybe he would but don't you remember what that letter from Austin did to Emma? I can't be real sure that the Lord's gonna' lead that direction."

Tom stretched his arms over his head as he put the subject to bed. "We'll let the boy call and see how it works out. Em's got a good head on her shoulders."

He cradled her chin in his palm, "Takes that from her Mama, don't she?"

Tom had arranged the land to change hands in late February so they weren't moving into what he described as a rickety house in the coldest months. The month of January was a blur to the whole family. The clouds gave way to some sunny days although the wind still blew and chilled every inch of exposed skin. Wrapped in shawls and wearing the thick socks Mama had given each child for Christmas, they sorted through the accumulated stuff of four generations.

Emma knew her mother was worried about her, for Jane took every possible opportunity to talk with and encourage her daughter. Emma did appreciate her efforts and she tried hard to be happy as she recognized everyone's excitement over the new adventure they were starting.

But something struggled within her. She couldn't help but feel that she was being pulled along by a rushing river and she wasn't even trying to fight the current. As she worked in the cellar trying to crate all of their preserved food, Jane joined her.

"Do we have many stores left Em?"

"Oh yes, there's a lot of pickles and the taters are holdin' out good."

When Tom announced the first wagon was loaded to capacity, Jane surprised him by announcing Emma would ride along to deliver the things and inspect their new home.

"Child you know there's no tellin' what the house may look like. I thought to write Lena but it will sure be a lot easier if you can set your own eyes on the place then we can discuss it. I'd sure love to see it myself but can't leave Gip that long and I wouldn't want to drag him along little as he is."

"Okay, Mama, I'll go with Papa." Emma couldn't help but wonder if there was more to her mother's plan than a simple look at the new house.

She didn't often ride on the board seat beside her Papa, and now Emma realized how much nicer it was to sit with the children in the back of the buckboard wagon with the wind hitting her back and somewhat shielded by her Papa's strong shoulders. As Tom slapped the reins over the backs of his team to turn them onto the Jonesville Road, Em thanked God for the weak sun that shone down on them and tried to burrow deeper in the quilt Mama had wrapped around her shoulders.

She'd never been to Martha Washington but she understood the lay of the land well enough to know they would be driving very near the logging activity in the Flat Woods. With the weather restricting their church attendance and no idea of taking the sheep to the creek, Emma had not seen Preston in weeks and then he'd been across the aisle at church with no opportunity to talk to him.

When Papa turned the wagon South instead of heading toward the logging camp, Emma inhaled sharply. It was enough to prompt an explanation from him. "Wagon's loaded heavy and the creek's roarin' now. I'm afraid to try to ford it while we're loaded. We'll go round the Turnpike then when we come home we'll ford the creek and see what we

Plans for Emma

think about the next load. I guess we'll have to make several trips considering everything your Mama wants to take with her."

"Well Papa, you can't very well expect her to move off and leave her whole lifetime behind, can you?"

He just shook his head as he stared straight between the two horses' heads.

When the wagon made the turn onto the Emory Turnpike, the first of the roads cut by the logging crews came into view. Emma peered down it knowing that Preston was working far away from this entrance. She didn't realize how much she had learned about logging from talking with Preston until facts about the business began to flow through her mind as though they were water in a stream bed.

She strained her ears wondering if the report of the axes against solid tree trunks would reach this far. Knowing that Preston would no doubt be hewing the big logs into the necessary square cross ties, she dismissed any thought of the men felling the tall trees. Preston would be located farther back and closer to the base camp and she bit back a tear as she realized that every turn of the wagon's wheels carried her further and further from that camp and from Preston.

Oh, that is if he's even here. It was an afterthought that occurred to her he may be off in Sunbright delivering a load to the train. With that thought, her head jerked out of the blanket and pivoted, hoping to see a wagon meeting them on the narrow path. She felt herself blush as she realized how desperate she was to see this man. And that realization brought renewed sadness. They had no permission to visit and very soon, they would not even live close enough if permission were ever granted.

Her desperation drove her to prayer again. *Father in heaven, this isn't real obedience to Papa, or to you, if I begrudge it so much, is it? Please give me the right heart and help me to trust in his decisions. I've been raised to understand that you'll give Papa special wisdom. Please help me to believe that with all my heart. And maybe help Preston to understand it too. I wonder if he's longing to see me like I am?*

Oh Lord, I guess I have to understand that you may have other plans. I don't know why you would have put this man in my life if you didn't intend us to have a life together. But help me to accept your will if he isn't in it. I do want to obey, and I will – I'm just having a hard time convincing my heart.

She tried to still her mind, knowing that this ride would last the whole day and should Papa take a notion to talk to her she mustn't talk about Preston or loggers or Sunbright. Ducking her head back into the warm blanket, she couldn't stop grinning and had to work to withhold a giggle at the thought of blurting out her inner thoughts to her father.

Lena met the pair at her gate and ushered Emma straight to the stove to warm herself. There was food already sitting on the table but Papa ate only a bite or two. "We've got all that junk to unload," he kept saying.

Charlie eased to the door and began sliding on his heavy coat, "You eat Mr. England and I'll water your team. Then we'll go together and get it all unloaded while Lena and Emma get caught up. She's been hoping Emma would come with one of the loads you're bringing."

Emma smiled at her sister, it sure was good to see her. Once the men were out of the house, they talked about every subject either could imagine. Emma realized it would be good to see her sister every day when they lived over here.

The Adamses were gracious hosts but Emma knew that her Papa would want to head out at dawn and waste no more time than necessary on this trip. He was planning to load the wagon again tonight and head back in a day or two with more of their belongings.

As they crossed the Clear Fork, Emma understood his fears for the water rushed before them frothing at the rocky edge.

"What do you think Papa, can we bring the next load this way?"

"I don't know Em, I'm wondering more about the stock. Could be we'll have to leave the hogs in the woods and come back for them at the first of the summer."

Plans for Emma

"Will the cows and sheep make it across here?"

"Yeah, I think the cows will be fine. I guess I'll try to sell all but a pair of the sheep and we can manage to get them across somehow."

Emma nodded and thought no more of it. Papa always knew what was best on the farm. It made her wonder why it wasn't as easy to trust him with her future.

Chapter 17

Because he was young, traveled by foot and was accustomed to working everyday out in the cold, Preston Langford was among the most faithful attendees at the Jonesville Baptist Church that winter. As the preacher cuffed his shoulder and congratulated him on his faithfulness, something in the glint of the man's eye told Preston he knew there was more than hunger for God's word that drew him to the little church in the worst of weather.

Preston gave him a smile of genuine thanks and prayed as he walked to his usual seat, *Lord, renew a right spirit within me. I need to be here for the right reasons.*

His prayer was sincere but he still looked around the room hoping that Emma was seated in deep conversation with one of her friends.

Each week as he walked through the barren woods he tried hard to pray and prepare his heart for the week's helping of scripture and admonition served by the circuit-riding man of God or on the off-Sundays, one of the aged saints from the congregation. However, he struggled to keep Emma from his thoughts. Frankly, Emma filled his thoughts most of the time. He had now sat behind her family's pew enough times that he knew every detail of her Sunday dress. He could see her profile each time she turned to speak to one of the little children that demanded much of her attention during the service and watching her this way, he'd memorized the details of her face. Oh, and her smile; she'd smiled at him at the creek, or across the congregation, or in saying a few words of greeting in the church yard. Preston had not counted the smiles but he was sure he remembered every single one of them. The very thought of her smile brought one to his own face.

Plans for Emma

Each week when he walked into the building, his eyes went straight to her regular seat. If she wasn't there, he scanned the crowd. When he couldn't find her, his heart dropped a little lower.

Somehow God had spoken to Preston on these long cold walks and made him to understand that should his dream of marrying Emma never come true, she had still been one of the greatest blessings in his life. Because of her, he had come back to God. Because he wanted to be worthy of this great lady, he heard God's word each week. Because she occupied his every waking moment, he remembered that God's gifts are perfect. Yet he faltered when he considered God might use his precious Em to teach him and never allow them to build a life together.

It was a hard lesson and he wanted to appreciate it even though it hurt. Preston remembered his own parents. He'd watched his mother continue to love the husband she lost fifteen years before. Through extreme hardship, she thanked God for the time he allowed with Harrison Langford and the children she had to remember him by. Looking back, Preston wondered how she hadn't grown bitter that her man had died off and left her with so many hungry mouths but Sarah Jane never let a day pass without praising God for something. Now Preston remembered he too must praise God.

Although he tried to be friendly, Preston didn't talk to many people at the little church. He had no desire to be matched up to one of the eligible girls and every greeting or invitation seemed a matchmaking ploy.

He watched for Tom England around the wood stove and only if he saw him there would he make a point to loaf for a while after the final prayer was said. Therefore, he heard little gossip about the community.

When the second Sunday in March dawned clear and sunny, Preston was sure he would find the Englands in their regular pew at church. As he walked he imagined seeing Emma's father and prayed for the right words to say to him.

His heart thumped in his chest in anticipation of speaking to this man and for fear he would again say no.

The ground was still cold enough that the mud did not hamper Preston's trek across the logging roads and the trip passed quickly.

Sure enough, lots of folks were out on this beautiful day and the church yard was overflowing with teams and young folks milling about before the service started. Preston greeted a few boys he'd gotten to know a little and scoured the crowd for that singular face.

Locating none of the Englands in the yard, Preston stepped into the building realizing he would need to stand through this service to allow the women and children sufficient seats. There was no sign of Mr. England in the back so he tried to find a place to stand that would not hinder the traffic as the children filed in to find seats with their mothers.

Surrounded by the men of the community, he listened as they talked about corn running low after the hard winter and spring plowing and the price of pork. He paid little heed to the talk until he heard the name 'England's and his ears perked up.

"I guess Tom's gone fer good now."

"Gone? Where'd he go?"

"Sold out and bought a place in Martha Washington. You know his girl married a man from there. He must'a had a big place 'cause Tom's bought a spread from him."

"Why, I can't b'lieve he'd leave. There's been Englands on that hill about as long as people's been settled in Roslin."

Preston heard little more of the men's chatter for his head echoed with bits of sentences, '...gone for good... bought a place in Martha Washington...'

Preston racked his brain wondering if he'd ever even heard of Martha Washington. His mother had moved the family from White Oak to Glades while he was so young and so grief stricken from his father's loss that he held few memories of living in the northern part of the county. And he'd had little business to go to Jamestown as a young man so

Plans for Emma

he was more familiar with Roslin and the Emory Turnpike route to Sunbright than the place he'd been born.

He walked home with his head low. A little breeze was kicking up and fighting against the warming nature of the noonday sun. Preston felt that wind through his whole being. His head spun trying to decide his next move, trying to figure a plan.

As he stepped from the scrub woods, that were left behind the logger's axe, into the camp clearing, he resolved to get himself to Martha Washington as soon as possible. Why, he did not know. Tom England had made himself very clear that he would not allow him to court his beautiful daughter. What could Preston do? Could he show up on their doorstep and make another plea for the father's blessing? Should he sneak around to see Emma and coerce her to run away with him?

Even as the thought of running away entered his head, Preston shook it away. One of the things he loved about Emma was her devotion to God and God's way. Even if he could talk her into it, she would one day resent that Preston had drawn her away from her godly family.

The thought made him smile. She was not 'high and mighty' like some girls who acted like they never even had a sour thought. No, Preston was sure that she was good through and through.

No further plan would come to him. He would find his way to Martha Washington the first chance he got and he would see where the Lord led him from there.

Despite his plans, Preston felt lower than he'd ever remembered as he made his way back to camp. The assigned bunk in the long building lined with identical beds seemed lonesome and empty despite the numerous grumbling, snoring or bantering men scattered through it. Even the bright spring day had paled.

Each day that week, Preston had to drag himself out of the bed when the triangle clanged to wake them. One day he didn't even bother going to breakfast, but sat on the side of his bed until he knew it was time to hear the day's assignments.

When the foreman asked him to drive to Sunbright, he even asked to be excused. The mornings were still quite brisk and no one else wanted the assignment so Preston agreed to go. As he left the logging road, he wondered if he could ever make Sunbright before dark if he went through Roslin and avoided the bridge creek altogether. He wasn't sure he could stand driving by that special place when he knew that Emma might never be there again.

Good grief man, you act like she's done gone on home. She's only gone to Martha Washington – wherever that is, it ain't heaven.

Despite the dread, when he reached the creek he felt joy when passing the England's former home. He didn't stop at the creek but looked at every detail of the landscape as the wagon slowed down the hill, flipping through the memories as though they were recorded in an illustrated book. He'd seen a book like that once when he was young and now he could imagine all of his memories were drawn for him to enjoy again.

Get your eyes off yesterday, Preston. It's okay to treasure memories, but you and Emma are going to make more, I'm sure of it.

Chapter 18

Every member of the England family was well aware of the struggles of a mountain farm and the hard work that came with springtime. But none of them had pioneered a farm for Tom was born to the Roslin home of his grandfather, Jane married and moved to the established home and birthed each of her children there.

This life in Martha Washington was a new kind of work. The house was rickety, drafty and far smaller than their home in Roslin. Jane remarked that it was no bigger than the log cabin Grandpa England had first built in Roslin but she knew her words were exaggerated. That was now a hundred years past and the Roslin home had grown with each generation into a sprawling farmhouse. Emma couldn't help but wonder how many years their new house had stood and whether it would survive even one more year.

Built of rough sawn board lumber, it had never been as sound as the England's notched-log house. Now it had been abandoned for an unknown time period and the wind and rain had seeped deep into the boards warping and splitting them.

Jane spent little time complaining about the house and responded to her family's complaints with tasks to improve it. Therefore, Emma decided right away that she'd keep her thoughts to herself in order to be free from the constant improvements. Still, she was happy to help her mother most of the time and even Lena found time to pitch in so that the sisters were able to work together as they had throughout their lives.

Things seemed even more remote here, but they all realized it was only because it was new to them. The mail came to Clarkrange at Peters' Store, and they traded in most anything the farmstead needed. However, it was four miles on the road and the roads were more often mud than anything else so Papa didn't go very often. But this week, he'd made the trip and returned with a tin of putty to re-seal the window panes and Emma and Lena set to work on them the first warm day they found.

Propped on makeshift scaffolding, the girls let their legs dangle as they worked and chatted.

"Em, it is so good to get to work with you like this. I miss spending time with you."

"Well Lena we see each other all the time, almost as much as before you were married."

"No Em, it's not the same at all. We never talk."

Emma shrugged and continued her work. "This old glazing is so cracked I don't know if we wouldn't be better off to dig it out before we put new in."

"Oh my, wouldn't the glass fall out on us? That would be all the colder then wouldn't it?" Lena giggled at the idea.

"Yeah, we sure don't want to make matters any worse, do we? Do you know how old this house is?"

"No, Charlie was pondering over that a few days ago. It's been here as long as he can remember. He doesn't even know whose house it was originally. Maybe his great grandparents built it because it's where his father grew up.

"Oh, I thought you were living in his grandparents' house?"

"Well, they built our house after all their children left home. I guess things were a little better for them and this house was too hard for the Grandma to keep up. So they built three solid rooms with a good stone fireplace. It's a funny story though, the old woman thought this was too much house for just the two of them but then she decided the new house they built was just too small so they added the kitchen onto the back within the first year they lived there."

"Ain't that the way it always is? We're never satisfied, are we?"

Plans for Emma

Lena studied Emma's eyes for a moment, "You sound like Mama, you know."

Emma could only nod. "Well your little house is not as drafty as this one, is it?"

"Oh no, it's as tight as a drum. Charlie is always puttering around filling cracks and tightening doors and such. Em, I am so proud of my husband," Lena beamed.

Now it was Emma's turn to pause; she admired her sister's beauty when she smiled. She dropped her eyes as she realized she had done little smiling of her own for weeks now. *Lord, please take away the jealousy. I don't wish Lena to be lonely or miserable, you know that.*

"What's wrong Em?"

She shook her head a bit as though clearing her feelings away. "Nothing, just admiring your happiness."

"Well that was a pretty miserable look for admiration."

"I'm sorry."

"You've been looking miserable a lot lately. Mama told me about that Langford boy in Roslin who asked to court you. Have you heard from him?"

"How would I? Did Mama also tell you that Papa refused to let him call on me? Then we moved off with no chance to even say 'good bye' to him. I guess he thinks I kind of fell off the edge of the world, if he even cares what happened to me."

"Why would you say that? Of course he cared or he wouldn't have talked to Papa."

"Well yeah, but once Papa said no, don't you guess he moved on? There's plenty of girls around."

"Ah, then you think you were just another girl to him? Is he like that?"

Emma dropped her hands into her lap and slumped her shoulders. "No Lena, he's the kindest boy I've ever spoken to. He would smile at me as though I was the most beautiful creature he'd ever seen. And he would say things to make me laugh and when I did, his eyes laughed with me. You know he has these big brown eyes, they are deep set in his face so he can look pretty serious but then when you look into them, it's like they are alive and dancing."

When she looked at her sister's wide smile, Emma blushed. "I got carried away a little, didn't I?"

"Well, maybe a little. I think we can get your mind set on happier thoughts. Charlie's brother Austin is coming for a visit in the next few days. Charlie sent word over a week ago that you were here and he could come visitin' anytime. Now, doesn't that sound like fun?"

After a quick gasp when Lena first mentioned her brother-in-law, Emma had held her breath.

"Emma, you are turning bright red. Whatever is the matter with you?"

She let out her breath in a gush and looked frantically to the ground. Had they not been propped so high or if the window could be opened, Emma would surely have run away. She felt a gentle touch on her shoulder.

"Em, did you hear me? What's the matter?"

Emma dipped her head. "Lena, I've prayed and prayed over this. I think I've wrestled with the Lord the same way the old prophets did."

After a long moment and seeing the color return to normal in her sister's face, Lena turned back to daubing at the glass with the flat stick Papa had given her and it took her a few minutes to respond. "Who won?"

"What? Won what?"

"You or the Lord? You said you were wrestling with the Lord."

Emma chuckled, "Yeah, like the old prophets. Do you remember a single story where the prophet won?"

Both girls laughed at Emma's joke but Lena was searching her sister's eyes for answers.

"Lena, I know Papa really likes Austin and thinks he'd be a good man for me."

Lena nodded, "The Adamses are fine people Em."

Nodding, Emma searched for the right words, "Oh Lena, I know they are. And Charlie is fast becoming like a brother

Plans for Emma

to me. And I can't say a thing against his brother. Austin wrote me you remember, back before Christmas."

Lena nodded slowly again without looking away from the window.

"But I just can't stop thinking about Preston Langford. Now I have come to understand that if God has chosen this man for me, he will also make a way for us to be together. And I know Papa's not trying to undo God's plans and even if he isn't being obedient in this, it's up to me to obey and wait for God to reward that. So I'll try to get to know Austin and I will try hard to yield to God's leading.

"Emma you could be a teacher. That was lovely."

"Oh you flatter-er. Get back to work," she giggled.

Emma's heart did feel lighter and she was truly able to enjoy Lena through the afternoon. However, as the sun headed toward the western horizon and Lena excused herself to go make supper for Charlie, Emma once again experienced a wave of gloom.

Lord, why do I keep feeling this way?

Jane carried in a basket of potatoes as Emma scrubbed her hands in the wash pan. "Did you girls have any luck with the windows?"

"Uh huh."

"I'll bet you enjoyed each other. You don't get much time to chat like you've always done growing up, do you?"

"Well, Lena has a whole other life now."

Jane picked up the paring knife and began peeling, "I am so thankful for Charlie. He's a good man and Lena seems very happy with him."

Emma bit her lip as tears welled in her eyes. She managed a nod and she grabbed the wash pan before stepping out the back door.

She remained on the porch a few extra minutes, allowing the evening's cool breeze to clear her head. Returning the pan to its place in the dry sink, Emma searched her mind for something to chat about that wouldn't send her bawling. She knew if she didn't talk with her mother about something unimportant then Mama would figure out what was on her mind.

"Em, you didn't have words with Lena today, did you?"

Too late. She already knows there's something on my mind. "Oh no Mama, we had a wonderful time."

"Well, okay. It's just that you seem quiet and I would have expected you to be gushing with stories this evening."

"I'm a little tired I guess."

Jane reached toward Emma's forehead and checked her temperature with the back of her hand, puckering her brow."You don't feel warm. It wasn't cold out there in the sun, was it?"

Emma chuckled softly, "Mama, I'm not sick. Like I said, maybe just a little tired. The sun was warm and beautiful today. That's one good thing about this farm, it's much flatter than our home in Roslin was. On that hillside we were half the time waiting for the sun to reach us."

"The land here is beautiful, isn't it? It will be home one day Emma."

"I know it will Mama."

"Of course by the time it feels like home you'll be moving into your own house and starting a family. Maybe even crossing the creek again to living in Banner Springs if Papa's hopes for Austin Adams come true."

Emma shut her eyes tight but could tell she would not be able to stop the tears this time. "Uh, I'm gonna' get a clean apron."

She rushed to the tiny room she shared with Almeta and Bessie. Sitting under the far window was the old sea chest that Papa had given her long ago to fill for a hope chest. She sat there now as she often did because the position under the room's single window made it the best place to sew or read.

As she looked out the window she opened her heart to God but she was somehow unable to utter the words of a prayer. All of a sudden she felt the chest under her. ·She thought, *My hope chest. I haven't touched it since we moved. Lord, my*

Plans for Emma

faith in you needs feet under it so I'm going to start working again to fill this chest because I know you have a future planned for me.

Rising temperatures and longer days brought out tiny green leaves, crocuses and jonquils. The path to the spring was carpeted with purple violets that led Bessie and Leonard to fits of laughter as they ran along behind their older sisters.

A trip for water became a much anticipated game and as Emma pretended to run away from the children, they all crashed onto the back porch laughing. Jane stopped her needlework to enjoy the sight and the sound of her children.

"There is nothing more glorious than the sound of children laughing."

Emma was panting as she dropped into a chair by her mother. "These two will sure keep you laughing, and running. They chased me all the way to the spring house and all the way back and they are ready to go again. Would you look at them?"

"Em, it's good to see you smiling too. I think you are getting past the pain you felt over that boy in Roslin."

"Preston. Mama, his name is Preston."

"Oh. I'm sorry. Of course I remember his name."

"It's okay, I didn't mean to sound so sharp. The pain is not so bad now, but I do still think about him."

"Well dear, you will doubtless always remember him."

"You talk like he's passed on to eternity. He's still over there in Roslin."

Jane chuckled as she squeezed her daughter's arm. "Now you know I didn't mean that."

Emma leaned over to look at the unfinished quilt top in her mother's lap. "Mama, that is going to be a lot prettier than we'd thought. Your points are as sharp as metal. Do you suppose I will ever piece as well as you?"

"Darling, your needlework is beautiful. We'll work on points again soon, it takes practice that's all."

"You're right and I'm going to practice right now. Stay here, I'll go get that Mariner's Compass I've been working on."

She was gone in a flash and skipped up the stairs to the old chest. Opening it, the scent of last summer's Lemon Verbena filled the air and brought a smile.

I want my kitchen to always smell like this. I wonder if Preston enjoys the smell of Lemons?

Despite the empty room, she felt her face warm as the blush rose up from her collar. With a slight shake of her head she pulled out the multi-colored fabric, and the bundle of her unfinished work and headed back outside.

Jane looked up as the door squeaked open, "Let's see how far you've gotten on this one. Is this your third quilt for your chest?"

Emma nodded as she unfolded her project.

"If your home has nothing else, it'll have warm beds."

Emma smiled, "And colorful ones too. Lena suggested I set the big center piece with flying geese surrounding it. I think that's a great idea but all of the background will have to be solid colors with the geese in print, don't you think?"

Jane nodded, "Uh huh. Emma the points are pretty good here. It really helped when you started joining several pieces together before you worked them into the bigger quilt, didn't it? For me the trick is slow and careful stitching and that's easier to do with less fabric in your lap. Would you like me to help you put some more of it together?"

"No thank you. I know you've got your own work as well as mending to finish there." Her eyes lit on the split oak basket at Jane's feet. "Maybe I should be helping with that."

"No dear, you work on your quilt. It's good for a girl to work filling her hope chest. It keeps her eyes on the future and the home that God is building around her."

"Thank you Mama. I guess I'll always need you to remind me that God is still working on my future; just like I'm still working on this beautiful quilt." She lifted the unfinished quilt up to admire it.

"Oh child, the good Lord will be working on you for your whole life. He ain't finished with me yet."

Plans for Emma

Emma smiled and blinked back a single tear. It was easier now not to cry all the time. *Lord, please help me to be pleasant while you're working on me. There's no sense at all in moping around all the time. That's not faith, is it?*

Mother and daughter worked for a solid hour with little talk between them. Emma enjoyed her mother's company and felt she'd wasted too much time worrying over the past months and hadn't had good time with any of her family.

"I guess I'd better get dinner started or your Papa will be pretty upset when he comes in from plowing and there's nothing to eat."

"I'll be right there."

"No no. You keep working. Enjoy the quilt and the sunshine."

Emma smiled up at her before returning her eyes to the pattern in her hands.

After stitching for another hour, Emma closed her eyes and raised her hand to rub the back of her aching neck. The bleating of two lonely sheep and kitchen sounds coming from the open window drowned out all other sounds. Emma had no idea she was no longer alone on the porch until a soft cough begged her attention.

Without opening her eyes she spoke to the child she was sure had joined her. "Honey why don't you climb up in the swing with me. I've about put my eyes out sewing."

With a smile she slowly opened her eyes to find neither Metie nor Bessie but instead Austin Adams smiling broadly.

"Oh my. I thought you were one of the children. Uh, that is, I had my eyes closed when I heard you and I guess I was talking to Bessie without even looking to see who I was really talking to. Oh that doesn't make a lick of sense does it?"

Austin's smile widened and the chuckle he suppressed was evident in his voice, "It makes perfect sense. I'm Austin, remember now?"

Emma's face warmed as she nodded, "Yes, I remember you Mr. Adams. Won't you have a seat?" She gestured toward a row of split bottomed chairs against the opposite wall.

He strode across the small porch and pulled one of the chairs out several inches. Emma unconsciously withdrew by cocking her foot under the swing.

"Mama will have supper in just a few minutes. I should tell her to set an extra place."

Austin shook his head but his eyes never moved from Emma's face. "No, I won't eat. I'm just now coming through and haven't even been to Charlie's place yet. When I saw this ole' place coming to life I couldn't help but stop here before I headed up their lane. It's good to see folks livin' here. My Pa is always sad when he comes by here. He was raised here you know."

"Yeah, Lena told me that. Well I'm glad we can save a piece of history."

"Miss Emma, did you get the letters I wrote you?"

"Letters? Well I got one before Christmas."

"I guess the second one never made it to you before your family moved over here. I had hoped you'd write back."

Emma's head dropped and her eyes darted from one edge of the porch to the other as though an answer might be hiding in a corner. "Oh, well that wouldn't have been right, would it?"

He nodded slowly but his eyes never broke from hers."Well, maybe not. But Mr. England he gave me permission to write – in fact, he may have suggested it."

Emma bit hard on her lip fighting the urge to run screaming at her father. She'd never spoken so disrespectfully to the man, had never even had a notion to do so. But now to hear him pushing her onto the man when he knew that her Preston was working and waiting for her. With a sharp intake of breath she stilled her thoughts. *You don't even know that he's waiting. Fact is, there's no reason to think he would be.*

"Miss Emma, the second letter asked if I might call on you but then I got word from Charlie that you'd be here soon. Then again he let me know just over a week ago that I could come on anytime to visit. So here I am. I come the first chance I got to leave the farm."

Plans for Emma

Emma tried to clear her mind, *Remember this is your Papa's desire and you owe him to keep an open mind to it.*

"Tell me about your farm Mr. Adams."

"Well, do you think you could call me Austin? I got just five cleared acres. But it backs up to the Laurel Branch so my stock have real good grazin' close to home. And they don't much venture beyond that water source."

Emma couldn't help but smile at his pride in the home he'd created. "Did you clear it yourself? We had a hilltop at the Roslin farm that we were working on clearin'. Takes a lot of sweat and sore muscles to clear new ground."

"Yes ma'am, it sure does. My little place was rough cut when I got it. My Pa had bought the land and we cut the timber off of it. He left enough for me to build a little cabin. Then I grubbed stumps and dug roots for two or three years. Well as a matter of fact, I'm still pullin' out roots!"

"Well I imagine the corn you'll take outta' there this fall will be worth it."

Her voice had grown so soft he leaned closer to make out the words. "Oh yeah, I can hardly wait to get my hands on them ears."

He cocked his head as though trying to understand her. With a deep breath he slapped his knees, "Well I'd better be gettin' on over to Charlie's. If I walk in there after your sister puts her supper on the table I'll be in trouble for sure."

Emma looked up at him as though she had forgotten he was there in the brief moment between their interchange."Oh yes. She'll want to feed you well after your trip over."

She stood with him and Austin looked long at her before stepping off the porch.

Emma gathered her quilting pieces together and headed into the warm kitchen.

Chapter 19

Austin grabbed the reins of his horse in one hand and cut through the corner of the open field toward his brother's farm. He usually enjoyed the walk into this property that he'd always known as his grandparents' home. Today was different. He didn't see the sun inching its way toward the western horizon nor did he see the well mended fences that Charlie maintained. He didn't notice the new boards on the old barn or the deep loamy soil turned and awaiting seeds. Austin's head was down and he concentrated on the next step his foot would take.

"Helloooo," jerked Austin's attention back to the present.

Seeing Charlie striding toward him, Austin stopped and held his hand up in greeting. As his brother came within earshot he returned the greeting, "Hidey Charlie. How are you gettin' along?"

"I reckon I'm doin' just fine brother. It's good to see you." He clapped the shorter man tightly on the shoulder. "I didn't expect you this late in the day. Did you have trouble gettin' started?"

Austin shook his head slowly and nodded his head toward the 'England home', "Nah, I stopped at the home place on my way. Been visiting with Miss Emma."

A smile spread across Charlie's face, "Not wastin' any time are you?"

As his cheeks warmed Austin defended the stop, "Well the old place just looked so inviting with clothes on the line and curtains in the windows. I probably would have stopped even if I hadn't known the girl was there."

Charlie arched an eyebrow up, "But she was extra incentive to be neighborly, wasn't she?"

Plans for Emma

"Ah Charlie. Let's get on up to the house before Lena comes lookin' for you."

They started up the dirt lane and Charlie quickly out paced Austin. "You're sure slowin' down. What's holding you back boy?"

Austin just shook his head.

"Now come on and tell your big brother what's on your mind. Emma hasn't rejected you already has she?"

"Well not exactly but I don't think she was as happy to see me as I was."

Charlie laughed, "That's not too surprising, she's a lot prettier than you are."

Even as he shook his head a grin escaped Austin's gloom. He waved off his brother's familiar teasing and kept walking.

Lena met the men at her kitchen door with a clean towel in her outstretched hand. "Charlie I've put warm water in the wash pan and here's you a clean towel to wash up with. Austin, I'm glad to see you; we didn't quite know when to expect you."

He doffed his hat with one hand and smoothed his hair with the other as he answered her, "Thank you Lena. I appreciate the invite. I won't be too much trouble to yu'ns."

"No trouble a'tall I'll put another plate on the table. Just cornbread, milk and beef with boiled taters tonight though. I hope that kind of food won't run you off."

"'Course not. I generally cook for myself you know."

With clean hands and faces the men entered the kitchen and hung their hats on the rack by the door. Austin's heart was heavy tonight yet he couldn't help but smile at his grandmother's kitchen. Charlie had been alone in this house well over a year before he married Lena and the kitchen always seemed lonely without his grandmother puttering between stove and work table. Lena was nothing like the rotund old woman but the same spirit filled the room again and Austin felt immediately at home.

"It sure does smell good Lena."

Charlie joined in winking at his wife, "This little lady keeps me well fed Austin. You just don't know what a woman brings to a home till you bring one in."

Lena smiled at Austin, "Is it hard for you to see another woman in your grandmother's kitchen?"

"Oh no, that's just what I was thinking, that it's like coming home again with good food cooking and clean windows and floors. Grandma would be proud of you – and proud of Charlie for marryin' so well."

Lena's smile continued to broaden with the praise and she laid a gentle hand on her husband's shoulder as she set the hot bread before them. Steam rose from the bowl heaping with potatoes in brown beef broth already on the table. Lena sat across from Austin and nodded to Charlie that he could begin the prayer.

"Father God, we thank you for this bounty. We thank you for the hands that have prepared it and pray your blessing on them. We thank you that my brother can break bread with us today and that you've delivered him safely to us. In the precious name of Jesus, Amen."

Amens echoed from Lena and Austin as Charlie reached for the meat and potatoes. Lena was more interested in hearing any news her brother-in-law brought than in the food before her.

After learning everyone in Banner Springs fared well and crops were getting planted in good time and no one close was near death, she turned her attention to Emma.

"I know Emma will be happy to see you. She told me you had written her."

Austin's fork froze in mid-air. "I stopped on the way in. Couldn't help myself."

Lena smiled warmly at him, "Well I'm glad to hear you're anxious to see her. She's such a dear girl that I really want someone to treasure her."

Austin returned the fork to his plate still filled with food. "I don't know Lena. I sat on the porch there talking to her for several minutes and I just don't know."

Plans for Emma

Concern clouded Lena's face, "She wasn't unkind to you, was she?"

"Oh no, nothing like that. I don't know that I can explain it – she was right there and talkin' to me but somehow she seemed to be somewhere else. Now that just sounds crazy, don't it?"

Charlie joined in, "Not exactly crazy."

"Well Austin, maybe she just needs to get to know you a little bit. I guess she was surprised to see you today."

"Maybe that's it Lena."

The trio lingered long at the table laughing as first Austin then Charlie shared stories of their childhood and memories from the house Charlie and Lena now shared. When Lena had put away the last of the dishes and blew out the wall sconce she patted her damp apron and announced, "I'm turning in. You boys visit as long as you want to."

Charlie stood stretching his long frame, "Nope, I've visited all I can. Milkin' will have to be done bright and early whether my lop-legged brother is here or not."

"Well Austin, I put a good straw tick in the corner of the front room. Charlie said you wouldn't want to sleep in the loft even though I'm sure it would be warm enough up there now."

"No, no. I'll be just fine in there where we always slept as boys 'cause Grandma thought we'd catch our death of cold in the upstairs. Never you mind that's where the lot of us ten kids slept at home. But things are different at Grandma's house, aren't they?"

As the door clicked shut behind his brother and sister-in-law, Austin stepped onto the front porch and found himself squinting toward the home place that the England family now occupied. Was that a flicker of lamp light still burning there? Would it be Emma still awake?

I wonder if she sits up reading until Mr. England has to remind her of the high cost of coal oil like my sister Martha always did?

Looking up to the night sky he turned his thoughts toward prayer, *Ah Lord God, this morning I was so excited to ride over here*

141

and see that pretty girl again. Why do I have such an unsettled feeling now?

No answer fell from the stars and after untold minutes Austin re-entered the house and settled down on the straw tick.

He woke to the soft shuffle of a woman's feet as Lena coaxed a flame in her cookstove and slid the coffee pot forward. Austin stretched on the pallet and after a moment slipped out the front door to visit the privy before greeting his hosts.

He looked into the barn but found only the milk cow who still stood in her open stall working at a bit of hay Charlie had put out during milking. Austin admired the neatness of his brother's tools and the smell of fresh hay. They'd been taught well how to tend to a farm and while Austin worked at it every day being here he realized Charlie might be the superior husbandman.

Stepping onto the front porch he noticed a wisp of steam rising from the wash pan and he smiled realizing Lena had put out warm water for her husband to use after his chores in the barn. Dipping his own hands in the wash pan a pang of jealousy hit him for he had to draw his own water to wash each morning.

"Austin, there you are. There's hot coffee on the stove."

"Smells good. I'll have some for sure. And do I smell biscuits?"

"Of course you do. We'll have salt pork cooked in a few minutes and the hens are laying well so you can have all the eggs you can eat."

"Umm hmmm. It is a blessing to be here."

Lena chuckled as she gently pushed him aside to pull the biscuits from the oven. "Sit yourself down there and eat up."

Charlie talked between bites sharing his plans for the day. "I'll be pulling in some rails I split to fence Lena's garden. You planning to help me or is this just a courting trip for you?"

Plans for Emma

Austin felt himself redden as he answered, "I'll do whatever I need to. But I do want to pay a call on the Englands at some point today."

"You let me get these rails stacked up and we'll all go over there for a little visit."

Austin smiled, maybe that was just what Emma needed – time to get to know him with other people that she knew and loved surrounding her. Maybe he was wrong to sit out on that porch alone with her yesterday. "I'll be finished before you are and we'll get that fence built in no time."

It was not yet noon when the three Adamses walked up to their family's old home place.

Austin had been quiet on the short walk but now chatted nervously, "Everytime I think of this place I call it 'the home place' but I guess we need to start callin' it the England home, don't we?"

Lena nodded with pride as she remembered all the work her mother and sisters had accomplished in the short weeks they'd been there. It really did look like a home now. She cracked the door and called ahead, "Mama, Em, are yu'ns in here?"

From the kitchen she heard a greeting from her sister, "Mornin, Lena. Come on in. Mama's changing little Gip and I'm in here finishin' up..." Emma had stepped toward the open doorway of the front room as she spoke and stopped short when she realized that Lena wasn't alone.

"Oh, good mornin' Charlie, Mr. Adams."

Charlie smiled, "You don't need to call him that Em, he's Austin to all of us."

She dipped her head and nodded without looking at either of them. "I was finishing up some bread. Papa bought some flour from the Todd's. We've not had any wheat flour in a few weeks and were pretty tired of cornbread. So yu'ns can have some hot bread – well it won't be ready till after dinner of course."

Again she dropped her head realizing she'd responded to them as though they'd be there all day long.

Lena turned back to the front door, "Well let's sit on the porch. The sun is heating the house and I guess you still have the fire going for the oven. It's really nice out on the porch."

Emma instinctively reached back to untie the flour-covered apron. "I think I'll grab a light wrap. Just one minute please."

By the time Emma stepped out the front door Jane had joined them and was talking with Austin. When she stepped onto the squeaking porch boards, Austin seemed suddenly uncomfortable.

"What's Mr. England into today?"

"Well Austin, I think he's layin' off rows for the corn crop. He plowed the last three days and he's just sure it's going to start rainin' again any day so we need to drop the seed today."

"I'll be happy to help with that. In fact, if you've got a spare hoe I'll go help with the layin' off."

Jane's eyes darted to Emma and back to Austin. "Well I sure hate to put you out in the field when you're on a visit."

"Don't matter to me. I'm glad to give a fellow a hand if I can."

Charlie stood up, "You're not gonna' leave me with the womenfolk looking like a good-for-nothing. If you've gotta be workin' come on let's get out there."

Lena watched her husband disappear around the corner before she turned to Emma.

"Emma, whatever's the matter with you? I don't think you said a word to Austin and he's come all the way over here to call on you."

"I did too say hello to him at the same time I greeted Charlie."

"Well don't you like Austin at all? He's a very good man and he works hard, just look at him heading out to help our Papa?"

"Lena I can't find any fault in Austin Adams."

Jane stepped close enough to loop her arm around Emma's shoulders, "But you don't show any joy in seeing him either dear."

Plans for Emma

"Mama, I will honor you and Papa. If you feel the Lord would have me marry him I will do everything in my power to make him a good wife."

Jane's lips pressed tightly as she looked into her daughter's eyes. She squeezed her again and stepped back into the house leaving the sisters to visit.

By the time Jane rang the dinner bell for the noon meal, better than half the field was marked by even furrows awaiting the golden corn seed.

Tom wiped at his brow with a dusty handkerchief as they walked slowly toward the house. "You boys were a lot of help to me. Three of us accomplished more than three times the work."

"Glad to do it sir," Austin answered without turning his head.

Tom had barely spoken to them beyond a friendly greeting when they first arrived with hoes in hand. Now he looked for a chance to learn more about Austin.

"Did you get your crop in before you headed over here?"

The question clearly embarrassed Austin. His last thought as he rode out of his yard the day before was that the corn needed to be in the ground. But his excitement to better know Emma England trumped the crop and he decided the planting could wait for a day or two. Now he had to answer for the decision. "No sir, I'm afraid I've put it off a little bit. But my fields are plowed and my sisters will come help drop seed so we can get it planted pretty quickly. I'm only going to stay with Charlie a couple of days then I'll get back to work."

Tom nodded. "Your land producin' pretty well?"

"Oh yeah. It's all new ground you know. I just cleared it in the past two years. Really last year was the first time I had it all tilled. It's just five acres but then again it's just me workin' it."

"I well know how that is. After we lost our boy George I thought I'd have to let some of the fields in Roslin go back to the brambles. He had really just got up to a size he could pull a man's load when the fever took him. If Lena and Em hadn't stepped in and worked like sons I don't know what I would've done."

Austin smiled with pride in this girl he hoped to marry. What a blessing it would be to have a wife that could work right beside him in the field. Even as the thought came to him he remembered the empty look in her eyes, the far away gaze even when she spoke to him kindly.

Tom continued on with his questions, "What about your stock? Did everything winter well?"

"Yes sir, of course my cows are a little on the thin order. It was a hard winter. But the grass is greening fast and they're eatin' good."

Tom nodded and quirked a sidways smile at Charlie as they stepped onto the back porch and each stuck their hands into the waiting pan.

As dinner finished Charlie begged off returning to Tom's field saying he needed to get Lena's new garden patch raked out and ready for planting. "You boys were plenty of help to this old man in the morning. Go enjoy workin' together and get my daughter a good place to grow her vegetables."

Austin looked from Tom to Charlie; he'd assumed he would return to drop corn with the Englands. However, somehow he felt dismissed and he rose to leave with Lena and Charlie.

As the screen door slammed shut Tom smiled at Emma. "Em, that's a good man. He's got his place well in hand even if he did put off planting to come courtin'."

"Oh Papa he's not courtin' he's just visitin' his brother."

"Emma Jane England, don't nobody think that boy come all the way from Banner Springs to see Charlie. He's come a'courtin' you. And you'd better just be happy to have someone that can read and can work and knows the Lord."

Emma stared at her plate and nodded almost imperceptibly. "Yes sir."

"Em, tell me what's on your mind?" Jane questioned.

"It's not my mind Mama, it's my heart…"

Plans for Emma

Tom cut her off, "Heart! The good book says it's desperately wicked! You can't trust your heart."

"Yes Papa." Emma sat a moment longer and the table was silent but for the chatter of her youngest siblings. Even Metie was quietened by her father's strong tone. Emma stood to begin cleaning.

As he announced the afternoon's plan his tone had softened only slightly, "Charlie and Austin have gotten us far enough ahead that you can come out and start dropping seed as soon as you're finished in here. In fact I'll take Metie and Leonard with me on the sled with the seed"

The children clamored out the door eager to ride on top of the big burlap bags. Jane watched her daughter as she moved silently about the kitchen but she said nothing more about Emma's future.

Chapter 20

Preston asked everyone he spoke with whether they knew anything about the Martha Washington community. He got plenty of questions whether he'd heard of a girl in Martha Washington or if there was work there and was he trying to get out of the logging business. He was glad to laugh off their teasing if it helped him learn where his Emma had gone. Sure enough, he came to understand the community was just about six miles due west and they did in fact have a church both in Martha Washington as well as an older church three miles further in Campground.

He didn't like hearing there might be two places he'd have to look for the England family, not when he didn't even know where in Martha Washington they may have settled. So, he decided he'd start with the Martha Washington Church and keep trying until he located them.

The very next Sunday, he left with the rising sun and set his back to the sliver of light that was the eastern horizon. The path he followed soon left the portion of the Flat Woods they had already logged and the thick, old-growth timber blotted out every speck of light. Until his eyes grew accustomed to the darkness he feared he'd have to sit down until the sun rose higher on the skyline, but it wasn't long before he could keep a steady pace toward his destination. Despite the well-used path, the travel was treacherous as he walked down, down, down. He began to doubt whether he could make it to the church in time for the morning preaching service. He was sure there was something at the bottom of this long descent and he only hoped that it would not be a gulf he couldn't cross.

This path's worn bare so I'll have to trust that all those feet walkin' it before me were able to get through whatever's at the bottom.

Plans for Emma

The path leveled out and he had several minutes of easy walking before he faced another hill. Preston stopped to breathe a moment at the base of the hill. He looked over his shoulder at the sun creeping higher in the sky and casting long shadows across the little cove he'd just crossed. Thankful for the sun and the old footpath, he looked up the next hill and resumed his steady pace already wondering what would be on the other side. He knew he was not more than halfway there for he'd been told he had at least a three hour walk.

At the bottom of the latest hill he heard the rushing water of a good-sized creek and hoped there'd be a bridge of some sort so he wouldn't have to wade ice cold water before church. He found a moss covered foot log and hopped onto it without a second thought. Based on his questioning, he knew there were two strong creeks to be crossed and he was happy to have found the first one.

The second creek had a rickety wooden bridge crossing a makeshift mill brake with another hill beyond it. Based on the sun's position now, Preston felt certain he must be getting close. He threw his hand up to acknowledge a woman feeding chickens near the little gristmill and saw some young folk cutting across a field to the south. There were a few houses along the road now and some well-kept farms. Two women joined him as he topped the hill and called a, "Good mornin'" to him. Preston spoke but didn't slow his pace to walk with them.

Soon he saw a steep bend in the road and heard voices long before he saw the little clapboard building set back among a patch of trees. He knew he was arriving well before time for a church service, but there were already people gathering in the yard and he was sure he'd found the Martha Washington Church.

Several boys introduced themselves to Preston and everyone seemed to carry the name "Baldwin". A flash of fear crossed his mind that he'd walked into a family gathering rather than a weekly service. As the squeak and jingle of wheel and harness announced each wagon loaded with families, he turned to search the faces. Finally, he saw the tall frame and angular face of Tom England seated beside Jane's ever-present smile.

Preston could have jumped for joy realizing he'd found the right place; he had found Emma. Jane spotted the boy right away and knew the look of sheer pleasure. Her smile broadened and she looked over her shoulder and spoke a quiet word.

The children were used to their mother looking behind with a soft word when they were riding in Papa's wagon. "Emma, I believe we have a friend from Roslin with us today."

Emma tried to look around Papa's seat as she asked, "Really, who is it?"

Feeling emboldened, Preston walked straight to the wagon. "Good Morning Mr. England. Miz England," he tipped his hat as he spoke to the lady. He determined not to look in the back for Emma but his eyes betrayed him and sought out her face among the children.

Emma's face bloomed with delight when she realized Preston was the friend Mama had mentioned, but she kept her gaze low. Her heart raced and as she studied the hem of her dress she willed herself to breath. Tears gathered behind her eyes and she blinked hard lest they escape. *Why are you all weepy Em? Here Preston has come all this way to see you – are they tears of joy? Or is it that you think things are hopeless? At least Papa has another chance to say yes to him.*

Preston knew Emma didn't want her father to see them making eyes at each other and risk a demand that they not even be in church together so he didn't question her or try to get her attention.

"Thought we left you in Roslin, boy," Tom had his back to Preston as he helped Jane climb down from the high wagon seat.

Plans for Emma

"Well Sir, you sure did leave me there but you know that I'm still a'wantin' to court Miss Emma and, well sir, I had to come see where you'd all moved off to."

Jane England's kind smile warmed Preston through and through. She took his hand between both of hers as she spoke to him, "Preston, we are so happy to see you here today. It's hard to move away from all your friends and I know that Emma, Metie and Bessie will be happy to have you with them in service this morning. Won't you sit with us?"

He looked at Tom before accepting the invitation and did not speak until the head of the house gave a nearly imperceptible nod. "Thank you ma'am, I'd be honored."

Jane took the baby from Emma and reached for Leonard's pudgy hand as they started into the church. Emma smiled as she walked past him holding Bessie's hand and giving Metie's back a gentle push to encourage her to move a little faster. The smile in her eyes spoke volumes to Preston's heart that he knew Emma might never be able to voice.

In the church, he and Emma were seated on opposite ends of the pew and Preston had to sit right beside her father. Yet he felt closer to Emma than he ever had. He hoped for an invitation to dinner but after the final "Amen," Tom gave him a brisk handshake and said, "Good to see you today." He then turned to lead his family away without any opportunity for Preston to speak to either Emma or Jane.

Preston took a deep breath trying to quell the anger brewing in his chest. He made his exit from the church as soon as the pressing crowd would allow and saw the Englands already loaded on their wagon despite several ladies around it trying to talk to both Jane and the children. Tom was about to hand the baby up to Jane.

Preston made eye contact with Tom and held it as he stepped from the porch and made a beeline for him. Something inside him urged caution. A quiet voice seemed to say, *Don't speak to this man in anger or you'll never get what you want.*

He forced deep breaths and waited until he was close enough to speak without raising his voice. Tom took two

151

steps away from the wagon as the boy approached him. "Mr. England, I don't mean no disrespect and I know you've told me your decision already but I've just got to talk to you again."

Tom's face first showed the real displeasure he felt at having to answer these questions the second time. But then he softened somehow and Preston saw the change and it gave him hope.

"Mr. England, did y'uns leave Roslin on account of me sir?"

Tom started to laugh but caught himself and lowered his head, clearing his throat. Preston pursed his lips in an attempt to obey the voice that kept urging him not to speak angry words. He was on the verge of losing the battle when Tom spoke.

"No son, I got a good offer on my farm in Roslin and an opportunity to buy more land here. It was a good deal, that's all."

Preston took a deep breath and started again. "Have you given any more thought to me courtin' Em?"

Tom seemed to catch his use of the familiar nickname and squinted his eyes. Preston saw the spark and tried to reason with the man. "I know there's got to be lots of boys interested in her because Emma is a fine girl but I would sure appreciate your telling me why it is you wouldn't want me keepin' company with her."

With a single finger Tom pushed his ragged hat higher on his head and looked Preston straight in the eye. "Like I told you at Jonesville, you're a good feller Preston. But I just want more for my Emma 'cause you're right, she is a fine girl. I want a man that has some land and can offer her some ease in her life. My girls can all read and write and I would like their men to have some education. Why, could you even read the Word of God to your children?"

Logic had failed for Preston knew he could not deny either of these points. He lowered his head and did not say

Plans for Emma

another word. As he turned he tried not to see Emma but out of the corner of his eye he caught her watching him.

The trip back to the logging camp took twice as long as the morning trip did. He'd eaten no lunch and by the time he crossed the footlog at the Clear Fork Creek he was shaking. He knelt and scooped water into his mouth then sat on a rock warmed by the morning sun. As he stared into the frothy water, he tried to reason with himself.

"You can't think bad of the man for wantin' something good for his kids. And you know Emma deserves better than you can offer her."

Still, something within Preston Langford screamed that this was the girl for him. If he was not naturally what she deserved then he would have to make himself into that new thing.

"The question then is how."

He looked around the dense woods feeling a little bit foolish for talking to himself.

Silently he thought, *I doubt she'd want anything to do with a man what talks to himself in the woods.*

As he stood to start the steep climb toward home he was able to smile. And he began to pray aloud. "Lord you've said that if I'm in you I'm a new creature. Well that creature ain't good enough for Tom England so I'm askin' for your help changing."

As he walked he cast his mind from one idea to another how he might somehow become good enough to satisfy Tom England.

"I wish I could talk to Em. I just wonder if it's only Tom I'm changin' for. Am I good enough for her?"

He shook his head in an attempt to shake off the doubt that wanted to settle upon him. "Now Preston, if you are going to make this happen then you can't be battlin' your own self too. God showed you the prettiest girl you ever saw so he'll show you how to win her if that's his will."

Chapter 21

The England wagon might well have been enroute to a funeral for all of the cheer the family expressed on the sunny winter day. Emma was fighting tears and only her strong conviction to honor her father and mother kept her from uttering a single word.

Tom hunched his shoulders and stared at the ears of his horses. When he did have to speak to the animals, he growled the commands at them. Even the horses held their heads low and plodded in such a dejected manner that the trip home seemed interminable.

Jane was as quiet as the rest of the family but it was her thoughts rather than emotion that silenced her. As she remembered the look of Preston Langford, it was obvious that he cared very deeply for her Em. *He's sure gone to great effort to see her and by the look on Tom's face it appears he's asked the second time if they can court. He's a handsome fellow so there would be any number of girls at Jonesville church eager to have him calling. What is it that draws him to Em?*

Jane realized she needed to know more about Emma's feelings.

The silence continued into the farmyard where the whole family peeled off the wagon and headed their separate ways. Tom drafted Metie to lead the team to water as he stored the harness. Both Bessie and Leonard had fallen asleep in the wagon's bed on the slow ride home.

Jane seized the moment to have her talk with Em.

"Em, me and you need to talk about this Langford boy."

"Yes Mama, what do you want to say?" Emma began dinner preparations before Jane asked but her words were lifeless.

Plans for Emma

"Emma Jane, I don't want you walkin' around here like some kind of scarecrow, head down and no emotion. That is not who you are, and I thought I was seeing you pull out of that. You should have really perked up when Austin called on you but instead you seemed to withdraw from the whole world.

I was happy to see the boy from the loggin' camp at church today and thought you'd be thrilled, but here you are down in the dumps again. Now, we need to figure out what the good Lord would have for you and get you focused on that and get a smile back on your pretty face."

With eyes glazed by unshed tears, Emma gave her mother her full attention.

Jane continued, "I guess I can see it in your face but I want you to tell me your thoughts about Preston Langford."

"How can I do that Mama? My every thought seems to be about him. I know that Papa has refused him and I also know that I have to honor my father. I guess the only way I can honor Papa is to marry Austin. I want to honor him but I just feel like Preston will always have my heart even if another man has my hand.

You know I will obey Papa and I don't want to think I know better but I sure don't understand him this time."

"Now, let's not worry about your Papa, or Austin Adams. Let's talk about Mr. Langford. You know very little about him, and we have no connections so that we can learn anything about him. How can he fill your head like that?"

"Oh Mama, I know it was maybe wrong, but he passed me at the creek one day – well you remember, I told you about it that very day. Do you remember?"

"Hmm, well child, you tell me so much that I can't say for sure I recall exactly that bit."

"Well, I did tell you, I promise you I did. I told you that a man stopped at the creek while I was down there with the sheep. And I told you that he was driving a load of wood or logs or cross ties. I don't remember what was on that wagon."

Jane smiled, "No, I don't guess you would remember that detail. But how would a passing start all of this?"

Emma smiled and blushed slightly, "Well it was awfully forward I know it was, but he slowed way down as he drove by and I looked up to see who it was driving, you know I thought maybe it was a neighbor that I knew. When he slowed down, I looked straight into his face and I just couldn't look away. I knew it was wrong, that it was rude but I couldn't help myself I stared right at him. And he stared too.

Well then he stopped the next time he came through because he needed to water his mules. And we talked for a minute. After that he stopped every time that he came through. It was maybe ten minutes a week that we talked but Mama it felt like my whole life. I would have driven that herd of sheep all the way to Sunbright for that ten minutes talking to Preston."

Jane didn't bother to scold her daughter's indiscretion in talking to a young man without a proper chaperone for she could see both the love that had grown between them as well as the pain of separation.

Now that she'd begun talking, Emma's words rushed out, "Lena said that the boys at the logging camp weren't church folks and you've taught me that I must be sure to marry a man what believes like I do. And Lena said the loggers were very rough, that they drink and carouse every time they go to Sunbright with those loads of ties. Now, I think she was wrong because Preston tells me he gets out of there quick as he can and that he doesn't frequent the tavern. But I wasn't real sure at first. Then when he started coming to church on a regular basis I kept waiting for him to speak to Papa. And when he did, Papa refused to let us court. What was the point of me saying anything then?" She sniffed and gulped air, "If Papa knows what's best and I'm willing to follow his leadin', then why do I feel so powerfully drawn to Preston Langford?"

Plans for Emma

Jane drew her daughter close in a warm embrace, "Dear Em. You are the one of my girls that I can always count on to fall back on her teaching. Neither Gustie nor Lena would deny themselves what they wanted just because their folks refused it. Remember the Bible teaches us that the heart is wicked and we can't always depend on its leading. That's why we have God's teaching to follow. But at the same time, there is a reason why a girl feels drawn to a certain boy instead of another one. There's some of God leadin' in that too, don't you think?"

"I did right, didn't I Mama? This might be the most important decision of my whole life – I sure want to get it right."

"Yes child, I think you did right. Now it's up to me and your Papa to do the right thing. Sometimes what's right isn't so very clear though. Here's what I know, we want the very best for you and your life. And you want to obey God by honoring his commandment to honor your parents. So I know that when the decision faces all of us who God has chosen for you to marry, then we'll all be agreein' on it. You let me talk to Tom."

Although her eyes blurred with tears Emma smiled at her mother, knowing that she could trust her to seek the very best for her children. "Are you agreein' with Papa about Austin Adams?"

Jane had removed her hat and turned toward the front room where her bed and big walnut dresser made a bedroom corner for the couple. She stopped in the doorway and turned halfway to wink at Emma and gave the tiniest shake to her head. "We won't mention the creek to your Papa."

Dinner was almost as quiet an affair as the drive home with the exception of the children who awoke from their brief naps with renewed energy. After the meal, Tom and Jane stepped into the front room while the girls tidied the kitchen. As Tom stirred the coals in the stick and mud fireplace, Jane scooted her hickory rocker a bit closer to him.

He turned his head and looked at her from the corner of his eye. "Well I can guess what you're a'wantin' to talk about."

"Now what makes you think I'd want to talk 'bout anything special?"

"Cause when you move that rocker, you've got something on your mind."

He settled into the straight-back chair and locked his boot heels in the front spindle, "Go ahead then, it won't go away; it's gotta come out of you."

Jane smiled. She loved this man and loved their ability to talk and even argue with love. Many of his neighbors did not know how good Tom England's heart was and she was thankful she did.

"I spoke with Em."

"About that Langford boy?"

"Yes. She cares very deeply for him."

"How could she? She don't know him. Austin she knows – he's called on her and we know his brother. We even know of his family in Banner Springs. That Langford boy, we don't know anything about him."

"A girl's heart doesn't need a lot of facts to love. You know that Em has had plenty of offers of suitors and she's never shown any interest in any of them. She's sixteen and while Lena's not even been married a half a year, there's lots of girls Em's age been married long enough to already have a child."

Tom shook his head as he studied the flames before him.

"I know she's special to you."

He turned to face his wife as he answered, "Now you know I love all my kids the same. Gustie is so full of life that she is like a gust of wind when she enters a room. And Lena can see the facts and lay them out like a Georgia Stock Plow. But Em, she's the best of both worlds. She's gentle and kind, yet there's a fire in her that gives her spunk. I believe she'd stand up to a black bear if she had to."

Plans for Emma

"That young Mr. Langford seems to have a little fire too. Otherwise he wouldn't have dared ask you about courting our girl after you'd already turned him down."

"Is that spunk or stupidity? Is he drawn to Em or just determined to get his way?"

"Now what is it that we know about that boy that would make you think he'd ever been spoiled to getting his own way?"

"Well he's sure respected in that lumber camp so I'll bet he gets his own way a fair amount there."

Jane snorted before she could stop the sharp breath she exhaled." A loggin' camp don't give no man his own way much."

"Well I guess you're right there. So I don't know why he's so determined."

"Tom England, have you ever been determined?"

He smiled and put a hand on his wife's arm, "I was determined to have you and I think Grandaddy Peters knew better than to argue."

She waved a hand at him, "Ah, he was just tired of us kids by that time. When you're number eleven in the family, the one time you can be sure to get your own way is when you want to leave home. With Mother's health slipping, I think he was just glad to get shed of me."

"Well I'd like to think that he knew you were going to be cared for."

She smiled and covered his hand with her own, "And I have been."

"That boy don't have much to give our Em. If we could turn her head to Charlie's brother, she'd have a right smart more. I don't know why she's so against marryin' Austin."

Jane shook her head and pushed the rocker a little faster. "Well Preston hasn't asked to marry her, he's only askin' to call. And living in that lumber camp all the way over to Roslin, he won't call often. Emma will obey you if you say Austin is the man she's to marry, but her heart is not in it."

"He don't know a thing about carin' for a farm; he'd no doubt run through or lay waste to the land I'm planning to give her. But the Adamses have a good spread in Banner Springs and they'll have taught their boys how to manage it. Don't you think Charlie does a good job?"

"Yes, Charlie does just fine and his grandparents left him with a good farm."

"Don't you think this Langford boy's a little like the pink eye? Just keeps coming around agin' and agin'?"

Jane smiled knowing that this banter meant she'd swayed his opinion. "He is persistent; doesn't that tell you he will stick to the work of the farm – and to Em?"

"He does work hard. Like I said, he's got a good name among the loggers. Guess he'll have to work hard, to overcome the simple-mindedness."

They laughed together now, "Tom England that was just awful."

They heard the back door open and the rise of voices told them Lena and Charlie had arrived for a Sunday afternoon visit.

"Guess we'll figure out just what to do with this mess at another time."

All of the children ran to greet Lena who had a basket on her arm filled with molasses bread and apple butter. Big pieces of the heavy cake topped with the spicy apple sauce were soon handed around the table along with fresh milk and hot coffee; the room was a'buzz with voices as everyone tried to catch up on news and gossip. This was becoming a tradition for the new Adamses had visited the Englands almost every Sunday afternoon since the move from Roslin. The children, accustomed to Lena caring for them as much as Mama, surrounded her, begging for love and attention.

Charlie was enjoying some time with his in-laws for he had barely known them when he took Lena as his wife.

In a short time, Lena found herself with baby Gip asleep in her arms and Leonard and Bessie playing a stick game at

Plans for Emma

her feet. Finally, there was time for the older sisters to talk a little and it was clear to Lena that Em was needing to talk.

"Em, you got something on your mind?"

Emma nodded her head, but didn't utter a word for a long moment.

Finally Lena prodded again, "I saw Preston Langford at church this morning, even saw him talking to Papa as we were pulling out of the yard. What was that about?"

"Well I guess you know what – there's only one thing it could be."

Lena nodded, "I didn't know who he was at first because I never would have thought of anyone from Roslin showing up at the Martha Washington Church."

Emma smiled now despite her heavy heart. "Can you even believe he would walk all the way over here and be here in time for preaching. Why, he had to have left at daybreak."

"Well I reckon you've got it pretty bad for this boy, otherwise you couldn't go from the dumps one second then glee the next. Look at that perty smile on your face."

Now Emma blushed and dropped her eyes to stare at the rough boards of the kitchen floor. "Lena, I'm just sure he's the man God would have me marry. I don't even know just exactly how I know that but know it I do. Yet Papa won't even let him call on me."

As Emma sniffed, Lena shifted the baby to free an arm to caress her sister. "Well Charlie was telling me about a girl down past Campground that run off with a boy last week. I guess that's an option."

Emma jerked her head up, wide-eyed, "Lena you bite your tongue. You know I'd never do that. Why, that would break two or three commandments and you know if God has this man chosen for me then I can't run ahead of him and elope with Preston, now can I?"

Lena smiled. This was the energy she was accustomed to in her sister and it made her happy that the girl wasn't so sad that she'd lost it altogether. "No, I don't guess that would be right. Maybe that means God will work it out."

Emma had to smile now too, realizing how Lena had duped her.

Neither sister had realized their mother was even in the room until she moved to take Gip from Lena. As she stooped down she smiled at Emma, "I'm happy to hear you regaining your trust in God. I think that's what we were talking about earlier, wasn't it? You can trust your Papa too you know."

Emma nodded. "I'm going to go out for a walk. I need some time alone I think."

No one argued with her for they were well accustomed to Emma's thinking time. Most of the time she liked to be outside and she always had to be alone whenever she needed to sort out any problem. She grabbed her bonnet and shawl as she opened the back door tying them on as she walked.

Both Lena and Jane stared at the door a long moment after it banged shut. Charlie came in to refill his coffee cup but tried not to disturb the women in their kitchen domain.

Jane turned to Lena with a thin smile, "Papa has agreed to let the boy call but who knows when we'll be back in Roslin to tell him. I don't expect he'll come all the way over here to church next week."

"Oh Mama, how sad. They will both be suffering for no reason."

"Now Lena you're not usually a weepy romantic. If either of them can't wait a few days or weeks then it's a love that will never last a lifetime. Still, I don't want to tell Emma until Papa talks to Preston."

Charlie smiled down at his steaming cup remembering facing the dour Tom England with his own request to call on one of the England girls. As he raised his head he caught his new wife watching him. He smiled and nodded at her as he turned back to the sitting room and his father-in-law's company.

Chapter 22

It had been a long day and a hard walk but Preston knew it was the disappointment that exhausted him. Returning to the camp, he went straight to his bunk and stretched out. Cradling his head in his hands he stared at the wooden braces of the bed above him. He tried to pray.

Father God... Gracious Heavenly Father...Lord...Lord... No words would come. He turned on his side and drew his knees up to his chin and he thought he would cry like a tiny little boy. Instead the tears just slipped from the corners of his eyes.

Help me Lord. Please help me.

As the men moved in and out of the bunk house they assumed Langford was sleeping as many of the men did on Sunday evenings. He moved no more than a dead man but his head was spinning.

In time, a plan began to emerge and Preston straightened out his long body and rolled onto his back again.

I'll just have to show him – convince him I'm worthy of his girl. I don't reckon I could go back to school, but I've been practicing reading and I'll keep working on that. Need to be in The Good Book anyway.

Land. That's what I do have control over. I don't have any idea what it would cost to buy a farm but I know I've not got it. This is good work here logging but Mr. England don't want to see his sons-in-law working for nobody else. He wants to see them on their own land. So the question is, how do I get some land?

Wonder if I could earn more money somewhere else? Okay that's the first thing I'm going to need God's help with.

It wasn't a plan exactly, but Preston had a purpose in mind and with that he was able to get out of his bunk and finish his evening, joining the crew for supper and taking his regular table near a lamp with his Bible afterward.

As he moved through the next days, he questioned the men he worked with about land costs and opportunities to earn more money than the logging company was paying. Some of the new men who came with their families to the woods had left farms and they talked about the cost of land and the joys of living at home and growing your own bread. As they talked, Preston's mouth watered imagining the taste of the gritted corn his hoe could produce. But the numbers shocked him. It seemed decent farm land was bringing twenty dollars an acre. One man told of a tract he was offered for just one dollar per acre; it was one thousand acres and could not be sold in part. A thousand dollars was more than he could imagine earning in his whole lifetime.

Preston had guarded every penny he earned in the woods for even before he saw the girl with the sheep he knew he did not always want to work with an axe. He also had a few dollars Mother had given him before she passed away. Secured to the bedrail nearest the wall of his bunk, he knew his leather pouch now held almost one hundred dollars.

He'd never before been concerned with money or property. He'd seen his mother happy in a squat little cabin and, after all, he'd spent most of his growing up years in a board room of a barn. Now, the idea of earning money and buying a farm consumed him. He started to notice the people in Sunbright and to wonder about work in town. He talked to the brakeman on the train and learned there was a railroad works in Monterey where pay was pretty good if you could get the work.

He also spent more time at the Roslin post office listening to the talk there. He believed that would be his best chance to learn of land for sale near here. And that made him wonder if Em would want to return to Roslin. While there was no talk of farmers pulling out in the springtime, he did begin to hear of a new timber operation in the Horsepounds.

He was studying over these ideas as he walked the team down the muddy road entering the Flat Woods as he returned from a delivery in Sunbright. All of a sudden he realized someone was calling his name.

"Hey, Langford. They's a feller lookin' for you. He's in the barn I think."

Preston nodded with a "Thank ya" and pulled the right reigns to move his team on to the barn. As he entered he heard voices near the smithy and stepped into the warm enclosure.

"Hello there Columbus. You toasty warm over that fire?" Preston greeted the blacksmith who came to the camp to tend to the iron shod feet that kept the operation moving.

"Preston, this here feller's been waitin' for you. His name's Charlie Adams."

Preston stretched out his hand as the stranger flashed a smile. "I married Lena England last fall."

Preston's eyes reflected his awakened interest. "Well I'm sure glad to meet you. Yeah, I remember hearin' your name and I think I saw you at Martha Washington church, didn't I?"

"Yep, I guess you did. Say, I was over to Tom and Jane's on Sunday and I think Tom's wantin' to talk to you."

He looked deeper into Charlie's eyes trying to see whether this was some kind of cruel joke. "I don't believe he's wantin' to say much to me."

"No, no. What I mean to say is that he's had a change of heart. See, I heard the womenfolk talking and Miz Jane said to Lena that Tom had changed his mind except he didn't figure you'd come back to church and there wasn't any way to get word to you."

Preston grabbed his arm with such zeal Charlie winced. "Can it be? Can it really be?"

"Yes it can be – and it is true. I well recall having to face that sour looking man myself and if Miz Jane can get him to change his mind – and I'm sure that's what's happened – then I didn't want you to have to wait a minute longer than necessary to know about it. What's more, that Emma looks like she may just break in half with grief and I can't stand to see that."

"Well what do you think I ought to do then? I guess I'll go to preaching at Martha Washington again this week and see him there. What is today anyway?"

Charlie laughed at the younger man. In fact he was so giddy now that he seemed like a little boy despite the three inches he had on him. "Today is Friday and yes, I think it's a good idea to come to church with us Sunday. I'm betting you'll get invited for dinner afterwards."

"Well praise the good Lord. You know he said I couldn't call on her because I had neither land nor schoolin'. I can't figure no way around the schoolin' at this point but I've been studying on how I could get me some land."

"We can work on that. There's land to be had in Martha Washington, though most of it would have to be cleared."

"You think Em would want to stay over there, close to her Mama and sister? I been wondering about that since she grew up over here and maybe she would still think of Roslin as home."

Charlie shrugged as he settled his Pageboy cap on his head and said, "Let's just get you to callin' before we plan the weddin'."

Preston's head wagged like an eager puppy and he pumped Charlie's hand in matching rhythm. "Yeah, yeah. You're right a'course. I'll be seeing you on Sunday then."

As Charlie set out at a fast pace headed westward, Preston called after him, "And I sure thank ya."

Chapter 23

Two days. It felt like an eternity. Whenever Preston was in the bunk house he looked at the old clock at least every hour. When he was in the woods he glanced at the sun's position every time he turned his log.

Lord, I know you've been moving that big ole' sun from the Eastern horizon to the West every day for a long, long time. And I know you're still moving it, but why does it seem so slow right now?

Preston had gotten into the habit of praying while he worked. The loud thud of blades against wood kept the men from much talk among themselves. But God could always hear. Preston smiled at the thought of it.

It seemed Sunday morning would never arrive. He took extra care as he readied himself for church. He shaved with great care, even taking a second look at the scruffy mustache he'd allowed to re-grow over the winter months. *Should you shave it? Aw, Tom England don't care what you look like, he's baulked over your prospects to give his daughter a good life.* He decided he'd leave it until Emma ever indicated what she preferred. As he left the bunk house he was smiling in anticipation of doing any little thing that would please his Em.

The long walk seemed shorter and the rough terrain couldn't intimidate him this time for he knew his way after just one trip since he was well accustomed to learning the natural signs of a trail. As he walked he tried to prepare his mind for the meeting with Tom England. Despite Charlie's assurances, Preston realized he didn't know what might happen today.

He smiled as he reported his emotions to the birds chirping all around him, "Well it's worth the walk. I'll cross this holler a thousand times if that's what it takes to win my Em."

A squirrel fussed at the intrusion of the man's voice and Preston mimicked a bark back at him. His heavy boots dug into the soft soil and he set a quick pace into the deep ravine. The creek roared with the extra water from spring rains. All of the forest seemed alive and Preston smiled at every sight and sound around him. His heart was overflowing with joy and the whole world seemed to mirror it.

It's Easter Sunday. I wonder if Missus England sets the same store by this day as Mama did? She always said it was the most important day of the year.

The rest of his walk was consumed by thoughts of the crucifixion of Jesus Christ. He knew that all Christian churches would be pausing in their routines of preaching services for a special remembrance of the Resurrection today. As Preston thought back to his first understanding that the crosses he saw on graves and alters, Bibles and song books all commemorated the sacrificial act and miraculous rebirth that they celebrated today. *Lord I thank you for what you done and for allowing me to learn about it. I've been trying to better educate myself by practicing my reading and by reading your holy word but you came to an ignorant boy and spoke to my heart that you would forgive me of my sins. If you ever allow me children of my own, I will teach them the same way Mother taught all of us about you.*

Memories of his mother flooded his heart. She loved springtime and welcomed all the hard work that came with it. She always told him that it was worth the mud and rain to get to see the green leaves and beautiful flowers. Preston looked at the forest that surrounded him and smiled as though he was seeing her in it. It seemed the birds started singing louder and the tiny blue bells at his feet seemed larger. He realized there were violets all along the border of the path that he had not noticed before. *Fine tracker you are Preston, what if they'd been snakes or hornet's nests?*

The whole walk was so wrapped in joy and memories that Preston failed to worry about Tom England or fret over missing Emma. Before he knew it, he heard the slow grinding

Plans for Emma

of the little mill on Slate Creek and knew the church would be right past the top of the hill.

Everything seemed beautiful at the church. Big bunches of yellow and white Easter flowers had been placed in each window and there were pink and purple tulips on the altar table. Several ladies appeared to be wearing new bonnets and many young girls' pinafores were so white he was sure they were brand new. Everyone had a smile on his face so that the whole crowd seemed to glow.

The Englands were already in their seats and Jane was the only one looking behind her as he stepped in the door. She threw him a warm smile and reached across Bessie and Leonard to tap Emma's knee. Emma understood her mother's gentle nod and shot a look back to the door. Her face lit up when she saw Preston but right away caution replaced the joy as her eyes darted across the room seeking her father's reaction.

Preston caught both of her responses and gave her a reassuring smile. He wondered if Charlie had shared the same news with her? She didn't act like she knew of her father's change in heart.

From the corner where he visited with new neighbors he was learning to know and enjoy, Tom saw the young man enter and made his way across the room toward him. Emma watched with baited breath fearing Papa might try to turn the boy out of the church house. Instead, Tom stretched out his big hand and placed his left on Preston's shoulder.

Emma bit her lip to control a gasp and yanked her handkerchief up to her lips in an attempt to cover her emotions. *After two rejections, why is Papa being so friendly to Preston? He even looks like he's glad to see him.* She smiled behind the handkerchief; *Easter is about new life, isn't it? Is it a new Papa I'm seeing?*

"Mornin' Preston. Glad you made it back this week. I think Jane's got a chicken stewin' if you'd like to ride back with us for dinner."

With a soft *whoosh*, Preston released the breath he hadn't realized he'd been holding since Tom first turned toward him. "I'd be honored sir; of course I'd be honored to eat with y'uns."

Tom led him to the pew and sent him around to the opposite end to sit beside Emma with little Metie in between them. Metie looked up at the tall man but dared not ask the many questions her face revealed.

Preston made himself watch where he was going instead of staring at Emma as he walked the six feet to the seat Mister England indicated. After he was seated he allowed one long look at her beautiful face which smiled at him with all the brilliance of the sun and the flowers he'd enjoyed through the morning's walk. Without making a sound, she reminded him of the singing birds and the rushing creek. He smiled and managed to say, "Mornin' Em."

Turning his eyes down to the younger sister, he greeted Metie. "How are you this fine morning Miss England?"

Metie's hand jumped to her chest, "Me? Am I Miss England? I'm just Metie you know."

Emma and Preston chuckled setting young Leonard to giggling then Emma had to quiet him before the service started.

Preston had never known a more beautiful preaching service. The sun shone through the little windows as though the Son of Man were ascending to heaven right there in Martha Washington. The congregation sang the hymns a Capella as though heaven's choir led them. While Preston could recall little of the sermon, he was sure Preacher Todd spoke as Peter had on the day of Pentecost.

With the final "Amens," the congregation turned as one to head out the rear door. Most families had special meals planned so the women-folk talked little and seated themselves on wagons or headed home on foot ahead of the men who lingered on the front porch. Preston spoke to a few boys he'd met last week and tried to be polite to the older men who

Plans for Emma

offered their hands in greeting. But he kept one eye on the England wagon as the children seated themselves in it.

As soon as possible, he made his way out to join them, speaking to Mrs. England first. "Mr. England asked me back for dinner, I hope that's okay with you?"

"Of course it is Preston, I hoped you would join us today. I've got a chicken stewin' and Emma baked a cake yesterday. There's greens cooked and sweet potatoes to top it all off. You think you can eat any of that?"

"Yes Ma'am, I sure can." Preston swung up into the bed of the wagon and stretched his long legs along the rear edge. Leaning against the low side board he smiled at the younger children as Metie, Bessie and Leonard stared for a moment.

Leonard sat on Emma's lap and made every effort to monopolize her attention. With his fat little hands holding her face he jabbered away in some language foreign to Preston's ears.

Metie fussed with Bessie in hushed tones as both girls stole glances at the stranger. Finally, Emma distracted Leonard with a wooden toy and tried to quiet her sisters. "Metie, Bessie, what are you whispering about? You'd think there was a snake in the wagon. Mister Langford, I was glad to see you made it back to church today. Tell me, what's the news in Roslin?"

A broad smile spread over Preston's face as he heard her attempts at courtesy. He wanted to pour out his heart to her but knew both of them needed to watch their words here. "Don't know that I've brought much news Miss Em. I made one trip to Sunbright this week but otherwise I've been in the woods with nothing but an axe and a log for company and they don't much gossip."

Emma's cheeks flushed pink, "I suppose I thought you would have news from the church. Have you been able to attend at Jonesville of late?"

"Oh yes ma'am. 'Cept for last week, I been to Jonesville every Sunday that was at all clear weather. A'course it's been a hard winter as you well know. There were some weeks that there was no way to walk down that woodland path."

"Of course. We were awful confined ourselves. We made the move over here at the end of February and we had good days but cold, real cold."

Tom climbed up in his seat without a word and didn't speak except to call on his team to start home. Talking was difficult above the rattle of the wooden bed and loud squeaking of the iron wheels.

As they pulled up to the little house Preston could see there was much work to be done on this new farm. While he'd never visited their home in Roslin, he had studied it carefully from the creek's view and he knew it to be a large and sturdy home. This house had a rickety porch in need of paint and wooden shingles with many hanging loose.

Preston hopped off the wagon before the wheels stopped and stepped to the front, reaching his hand up to Jane. It was awkward to climb down with one arm wrapped around baby Gibson. "Thank you kindly Mr. Langford."

"I'd be obliged if you'd call me Preston, ma'am."

"Preston it is," she smiled and passed into the little house.

Preston returned to the back of the wagon in time to give Bessie a hand and to take Leonard from Emma. By the time he'd set the toddler on the porch, Emma was behind him leading the children toward the door. Before he could wonder what to do next, Tom called him, "Gimme a hand with the team, would ya?"

The barn seemed to be in no better condition than the house, although Preston could see that Tom was already working to brace the walls and patch the holes that allowed the rain to blow inside. Preston worked with practiced skill unharnessing the horses, speaking to each one in turn. Tom propped himself against the loft ladder and removed his hat.

"I's glad to see you come in this mornin'. I wasn't sure when we might see you agin'."

Preston had already decided against mentioning Charlie Adams's visit. "Well sir, I didn't mean no disrespect but I'm

Plans for Emma

hoping you'll change your mind about letting me call on Emma."

Taking his time with his words, Tom nodded his head. "Well I guess I have. I'm willin' to let you call on her. You're a hard worker and you're provin' you'll stick to a thing since you've asked me again and again about seeing her. But now I still want you to know that I can't be giving my blessing to any marryin' if you've got no way to provide."

Preston hung the second harness on wooden pegs and grabbed a coarse brush as he answered, "A livin' is a hard thing to make on this mountain, Sir. But plenty of families have done it and I sure wouldn't want to let Emma down."

Tom turned to rubbing down the other horse, "I know you wouldn't son."

By the time Preston and Tom entered the house, it was filled with the aroma of a feast. The big oak table was not what his sister's would've called fine but it was clear it had been crafted with an intention to feed families for generations. Lena and Charlie had arrived and joined those already seated around steaming bowls of chicken and dumplings, collard greens and carrots. As Preston took the seat Tom pointed him toward, Emma arrived at the table with a golden pone of cornbread. Glasses were filled with rich milk and Jane carried a coffee pot to the table as she seated herself.

With a nod from his wife, Tom announced, "Let's return thanks. Heavenly Father, we thank you for this meal and for your continued blessing on our home. On this day when we remember the resurrection of your Son, we thank you especially for him. We ask your blessin' on this meal, on the hands that have prepared it and on the guest who shares it with us. We pray in the name of our Savior, Jesus Christ. Amen."

Everyone echoed his "amen" and hands reached out in unison for the food. Jane was quick to remind them of their manners, "Children, make sure our guest is served first."

With a repentant, "Yes Mama," Metie handed the dumplings to her left and Preston smiled his appreciation.

There was little food left at the end of the meal but everyone was very satisfied. Without a single spoken word, Jane nodded to Emma who stepped through a low door behind the kitchen and reappeared with a stack cake.

Preston had not had apple stack cake since his mother passed away and he felt almost lightheaded seeing it. The dark cake layers were smothered with deep rust-colored apple butter seeping from between them. Emma sat the cake at her place and stood as she sliced an ample portion and handed it to him.

"I sure thank you for this. Haven't had stack cake since my own mother made it."

Jane seized the opportunity to hear about his family, "Emma told me you lost your mother not too long ago. I'm so sorry to hear that."

"Thank you Ma'am. She was a dear, dear lady. She had to face a lot in her life here and I miss her but I'm sure glad she's in a better place now."

"Yes, the promise of heaven makes a loss a lot easier to face. She was a good cook?"

"Well I guess every boy thinks his Mama is the best cook of all. But I didn't get to eat with her much except on Sundays so I guess that made it seem all the better. She was always poor, having all us young'uns to raise after Pa passed away. But she could set a table out of nothing it seemed like."

Jane smiled, appreciating that he wasn't embittered by the hardships he'd known. "Emma made this cake. I hate to admit it but she's better at it than I am. I get distracted and manage to burn the layers. A stack cake requires patience and our Em is blessed with that."

Preston smiled, his pride in Emma impossible to mask.

The meal ended in another bustle of activity as dishes were cleared and babies were whisked away for naps. Charlie and Tom dragged straight chairs to the fireplace for a moment's relaxation. Preston couldn't hear what was said as Tom spoke

Plans for Emma

to Emma then he gave a quick nod to Preston and Preston decided this must be permission for them to talk alone.

Emma seated herself at the end of the table and Preston took the chair nearest her. She smiled at him and he was transported back to their creek side visits. "Papa says we can visit for a few minutes here. Is that what you'd like or do you want to visit with him and Charlie?"

Preston sprouted his mischievous grin, "Do you think I would ever go talk to them men instead of looking at your pretty face?"

She giggled and mockingly chastised him, "Now don't talk foolishness. I do want you to know how happy I am to have you here. When I heard Papa saying last week that he'd refused you when you asked if you could come callin' - well I din' guess I'd ever see you again."

"Emma, I couldn't give up on you. Anyway, when Charlie came to the camp this week..."

"What?" Her question was louder than she meant and her eyes flew toward Jane and Lena to make sure she hadn't alarmed them. "Charlie! What was he doing at the camp?"

"Came to tell me Mr. England had a change of heart. That he was going to let me call on you."

"So they knew. It was a conspiracy, wasn't it?"

"Nah, I don't think that. They were just tryin' not to get your hopes up. They don't know me, don't know whether they can count on me. But I'll show them they can trust me – can count on me."

"I know you will Preston, I know it."

"I don't know if I can make it over here every week for preaching. Would you let me write to you?"

"Oh, would you write? Of course, I wouldn't expect you to come all the way over here every Sunday. I guess I just wondered, will you go to Jonesville instead?"

"Oh yes. I'm gonna' be in church. The Lord has made it plain to me that I have to be faithful to him first."

"I'm so happy to hear you saying that. And I will look forward every day to a letter from you – well, we have to go all the way to Clarkrange to get mail. That's about as far as Roslin so we don't get it more than once a week."

"Well you can know the letter's coming."

Their visit seemed far too short when Charlie called him across the room, "Preston, if you don't get yourself down the road, you'll be crossin' that creek in the dark. The way it's been rainin' I wouldn't want to try that. Could be you're braver than me though."

The sun was still shining and the birds still sang as Preston made his way back down the deep hollow toward the roaring creek. He savored each word he'd had with Emma, memorized every detail of her face. Yet he was burdened by Tom England's warning that he couldn't bless a marriage until Preston could provide for his daughter.

He tried to pray as he had before, giving this obstacle over to God's care. Yet still he thought about it. His mind whirred with ideas. How would he buy a farm?

He considered the families that had begun moving into the logging camp. Most men didn't bring wives and children along until a camp was well established, and truth be told, the company didn't much want the families there. But they preferred to tolerate the families rather than to lose reliable loggers. So little huts sprang up at the edge of the tract of timber, where the best trees had been taken and the company buildings moved out.

Preston wondered if Mr. England would permit this; would he consider a logger's pay proper provision for his daughter? Preston dismissed the idea, realizing this was not the life he wanted to give Emma. Living on company land, in a company house, he felt he'd be no better off than when he was indentured to Dr. Apple.

Unable to find the answer to his money worries, his mind turned to his lack of schoolin'. He'd promised to write Em without thinking through his ability to write a letter. Now he worried that writing to her would show his ignorance. Even as the thought passed through his mind he knew his vanity threatened his best connection to her. He had been working

Plans for Emma

through passages in the Bible and he knew his reading was improving. He'd even started picking up pieces of newspapers left in the dining room, or reading the tattered papers that lined some of the walls in the bunkhouse despite their faded lettering.

Preston was often entertained when he'd work his way through a story only to look back at the date of the paper and find it was months old. Still, he was amazed at the things that were happening in the world beyond these logging woods. Two Dayton boys had taken flight in a machine they built themselves and telegraphed their father of their success. And a great fire in Chicago had taken the lives of more than six hundred people in a 'theatre' – which was a word Preston did not know. He did understand 'screams' and 'panic' and his heart went out to those people so far away from Tennessee. He read about a federation of labor unions and worried about workers whose lives were made harder by their employers; he was thankful for a decent job among pretty decent folks. And his foreman treated him well.

As Preston labored through the printed word that he found around him he prayed that God would allow him to develop this skill. Time and again he shook his head in frustration and flexing his big hands he questioned, *How can the axe come so easy to me and yet reading is one of the hardest things I've ever undertaken?*

He found the papers harder to read than the Bible and wondered if God granted him better understanding of the Holy Word. In the Bible, he could follow the preacher and reason out the words he didn't know; there was no reference point for the newspaper. Each week in preaching service he placed a scrap of paper in his mother's Bible to mark the preacher's text. Those verses would still be fresh in his memory as he returned to the dining hall and read them again, closing his eyes and trying to remember just how the new words looked.

This was the area that threatened to deter his plans. He wondered if it was fair to ask Emma to join her life to someone who was hard pressed to read the news of the day. Again, the still small voice he now heard more and more often checked his thoughts.

You've given this whole thing to God again and again. Don't you think he would have shown you by now if this was not his will. God isn't going to answer that you aren't good enough – you are his child after all.

For weeks, he mulled over the possible solutions to this dilemma. In his letters to Emma he tried not to show her this concern but there seemed to be no way to hide it. He listened to every conversation around him hoping someone was talking about good work to be had. He talked to anyone that seemed to have information. One thing was clear to him, working in this logging camp was not going to earn him the money he needed as fast as he wanted. No one in the camp had any ideas for him. There seemed to be no more wisdom at the Roslin post office. However, the men at the railhead in Sunbright encouraged him to seek work on the railroad. They advised the railroad always needed men and a stout young man willing to work hard would do well there. The Tennessee Central built a round house in Monterey where the trains would be repaired. That seemed the best place to seek work.

He also heard rumors of homestead land still available in the west. If there was no work to be had on the railroad, he could head west. It would be the wrong time to set up a homestead but he would figure that out along the way. After all, he couldn't expect to have all of the answers before he even started out.

He hit on the plan while driving home from a Sunbright delivery. It was Tuesday and he knew he needed to let Emma know as soon as possible. When he stopped to water the team, he pulled out some scraps of paper he was carrying and a piece of pencil and laid out his plan in writing.

Lord, I may be asking a lot of her, to wait on me for who knows how long – well of course you know Lord - then maybe we'd have to go off to a land neither one of us know anything about. But this plan seems right to me – well at least it seems like you're meaning for me and

Plans for Emma

Emma to build a life together. And this is the best way I can figure to start that life. So I've got'ta ask you to speak to Em's heart when she reads this letter. Make her understand more than I can write words to say. Make her know I love her and I'm wantin' to do this for her.

Chapter 24

Papa returned from Clarkrange on Friday afternoon with two letters from Preston. Emma was on her knees in the garden when he drove in. He couldn't resist the urge to tease her and urged the horse right up to the split rail fence. "Em, why don't you scrape that dirt off your hands and read this boy's letters. He's going to wear out the postal system I guess or else he'll go broke buyin' stamps."

Emma jumped up so fast her bare toe caught the hem of her dress and pulled her back down. Both she and Tom were laughing as she struggled to get up and take the letters, trying not to soil them. She jogged to the watering trough and scrubbed away the moist soil.

Still patting her hands on her apron, she took her now familiar place under a big maple tree on a log that had been left there from some forgotten project. Checking the postmarks, she read the oldest letter which talked about logging and the boys he worked with and the preachin' at Jonesville. Next she turned to Preston's most recent thoughts.

Dearest Em,

I trust you and your family are all doing well. I am missing you and recount the time we spent in your mother's kitchen, and every visit by our creek. I have worn your letters to tatters reading and re-reading them.

You know my heart, that I long to marry you. Em, that's not too forward a thing to say to you is it? But your father has said he cannot bless a marriage if I have no way to provide for you. And I don't blame him one bit for that. So I've thought day and night of what I must do.

Plans for Emma

I've prayed too Em, really I have. And it sure seems that the good Lord has provided a way for us to see each other and to be able to write.

Well now I write you with a lighter heart than I've had in many days. We need a farm and I have seen that working in this logging camp will not allow me to save enough for many years. I'm hearing that the railroad needs a lot of men and they've built what they call a roundhouse in Monterey where I might get work. So, I've decided to go there as soon as possible and try to get some work.

If I can't get work there, I can catch a westbound train and see can I settle a homestead somewhere out west. I am hearing there is still land to be had, although it's more scarce than in years past of course. I suppose that decision needs to be yours in part. Would you be willing to go west with me if that's where I could get land?

I will plan to see you in church on Sunday and maybe we would get to talk a few minutes before I head on to Monterey. I will wrap things up here and plan to be in Monterey first thing Monday in hopes of getting work.

Take care dear Em. I will see you soon.

Emma's hand fell to her lap. She was thrilled to hear she would see him on Sunday. But the idea that he would go out west, even though he was going there to allow them to marry, was almost more than she could bear.

Emma wandered across the grassy field and along the garden's edge. She didn't know how long she walked, nor what she'd been thinking. She wanted to pray. She tried again and again to pray but the words would not come. In the end, she found herself in the kitchen where Jane and Lena were shelling peas together.

"Child what's happened to you? You look like you've seen a haint," Jane stood and placed a hand on her forehead to check for fever.

Emma rustled the letters in her hand. "I've had a letter from Preston."

Jane and Lena exchanged an anxious glance. "What has he written, Em," Lena asked.

"Well he'll be in preaching service with us on Sunday." Emma offered a weak smile to allay the fears she saw in their face that proved they'd thought Preston had broken her heart in that letter.

"And?"

The words gushed out now like a rushing river, "Well he's determined to get us a farm so Papa will let us marry. But there's no money. And he's desperate to find a way to earn it. So now he's hit on the idea that he will get work with the railroad. And that wouldn't be so bad since he's going to Monterey to the train works there. But if he can't get work in Monterey he says he'll catch a westbound train and keep trying on down the line. But that's not the worst of it all. If there's no railroad work he says he can still homestead a farm out west. Oh Mama, what are we to do?"

She fell on her mother's shoulder sobbing quietly. "Do you think it's God's plan to take us so far away? Did he move us from Roslin to prepare me for a bigger move?"

Jane patted her shoulder and prayed for wise words."Lord, show us the way." Patting Emma's shoulder she tried to encourage her, "It's a good test for you Em. Are you willing to leave everything and go so far away with him?"

With a sniff Emma faced the challenge, "Well yes, I believe I would be willing. Only it would be hard to leave you. Why, little Leonard and Gip wouldn't even remember me. But there is a time when we have to accept what God has given in our individual lives. After all Lena didn't know that we would be coming to Martha Washington when she married Charlie. Oh but that's not the same at all, is it?"

Jane smiled at her daughter's wisdom even as she tried to comfort her. "Shh, shh. Don't borrow trouble from tomorrow. We don't know but what he'll get the work in Monterey. In the meantime, we just need to give this over to the Lord. God knows what he's about in your life darling."

Plans for Emma

Nodding and sniffling, Emma made her way up to her room to store the precious letters in the growing pile.

As she left, Jane looked to Lena, "Do you think I ought to tell Tom what the boy has in mind?"

"No mama, we've got to give it to the Lord the same as you told Em to do."

Kneeling by her hope chest, Emma caressed the letters as though they were the very flesh of her beloved. She smiled knowing that Preston had held them, had written each word of the letters to her. She always remembered that writing wasn't particularly easy for him and that made every little note she received as precious to her as if it were written on bank notes.

I wonder if he'll be able to write from a homestead. How long will that all take? Lord, here I am again. I've surrendered to you so many times I guess you're getting' tired of hearing it. It does seem like the issues get bigger every time I come to you. Now, I know that you have a plan and I know that you're going to take care of me and my Preston. Thank you for that. Make me strong for him Lord. I can't break down and make him think that I won't support what he thinks is best. Only, please Lord show him what you know is best.

Her eye was caught by the colorful quilt that still needed work and she picked up the quilt top. Automatically, she turned it to the unfinished corner and reached for the cut pieces wrapped in brown paper. In her mind's eye she flipped through the things she'd placed in this chest over the years and a realization settled over her that what had only been a dream for so many years now seemed like a real possibility. She carried the quilt top with her and resolved to finish it by the week's end.

Each day Emma picked up her needle, pinned and stitched the colorful pieces into the compass design. She could see that her stitches were neater and the sharp points of fabric more obvious in the design. She smiled as she thought of sharing this work with Preston, thought of him feeling comfortable and at home among these things she'd made with her own hands.

Beth Durham

Lord I know this will all work out in your perfect time. The time just seems so long to me so please keep reminding me that your plan will work out.

Chapter 25

Preston spoke to the foreman and explained he wanted to try to get on with the railroad. The man was sorry to lose such an eager and skilled worker but could not argue that he could make more money elsewhere – if he could get the work. "You'll always have a place on my crew if it don't work out," he promised.

On Sunday morning, Preston prepared to leave the camp for good. The pack he made was small for he had little to carry with him. He spread out his working clothes and wrapped within them his mother's Bible and the few letters Em had sent him. There was a single picture of his parents and older siblings taken before he was even born; he nestled the thick paper board between the Bible and letters. He wrapped the pack with leather strips leaving a loop big enough to swing on his back. He buttoned the leather money pouch inside his pants' pocket to keep it safe, said a brief farewell to the boys that were awake and stepped into the crisp morning air.

Making a quick stop by the tool shed he swung his axe on his shoulder and set his face toward the still gray western horizon.

The mornings were warmer now and the walk very pleasant. He walked with a new purpose for he didn't intend to cross this holler again in the foreseeable future. He would be moving forward from now on. He tried not to plan further than the walk into Monterey, but he couldn't help but look forward to a life with Emma England. He chuckled as he corrected himself, "That will be Emma Langford when you start that life."

Everyone at the Martha Washington church welcomed him warmly. He took his place at the end of the England's pew without waiting for an invitation. Charlie and Lena were seated in front of them and Charlie reached back with a hearty handshake. He felt like everyone was sharing his excitement even though they knew little of his plans.

Emma's attention was divided between the baby on her knee and Leonard pulling at Metie's braids as Preston folded his lanky frame into the wooden pew. His letter had been both specific and vague with lots of details about his plans and dreams but no real timeline. Therefore, she hadn't been sure whether to expect him at church today. To be safe, she'd spent an extra few minutes on her hair and had tied a ribbon in a big bow around her head instead of the homemade bonnet she normally wore to church. She couldn't help but smile when she realized who was sitting at the end of her pew and she could feel her cheeks pinking. Somehow, it was hard to hear the preacher whose voice she always thought bellowed in the tiny room.

As the service ended, Jane looked to the end of the pew. "You will be joining us, won't you Preston?"

Pleased that she had taken up his first name he smiled as he nodded enthusiastically.

In a bold move he fell into step beside Emma as she led Bessie and carried little Gip from the church. He helped everyone into the wagon and climbed aboard himself. The whole family chatted, but Em seemed quieter than usual.

Arriving at the little farm house, he saw many improvements were being made. The porch no longer sagged and a swing had been added to the end. Jane pointed to it as she ushered the little children inside, "Emma why don't you and Preston enjoy the sunshine for a few minutes while I get dinner on the table."

Preston was thrilled with a moment alone with her and stepped aside to let her seat herself first.

"Did you get my letter? You weren't surprised I was there in the preaching service this morning, were ya?"

"Oh no, I was very pleased. I got two letters from you on Friday and I've been looking forward to today."

Plans for Emma

"Me too. You see that I've got my pack with me?"

Her voice was so soft Preston found himself leaning closer to hear her clearly. "Yes, I see. So you will go on to Monterey tonight?"

"Yeah, I want to be there very early in the morning so they can tell that I'm a hard worker and won't keep 'em waiting."

"Oh Preston, I know that if there is any work to be had at all then they'll see you're a good man for it. And I do hope that you get on with the railroad there."

"But I guess we need to talk about the other possibility."

"Going west?"

"Yeah. What do you think about that idea? I know it's not what you would have expected. I mean, I hate to take you away from your family. But if I can't get the railroad work then I don't see any other choices and I've tried to look at this thing every which way."

Emma nodded, unable to find the words to answer him.

"Are you willing Emma? Will you move out west with me?"

"Oh Preston, I'm scared and I've got no lie to tell you about that. But I would go anywhere with you. I know that God has chosen you especially for me and so it's like following him, ain't it?"

Preston stayed the hand that reached out to her – he almost put his arm around her shoulder to draw her close to him but Almeta threw open the screen door, "Dinner's on the table. Y'uns gonna eat?"

Emma's warm smile broke into laughter as she tried to scold her little sister, "Metie you get in that house."

Preston hadn't asked whether Emma had shared his plans with Tom and Jane. He felt that it was his responsibility to announce it. The meal was almost finished when Lena and Charlie stepped through the front door.

Charlie was jovial as usual and came in talking about the rhubarb pie Lena carried. "Boy it smells good. I had a terrible time keepin' my fingers out of it while we's walkin' over."

Lena feigned smacking his hand as she turned so the basket was out of his reach. "Well if you don't keep your fingers out then you won't get any at all."

As everyone settled down with the sweet dessert, Preston sought an opportunity to share his plans and Charlie provided it.

"Is that your pack on the front porch, Preston? You carryin' your axe with you these days?"

Preston smiled, thankful for the opening. "Not generally but when I left the camp this morning, I didn't intend to return."

Tom spoke up now around a mouthful of pie, "You had trouble there?"

"Oh no sir, nothing like that. The boss, he said I'd always be welcome back. It's just that I'm feeling like I need to find something a little… better. I'm going to go to Monterey and see if I can get on with the railroad."

"Railroad? Well I guess that's good work but they may ship you out of here."

"Yes Sir, I know that could happen. Fact is, if I can't get work in Monterey, I'm prepared to head on west until I find either good work or land available to homestead."

Tom's eyes shot first to Emma then Jane. He was suspicious that neither of them showed shock at this news. It appeared they had heard about it already.

"Homestead? Why all the best land is already homesteaded."

"Yeah, I've heard that. But the fact is, without good work that may be the only way I can get a farm."

"You got the idea you're going to take Em with you?"

Both Tom and Preston were looking at Emma now. "I would sure hope to send for her once I had some land."

Tom gave a heavy huff and returned his attention to his pie. An eerie silence covered the table as the news settled upon everyone.

As forks tinkled against plates and the young children were permitted to leave the table with heavy eyes, Preston looked

Plans for Emma

at Em with unspoken pleading, "I guess I'd better be gettin' on down the road now."

Understanding, she swung her legs across the wide bench that provided extra seating at the table, "I'll walk you to the porch".

Preston turned to Jane, "Miz England, thank you for another good meal. If I got to sit at your table every week I reckon I'd get as fat as this winter's hog."

Jane giggled and reached out to take his hand, "You are always welcome at my table Preston. Take care of yourself, okay?"

"Yes Ma'am, I'll sure try." He stretched his hand to Tom, "Mr. England, I hope to write to you with good news before long."

"Can't imagine what good news would have to come in a letter." Tom grasped the extended hand and gave it a firm shake.

Emma stood in the doorway and Preston let a quiet sigh escape when he turned his eyes to her. In two long strides he crossed the tiny front room and stepped out behind her. "May I take your hand Miss Em?"

She smiled and dropped her eyes but did not tug her hand away from his grasp.

They both studied the hands, tanned golden brown and showing the wear of wind and work despite their youth.

Preston caressed her fingers with his thumb, his touch as gentle as the calloused hands could be. "It may be a long time before I see you again but you can be sure you'll be getting letters. I know I don't write so good. Can you make any sense out of them?"

"Oh Preston, you write just fine and I treasure every word."

After another long minute she continued, "Are you sure you'll have to go further west than Monterey?"

"I can't figure any way to get a start here. My Pa worked another man's land until he died and that left Mother without even a home to raise the children he left behind. Your Papa expects more for you and I can't blame him for it, fact is that I want better for you.

Emma, God has blessed me with your friendship already. Because of you, I've got myself back in church like I ought to be. And I've been practicing reading in the Bible. Like you said, I know God intends us to marry." He took a deep breath and let it out with a 'swoosh', "So, I've got to be about finding a way for that to happen."

She had to sniff as the tears threatened to spill out. "I know Preston, I know. I'll miss you but I'll be waiting for word from you."

With a squeeze of the hand he still held he hoisted the pack onto his shoulder and stepped off the porch.

As he reached the road, Preston fought the urge to look back for he feared if he saw sadness in Emma's eyes he would never even walk the sixteen miles to Monterey. As he stepped onto the hard-packed dirt road he saw movement in the fence row.

"Charlie, how did you get out here? I thought you were still at the dinner table."

Charlie grinned at him and spit out the straw he'd been chewing. "Don't you worry, I wasn't eavesdropping on you and your sweety."

"Well what are you doin' then?"

"I thought I told you there was land to be had right here in Martha Washington?"

"Yeah, I remember that. But I've got a pitiful little saved despite the fact that I've held onto about every penny I earned logging. I don't reckon I can afford cleared farm land."

"Boy, look around you. There's not a fraction of this mountaintop cleared. I hear that there's some good farmland out west but I'm afraid it wouldn't come much cheaper than this would."

"Well do you know of land for sale around here?"

Plans for Emma

Charlie looked down the road to the south and nodded, drawing Preston's eyes that direction. "I could let you have maybe ten acres on the south side of my land."

Preston's eye squinted at his newfound friend. "How could you do that?"

"I got my Granddaddy's farm and that side ain't cleared yet so it don't do me too much good."

Preston looked down the road as though he might be able to see the land in question. "Well that don't change the fact that I couldn't afford it."

"Look here Langford, I can see the way you and Emma are looking at each other and I been hearin' from Lena how broken up her sister is thinking that you won't be able to marry for years and years. I can let you have that land for ten dollars an acre. How long would it take you to save that?"

Preston's eyes widened in awe then squinted again as he searched Charlie's face for any sign that he was trying to trick or mislead him. "I got that much now."

Charlie's face split in a broad grin and he dropped a hand on Preston's shoulder, "Well then have we got a deal?"

"You don't reckon I ought to go on to Monterey and see if I can't get on with the railroad?"

"Why would you want to do that? Are you dreamin' of bein' a railroad man or a farmer?"

"A farmer of course."

"Okay, then that settles it."

Charlie turned the younger man around with a hand on either shoulder and they took two steps toward the England house when Preston froze. "No, that don't settle nothin'."

"Huh?"

"I got the hundred dollars to pay you but that's about all I have got. Wouldn't leave a penny for building a house or setting up housekeeping. Why, I couldn't even buy a milk cow."

Charlie looked long at his new friend, unsure how to respond to him. "Let's worry about one hurdle at a time."

"You keep saying that but I can't help but see mountains before me a'waitin' to be climbed. I thank you for the offer of the land and I will be takin' you up on it. Would you allow me to go on to Monterey and see what kind of work I can get at the railroad?"

"Of course. You go on and we'll just keep this between us."

Preston put a big hand on Charlie's arm, "Thank you friend."

Charlie dipped his head and turned back toward his father-in-law's house.

Heading out of Martha Washington, Preston set his eyes on the road and his heart on heaven. *Lord, I thought for sure that you were sending me out of here and that Emma and I would leave to make our own way. Now I have to ask whether you've sent Charlie to help me out? It'll be every penny I've saved but I've been penniless more than once. Oh Lord, to be penniless on my own land seems downright rich.*

Preston grinned at the thought of a rich man with no money. Yet the thought stuck with him for the rest of his long walk. Maybe riches didn't always come in silver and gold.

He passed the night with a lighter heart than he'd had in weeks. He walked into the little town as the sun was winking out its last bit of light. Despite the late hour, Monterey was far from sleeping. The hiss of an idling locomotive could be heard from the town limits and led Preston to the freight depot. There he found a beehive of activity as men moved all sorts of barrels, crates and sacks on two-wheeled wooden carts. Further down the line of waiting cars, stacks of lumber were loaded onto open cars like he'd seen so many times in Sunbright.

This was the first time Preston had been to Monterey and he did not know a soul here. He looked around for a place to catch a bit of sleep before seeking work for he was certain no one around at this hour would be able to hire him. A separate building several feet away had trunks and luggage stacked around and Preston decided that must be where people

Plans for Emma

boarded the train away from the freight. He saw the clean red brick of a building sitting east of the passenger depot and sporting a sign 'Imperial Hotel'. Preston knew he could get a room there but didn't dare spend a penny of his precious savings, knowing he'd committed every bit of it to Charlie for the land. One end of the freight depot was dark and no one seemed to be heading that way with their little carts so he propped against the wall using his pack as a pillow and pulled the floppy brim of his hat over his eyes.

He had just drifted off to sleep when the locomotive blew out a burst of steam and every part of the long train began to shudder, shake and clatter. Preston sat bolt upright, his heart pounding in his chest. As his mind cleared of sleep he remembered where he was and realized the train was pulling out of the station. Sure enough in a few minutes, it was gone and the sound quickly faded into the western horizon.

He settled against the rough board wall and was soon asleep again; the next time he opened his eyes the dusky light told him morning had arrived and he needed to be about his purpose here. There was already plenty of activity around the depot and he wondered if the place was ever silent. After asking a couple of men who might be able to make a hiring decision, he found Fred Ray and introduced himself.

"Mr. Ray? I've been told you're the man what makes hiring decisions around here. I'm wondering if you could put me to work?"

Fred Ray held a clipboard thick with tattered papers, he slid a pencil behind his ear and ran his eyes over Preston's long body. Preston had the impression he was inspecting him as though he were a piece of livestock.

"Hu-hmm," he cleared his throat, "What can you do?"

Preston smiled at the direct question. "Well Sir, I'm strong and healthy. I can give you a long day's work day in and day out."

"You got any railroading experience?"

"Well, no Sir, I can't say that I have. I's raised on a farm and can do most anything with stock or crops. Lately, I've been working in the logging camps over in The Flat Woods near Roslin."

"We don't keep any stock and sure don't raise crops. We need a brakeman, you know he'd have to ride with the train. It's an awful important job, because he's got to go from car to car applying the brakes on that long roll off this mountain. You ever been off the mountain boy?"

Preston was not liking the way this man looked at him. Somehow he reminded him of Dr. Apple and he was not at all sure he wanted to work under that man again. *Remember Emma. This is for her.*

"No Sir, I've been making deliveries to the railhead in Sunbright for a while now, but that's about as far as I've been East of here and Monterey is the furthest West."

The trainman shook his head and continued to study Preston. "Brakemen have to have pretty steady nerves. Don't believe that would be the best place for you. You look strong enough though."

"Yes sir, I can tote a cross tie on each shoulder if I can get 'em up there."

"Well, it sounds like you'd make a good enough Juggler. Can you read?"

Preston felt his neck warming. "Some. What's a juggler?"

"Jugglers are these fellows running around loading and unloading. The men that can read the manifest and the labelling on the freight can work by themselves or lead a crew of other men. But if you can't read the owners' names you have to be directed with every cart-full."

Preston shifted his pack, shuffled his feet and cleared his throat. "I can read most of the scriptures - what I've heard read in church. I been trying to read from the newspapers some. I b'lieve I could make out names on crates and sacks."

The foreman shook his head, looking into Preston's eyes as though he could read there whether the boy was telling a lie. "I could use you when the hogs start coming in. Check back with me about August; you'll know it's time because everyone knows when the hogs start coming."

Plans for Emma

With that the pencil was back in his hand and he turned his back on Preston as though shutting a door.

Preston's heart sank as he stared at the dusty coat of the freight manager. He turned to face the rails, studying the criss-crossing of the iron with the evenly spaced crossties between them. He stared at those wooden timbers like they were old friends and he wondered if he'd hewn any of them. He shook his head and glanced into the west where the rails disappeared into the horizon.

What are you going to do now Preston?

No answer to the silent question came. The activity of the freight office was picking up and he realized he needed to move out of the way of the jugglers.

Hmm, and you already learned something. When you walked in here you wouldn't have known what to call these men.

His hand unconsciously tapped the pouch at his belt and he wondered if he should get a ticket to the next town. Another tap reminded him that there was enough money to buy the land from Charlie. He didn't even know the man yet Charlie Adams had shown him uncommon kindness. A fleeting thought wondered if he could trust him. Then somehow he knew that he should place complete trust in this offer not because of Charlie but because God was directing it.

As he stepped off the depot's wide porch he felt calmer already. His stomach growled, reminding him he had not eaten since Jane England's hearty lunch yesterday. That pretty red brick building was behind him and he was sure breakfast could be had there so he turned around hoping his mind would be clearer with his stomach satisfied.

With his hat he tried to knock off as much dust as he could from his pants legs before he stepped between the white posts that held an upstairs balcony. The doors of The Imperial Hotel were already opened to the morning air and he could smell ham and steak cooking inside. With another rumble from his gut he allowed his nose to lead him to the dining room. There was only one other customer, a polished older gentleman engrossed in a newspaper. His handlebar mustache was waxed into such elaborate curly-queues that Preston couldn't help but rub his own unshaven jaw.

The man looked up at Preston and nodded a greeting as he turned the page of his paper. Preston sat down at the table next to him and in seconds a steaming cup of coffee appeared on the table.

"Mornin'. You wanting anything special this morning?" The question came from the starched white apron parked beside his chair and Preston tilted his head to see the woman behind it.

"Whatever I'm smelling would be all I'd need. Is it ham?"

"Yes Sir, we got ham. I'll be right back with a plateful."

Preston dropped his head thinking he should pray but somehow unable to begin. He heard the scuff of a chair behind him and glanced back. The voice that greeted him did not carry the melody he was accustomed to and he assumed his neighbor was a foreigner to the mountains.

"I would think it's too early in the morning to look as down as you do. Is this because of a riotous night?"

Preston couldn't help but smile, "No Sir, I was just trying to figure which way I ought to go next?"

"You didn't get off the train without a destination in mind, did you?"

"Oh, no Sir, it's nothin' like that. In fact, I didn't come off the train at all. I's looking for work but it'll be months before I can get on here. And I'm just wondering if I ought to head out west and see if something comes up."

Polished boots turned out from the table as the gentleman crossed his legs and settled himself back in the chair. He reached for his coffee as he offered his advice. "Well if there's no work here, what's the other choice?"

"You see, I have had the offer of some land I might buy here – or at least back in Martha Washington where I've come from yesterday."

"Land, oh well that's always the best bet. Have you any means to buy this land?"

Plans for Emma

Preston gave a single shake of his head, "Yeah, I can swing it. But that's about all I can do."

"Well I have had good luck in land deals and found that I much prefer it over working for another, even for the government."

This piqued his attention, "You been a government man?"

After another sip of coffee, then a chuckle, he nodded, "Some. Soldier of course. That's a kind of government man. And then I held an office in Chattanooga and later took an office in Knoxville but none of that suited me. I guess I've slowed way down now but I saw the need for a nice lodging house here in Monterey and my young wife certainly enjoys the town."

Preston realized his food had arrived and he dug into it, trying to talk between bites. "You the owner here?"

"Yes, and I'm quite proud of the place. I suppose I should be getting back to the business of it now. My name's Wilder, Colonel Wilder. Enjoy your breakfast."

Preston stood and caught the chair that threatened to topple behind him with his left hand. He offered the other to Colonel Wilder, "My name's Langford."

Colonel Wilder shook his hand, "I'd tell you to buy the land, but you didn't really ask me, did you?"

"Well I sure appreciate your advice though. Thank you Sir."

With surprising grace, the genteel old man walked toward the desk Preston had passed on his way in. He seemed to be evaluating every element of the room as he walked and Preston wondered what kind of land he'd bought that led him to government work and now owning this fine hotel.

Preston crushed a bit of biscuit under his fork and sopped up the remaining gravy before looking for the waitress. Leaving the ten cents his waitress asked for, he unfolded his long frame and picked up his tattered hat. As he stepped off the polished wooden floors of the lobby he settled his hat on his head and squared his shoulders.

Beth Durham

Lord, I don't know what you're a'planning but I'm gonna' go buy me a farm and trust you for the next part.

As he walked he prayed. Several times he stopped himself – sometimes he stopped walking – as he found he was simply repeating, *I need your help Lord, help me, show me,* or some variation of the same words. Still his heart was settled and he had little doubt that he'd made the right choice.

Colonel Wilder I wonder if you know you were God's messenger today?

With a couple of stops for water as he saw a spring bubbling up along the dirt road, his walk should have taken till supper time. However, as he turned at a rough wooden sign labelled 'Campground' he saw the sun still sitting high in the sky and guessed he wasn't much past noon. A man stopped his mule and looked as though he would come to the fence to speak to the stranger but Preston just threw his hand into the air in a hearty greeting and never slowed his pace. There was no traffic on the road but he saw a few children in gardens surrounded by split rail fences, and the wood smoke that kept reaching him reminded him this was wash day in most homes.

He stopped at a trickling branch that crossed the road and looked longingly on toward the England home. He wanted to go to Emma and assure her he would not be expecting her to leave her home and move west with him. Instead he started up the little hill he knew led to Charlie and Lena's house. He had business that must be attended to and he knew that Emma would have a double blessing when he was able to tell her that he was both home and that he'd bought land for their shared home.

Chapter 26

As Preston approached the yard surrounded by the familiar split rails positioned to keep out roaming stock animals, each step was echoed by the random flapping of Lena's clean laundry. She was at the line, running her hand across the coarse flour sack sheets checking for anything that was dry enough to be folded into the oak basket waiting at her feet.

"Helloooo," he called while still several yards away.

Lena turned to the sound, squinting to make out the face of their visitor. "Is that Preston Langford? Well I never thought we'd see you today."

Lena met him at the fence. "I was hopin' I could talk to Charlie. Is he around at this hour?"

Lena nodded, peering into his eyes for some clue to his unexpected return. Then she smiled and Preston saw that her resemblance to Emma was unmistakable. He had found her to be more reserved than Emma and had thought her to be almost surly but now he saw real friendship in her eyes. "I'd think it would be Em you'd be asking after, but you'll find Charlie not far from the house here. We've got a young milk cow with a new calf and he wanted to start milking her tonight but she's not used to coming home in the evenings yet. I thought we should'a penned her up this morning but he'd rather hunt for her."

Preston tipped his hat with a smile at Lena's assessment of Charlie's farming decisions, "Thank you. I'll see can I find him."

"When you do, bring him on home and I'll have pone of hot bread and cool milk for you. I'm afraid we're out of coffee."

"The milk would be a fine treat."

It took little effort to locate Charlie for he was calling "Saaaauuuu, saaaaauuuu," from the corner of the open field. Sure enough a young cow and three day old calf cleared the tree line and made their way toward him. Since the animals didn't know him, Preston eased up beside his friend trying to be careful not to spook them.

"That's a fine looking pair Charlie."

Charlie had been so focused on calling them he had not noticed Preston and he turned to him now. "Well Langford I don't know why I'm surprised to see ya', but I am."

The men shook hands and turned back to watch the cow mosey across the field, her bell tinkling with every step.

After a long quiet moment Charlie asked, "No luck with the railroad?"

"Well, they said they could use me – in August."

"You gonna' go back then?"

"Guess that depends on whether your offer of land is still open."

Charlie grinned without turning his head, "A'course it is. I couldn't rightly withdraw the offer once I'd made it, now could I?"

"Still your land. I wouldn't give you a bad name if you did."

The young mother was close enough now to try to catch their scents and she knew that Preston was strange to her. Charlie had a little wooden pail with an ear of corn shelled and he held it out for her to smell. "Come on now Daisy, Preston ain't gonna do you no harm."

The corn piqued her interest and she took another step toward the men. Charlie turned and Preston stepped out of the way knowing the cow would follow both the corn and the familiar farmer. They walked in silence back to the big barn behind Charlie and Lena's house. Preston admired the setup as he neared the building. It was old, maybe one of the oldest barns he'd seen but it was in good shape. He could see new boards here and there where repairs were made as rot took its toll. The roof's wooden shingles appeared to be sound and he could see a square of yellow where new shingles had been added with little rain on them to blacken them.

Preston couldn't help but wonder how long it would be before he had such a place to house his own animals. Then he stopped walking as he reminded himself, *You ain't got the first animal to put in such a place.*

Charlie bent to slide a draw bar across the opening after the cows passed into a little pen built on the back side of the barn. "Will you grab the next bar Preston?"

With a nod he put the top bar in place then leaned on the closed gate to watch as the young calf began to nurse.

"You ain't gonna try to milk her Charlie?"

"Nah, calf's only a few days old, it'll still be new milk and you know that's no good. Lena got some milk from her mother so we'll let him have it tonight. I just wanted her to get used to coming in so maybe I won't have to hunt her too many days."

Preston nodded. He was eager to talk about the land but didn't want to push his friend so he waited in silence and watched the sweet scene as the mother turned her head and licked her calf.

"You want to have a look at the ten acres?"

"Guess I should. But I think Lena was looking for you. She told me to bring you in when I found you."

Charlie whacked his back as he chuckled, "I brought the cow and you brought me. Pretty good I guess. She'll have something ready to fill our bellies. Let's have a bite of that then we'll walk over your land."

"Yeah she said something 'bout cornbread." Preston's hand moved to his belt and the thick pouch buttoned there. I've got your money."

"There'll be time for that. Them Englands can sure make good bread and she can churn butter that's white as cream and sweet. Ooohy I sure am proud of my little wife."

Preston's heart swelled with pride in the family he hoped to join. He was almost as proud of Emma and he'd never seen her churn butter, didn't know if she could bake bread and she certainly wasn't his wife. Still he was proud of her. He chose not to mention this to Charlie as they swung open the kitchen door.

"Lena I could smell that bread plumb to the barn. I can eat the whole pan myself."

The half-filled basket of clean laundry sat on the worn table and Lena reached for it as they moved into the room. "Well come on in here. I set out some cold meat and cheese because I'm betting Mr. Langford hasn't eaten much today. Did you even make it to Monterey?"

Preston removed his hat and placed it on an empty peg on the wall, "Yes'm but didn't have much luck at the railroad. I had a good breakfast, but my stomach's telling me that was too many hours ago."

"Well I'm glad you came back here instead of heading out west. I wasn't much looking forward to my sister heading off into the sunset."

He ducked his head with a slight blush, "I guess I ought to be ashamed of myself for even mentioning it. Thing is, I just couldn't see any other plan. Not real sure I see anything else now but we'll see what works out."

Lena rolled her eyes to look at her husband, "I think you two are cooking something up. You help yourself and I'll go take care of the wash."

She disappeared through a curtained doorway into what Preston assumed was their bedroom and they heard her begin to hum.

Charlie passed a bowl of cold ham and a chunk of pale cheese. Preston took the still warm bread and piled it with meat. His stomach rumbled when he smelled the meal and he realized how hungry the day's walking had made him. The men ate in silence and as he reached for the last half of his cup of milk Charlie leaned back in his chair.

"Like I told you yesterday, there's about ten acres on the other side of this Keytown Road," he motioned with his free hand out the front of the house. "None of it is cleared. There's a decent spring but I don't know how it would last in

Plans for Emma

a dry season. To tell the truth, I've never checked it since there's a strong well here near the house. The land rolls a little but there's none of this farm real flat. I think you could get one good field out of it and another that wouldn't wash too bad."

"Charlie, I grew up on a hillside farm so if I can plow without fear of rolling down to the holler, I'll think I'm plowin' heaven's fields."

Charlie was laughing as he pushed away his dishes and stood to his feet. "Lena, we're headin' out. That was a good little meal and you're a fine little woman."

She stepped through the curtain with a stack of kitchen towels in her hand which she now fluttered toward her husband. "Oh shoo. Where are you two headed?"

He pointed with a jerk of his head, "Over to that patch of woods the other side of the road. I think Preston's bought him a farm."

"Farm? What farm?"

"Well, it'll take some doin' but he's been in the log woods the past year. He'll have that timber cut and stumps grubbed out before next spring."

Preston's eyebrows shot up and he jerked his head. *Wish I had that much confidence,* he thought to himself.

Charlie led him along the dirt road, pointing out elements of the land he'd known from childhood. "I"ve been trompin' over this land my whole life. My grandaddy built that house me and Lena are livin' in and I stayed with him and grandma a lot because they were needin' some help by that time. When they passed-on the house was given to me. This little piece of land is the back corner of the farm on the south side of this road. It's got one low spot on the far corner, we'll walk across it so you can see. I want you to know what you're getting."

Once they stepped past the sharp rock that Charlie indicated would be the corner-marker, Preston paid close attention to the lay of the land and the timber that covered it." Why Charlie, there's a lot of good timber here."

"Yeah, I was thinking about that last night. You could probably build you a house out of what you are clearing."

"Oh, Charlie, I can do more than that."

"Well good then. I want it to be a good deal for you but I couldn't let it go for less than ten dollars an acre I don't think."

"I think that's a fine deal. You want your money now?"

"Boy you sure are eager to part with that money. Let's walk the rest of it."

Preston didn't want to step off of the patch of land. He thought he could live out the rest of his days on this ten acres and live a happy life – if Emma could join him there. He felt a little giddy and tried to restrain himself while Charlie was still with him. He would give a good 'hoot' as soon as he was alone, and a land owner.

The business was complete by sundown and Preston excused himself when Lena offered supper, "I think I'd better let Emma know what all's happened. Don't you?"

"Yeah, she'll skin me and Charlie both if she finds out we've kept you here all afternoon without a single word to her."

The couple walked with him to the front gate and pointed out a path that was developing from repeated trips to the neighboring farm. Preston felt he could follow it even though the woods were now quite dark.

As he made his way into the England's side yard there was already lamplight from the kitchen window. He could see no one in the barnlot or on the porch despite the day's warmth that still lingered. "Hello the house," he called before he opened their gate.

The door opened with a loud creak before he could step onto the porch. Tom's pipe glowed but he remained hidden in the deep shadow. "Howdy. Who is it?"

"Preston Langford, Mister England. Can I come in for a spell?"

Plans for Emma

"Well I never thought we'd see you today. Sure, you come on in. Jane's clearin' the table. Maybe there's some scraps left for you."

"Thank you sir. I appreciate it."

"Have you just got back from Monterey? Weren't no trains headed west?"

Preston smiled at the dry humor. "Well Sir, I decided there was nothing off this mountain I needed to see. Fact is I've bought me a farm today, right here in Martha Washington."

Tom England stepped into the lamplight and tried to get a clear view of the young man. "You tellin' the truth boy?"

He nodded, "Oh yes. I wouldn't dare tell you no lie."

"Well that'd be best. Get on in there and sit yourself at the table. We need to hear this story."

Seeing the visitor, Jane added water to the coffee grounds and quickly brought it to a boil on the front of the stove.

There was some cornbread left and Emma put the butter back on the table beside it as she took a bowl of turnip greens that were topped with chunks of white fat that had cooled on them. She opened the draft and lifted the stove eye exposing little flames that licked up the fresh oxygen pulled into the stove. Settling the cast iron kettle into the opening, it took only a moment for her to return the greens to the table with a bit of steam wafting from the top. There was a spoonful of beans left and Preston poured all the remaining juice over his bread.

"I thank you for the meal Miz England. I wasn't thinking about food when I come this way."

"I know you weren't son, I know you weren't."

Preston couldn't hide the smile despite the mouthful of food he was chewing.

Emma sat down across the table from him and her eyes questioned him even before her father began.

"Well if you've had enough to eat that you won't fall out on us, tell us what's happened."

With a deep breath, Preston began at the fence row when Charlie met him the day before. In a few minutes, he wrapped up his story, "I guess I just realized that I couldn't ask you to give Emma up to the west and an unknown future."

Emma could no longer hold her questions, "So you bought the land from Charlie? Did you say ten acres?"

He nodded. "Now, it's all trees of course but that's no problem for me you know."

"There's no house on it," Emma seemed to say it to herself.

Preston stopped the hand that tried to reach across the table for hers. He didn't want to tell her in front of her father that there was no money left for a house.

Chapter 27

Preston awoke in the England's barn with cold feet. The blankets Jane had sent along with him didn't quite cover his long frame and the June mornings still held a chill. The temperature got him moving and he was trying to comb out his hair with his fingers when he heard Tom come in for the morning milking.

"You awake up there?"

"Yes Sir. You milkin'? I'd be happy to do that for you, it's the least I can do since you gave me shelter for the night."

"Well I'll let you do it. Em's been doing the milkin' for me for years now but I couldn't have her out here with you, now could I?"

Preston smiled shyly and took the bucket from him. As Preston positioned the milking stool, Tom dropped a handful of hay into the manger. "Not much hay left since we didn't get to lay in our winter stores here. But she'll stand pretty still for you."

Preston made quick work of filling the bucket with little chatter between the men. Tom pointed him to the kitchen with a promise of hot coffee and some kind of breakfast. "I never know what the womenfolk are cooking but they never leave me hungry."

Careful with the frothy bucket, Preston stepped onto the porch and gave a light knock. "Okay to come in if I bring you your milk?"

Emma met him at the door and took the milk from him. "We were waitin' for you. Did you get any rest?"

"Slept like a log. Don't know when I've felt so rested, only there was a chill this morning."

"Go warm by the stove. I'll get you a cup of coffee."

They exchanged a warm smile and turned to different corners of the long kitchen. The room was alive with activity as Almeta worked to keep the toddlers away from the hot stove, Emma strained the milk and Jane filled the table with corn light bread and apple butter, boiled eggs, fried pork and gravy.

Like a well-orchestrated dance, the girls and children settled themselves at the table about the same time Tom appeared in the back door." Preston, have they taken care of you? Let's sit down and eat a bite, I expect you've got work to do today like I know I do."

They sat and ate in what Preston was learning was their customary silence. Every time he looked across the table Emma seemed as though she would burst with questions. Preston grinned down at the plate he'd been served and tried not to show the family how much he was enjoying Emma's excitement.

In the end, it was Jane that relieved her daughter's burden by allowing the pair to talk. As she rose and gathered empty plates and bowls from the table she looked at Emma, "Do you want to start shelling the peas we picked yesterday evening, Em? I guess Preston might like to talk for a few minutes before he heads off on his day and that's good work to do when you want to talk."

Emma only nodded and did not look at Preston as she scooted off her bench, pushing Almeta out of her way.

Preston assumed he was permitted to follow and did so before anyone could correct him. However, he caught the slight scowl of Tom England's heavy eyebrows.

Em took a seat in one of the ladderback chairs by the fireplace and put the basket on her lap. Preston took the matching chair.

"Can I help with those?"

She smiled at the basket, "I can hull these things so fast there's no need for help."

"Well I do imagine you're little fingers would be faster than mine at it."

Plans for Emma

"Little? I do wish I had petite little hands like Lena but I just don't. Mine work and I am determined to be thankful for that."

Preston smiled, admiring the wisdom of her attitude.

She looked at him as she spoke and her hands continued their work. "What will you do now – I mean now that you have the land? Will you try to go back to Monterey when the jobs are open?"

"No, wouldn't be no profit in that. I've got the land now I have to get it fit to work. There's a lot to be done."

"But there's no house. Will you build one now?"

He dropped his head studying the corner of the flat rock that formed the hearth of the fireplace. "Em, it took everything I had saved to buy the land. Now, don't think Charlie has cheated us or anything because I do think it was a good price but it was everything that I had."

Emma was nodding with understanding and Preston looked deep into her eyes. "Have I disappointed you too much?"

Her hands stopped, "Preston, of course not. I'm finding it hard to believe you were able to buy a farm at all. It will work out, I'm sure of it. Look at what God has done so far. Just tell me what you are thinking you'll do."

"Well, Charlie offered to let me stay with them until I could get some money put aside to build something but I wouldn't want to do that. I won't never get ahead by leanin' on somebody else."

"I understand that, but I'm sure they would be happy to have you."

"Well, Charlie tells me there is a good sized bluff - it's not actually on our land but it's a close walk and it's on the backside of his fields. The Cherokee Indians used it. He says there's all kinds of arrowheads down there. Anyway it's a good shelter."

"Oh Preston, we can't let you live out under a bluff. Why, you'll get pneumonia before you've passed a single winter there."

He chuckled, "You don't think I'm too strong, do you?"

"Of course I do, why you're as fit and strong and..." She blushed as her voice trailed to silence. "What I mean to say is nobody could live out like that and be healthy."

"Well it appears the Indians did for they've left their sign there. Me and Charlie walked down there after we looked over the land I was buying from him. Anyway, it won't be for long, not even through the winter. I think I can have a spot cleared for the house in a few weeks. It's a good thing I've got logging experience, ain't it?"

Sharing a laugh, Emma's hands resumed their work with the peas and Preston stood, stretching his long legs. "I keep calling this place 'ours' and before I start working on a house I would want you to look at the spot but Emma it occurs to me that I might be takin' some things for granted."

He turned to her but could only see the top of her head as she stared at the basket. She'd been waiting for this question but now that she was sure it was coming it almost frightened her. With a deep breath she looked up at him, waiting for him to finish.

"Em, are you willing... I mean, do you want to, urr are you thinking... no that's not what I'm meaning at all. Do you know what I'm tryin' to say?"

"Yes Preston, I believe I do but I believe I need you to actually say it."

He took a deep breath and sat down again. "Miss Emma, I guess I should have talked with you before I bought ten acres next to your sister and so close to your folks. But I'm sure hopin' you will be my wife and I'm working to make a home for you. Are you willin'?"

The smile crept from lips she'd pursed to hide her enjoyment of his struggle. It grew to encompass her whole face and fill her eyes. She set the basket on the floor and reached both hands to him. "Preston Langford, you'll have to speak to Papa but I would be honored to be called your wife."

Plans for Emma

"Whew. That was harder than hewin' a cross tie from a wild cherry tree."

She continued smiling up at him, hoping he was planning to speak to her father right away. Preston seemed frozen in place until they heard Jane's voice coming toward them.

"Em, how are you a'comin' on the peas? I was thinking we could cook them for dinner."

Preston dropped her hands the instant he heard the voice; Emma suspected her mother was announcing her presence.

"Oh, it doesn't look like you've made much progress. Mr. Langford do you know how to shell peas?"

"Well, uh, yes ma'am, I reckon I could manage it."

Jane was smiling at him. "Why don't you let Emma do it. She's very quick."

"Yes ma'am. Uh, do you know which direction Mr. England went?"

"I believe he's got plowing to do this morning, you can probably still catch him in the barn. You come on back in at noon and enjoy these sweet peas with us. We've got greens too and there's some side meat left so it will be a good dinner."

"Yes Ma'am; thank ya' ma'am." He rushed from the front room of the house almost hitting his head on the low doorway and leaping from the porch to keep from stumbling.

Jane laughed out loud. "I never seen him be so clumsy. What was he running from?"

Emma was already back at work on the peas, "I sure hope he was running to Papa."

Tom was leading out his big mare and heading toward the turning plow positioned at the corner of the barn when Preston rounded the back side of the house. He slowed his pace, not wanting to run up to the man or to spook his horse.

"I'm glad to see you Preston, hold this plow upright so I can get the trace chains on it. Sure is easier to do this with a second set of hands."

"I'm happy to help. Glad I caught you 'cause I'm needing to talk to you."

"Can you talk and walk at the same time? Day's getting away fast and I'll be lucky to get this patch turned before dark."

"Yeah, I can walk with you. Like I was tellin' you last night, I've bought some land from Charlie and I'm gonna' be working on it. I'll have to get some kind of house built and clear a right smart of the land so it will sure keep me busy. But I'm hoping to do all that to make a home for me and Emma. I'm hoping you will agree to her marryin' me."

"Marrying? I only told you it was okay to court her a few days ago."

"I don't mean any disrespect sir, but what would be the point of the courtin' if there wasn't going to be a weddin'?"

Tom stopped and the horse stopped. He chuckled low and long. "I can't argue with you there. But neither can I let her go marryin' somebody that don't even have a roof to put over her head."

"Sir, I will have a roof over her head. I told you what I'm planning to do."

"Well son you just get to doin' and we'll see about the weddin' later on."

Preston's fists involuntarily balled and he forced them open. He had no intention of brawling with this man he wanted for his father-in-law but he was beginning to feel like the man couldn't be pleased. With a quick nod of his head, Preston set off across the open field toward Charlie's house. He'd left his pack there and all he could think of was getting his axe in hand and felling trees.

Chapter 28

Preston walked onto his own land with an awe he had never known. Every tree seemed taller and greener and stronger than any he'd ever seen. He turned his heel in the thick layer of leaves and kicked back a clump of the richest soil he could imagine. *We could grow anything here, and this timber will make the finest house on the mountian,* he thought as he let the pack drop to the ground.

He turned his head from side to side, taking in the lay of the land and orienting himself to the directions. *Where to start?*

Preston soon realized that clearing his own farm was very different than felling and hewing trees in the lumber camp. There was no foreman here to point and direct him, no team of men and animals to limb the trees and load the logs. When he hired on in The Flat Woods, the operation had already been going for many years so he never saw the vast, untouched timber that would have challenged the first group of loggers. *Your thinkin' foolishness Preston, even comparin' this little ten acres to that big tract of timber.*

He smiled, and renewed pride swelled in his chest as he thought again that he was a land owner.

"If you don't get to swingin' that axe, this ain't ever gonna' look like a farm." Now he laughed out loud at himself.

Walking back to the dirt road, he paced out what he thought would be the center of his property line and turned his back to the road. Spotting a small area with no trees he went to its edge and set to work on the first tree, notching it to fall into the clearing.

This solitary work allowed his mind to spin with plans and dreams. Over the past months he'd disciplined himself to spend this time in prayer but today he could think only of Emma and to remember her father's taunting words.

Each swing of the heavy iron axe relieved a bit of the anger. The Holy Spirit seemed to speak to his heart that God was in control. Preston countered, *He doesn't believe I will even build her a house.* In that familiar and gentle way, the spirit reminded that Preston's anger would do nothing to convince Emma's father.

Thud! The iron head rang against the solid wood. *Why couldn't he be happy for us? I know that I don't deserve a girl like Em, but does he not believe I can care for her?* He knew the answer before the axe could again ring against the tree; the same internal voice seemed to say, "Emma believes her father to be a godly man, can you believe God will guide him the same way as he's guiding you and her?"

With a loud crack the tree's weight carried it downward and all of the forest seemed to freeze for a long moment before it crashed to the ground. Preston straightened his back and wiped a line of sweat from his brow. "Lord, I know you can lead this man. But how do I know that he'll be following you?"

Swinging the axe onto his back, he walked up the bare tree trunk toward the broken limbs. This time, the small voice had not needed to prompt him, "Guess my faith has to be in the good Lord and not in Tom England or any man."

By the time the sun stood straight overhead, Preston's thought had turned toward the future, of a life with Emma that he again felt certain was destined to be. He looked around him. Three giant oak trees lay on the ground and he moved now to chop off the limbs of the last one that had fallen. He was trying to figure the diameter when he heard voices approaching and turned to the sound. Emma and Lena walked side by side talking and pointing as they moved.

"Preston, you are making quick work of these trees. At this rate you'll have this farm scalped by the end of the summer."

He laughed at Emma's joke, "Well I don't intend to drop 'em and leave 'em you know. In fact, I'm limbing this one now and will start hewing all three next."

Plans for Emma

"You need some food in you. Mama thought you'd be at our house for dinner. But I brought you what we had left."

Warmed by her kindness he smiled, "Thank you Em." There was so much more to say but never any opportunity to say it. He willed her to read his thoughts as he looked deeply into her eyes.

Lena turned around, cocking her head to see her own house in the distance. "Em we'll be next door neighbors. Won't it be wonderful? We'll be able to share garden vegetables and our children will play together."

"Lena!" Emma scolded her sister widening her eyes.

"Well, children are a reflection of a blessed marriage. There's no shame in talking about them."

"Not before the marriage I think," Emma's glance darted to Preston as her cheeks reddened and she dropped her eyes. With a deep breath she tried to change the subject, "Anyway, we don't even know if Papa has agreed." She spread out a small blanket and sank to her knees to unpack the basket.

Preston picked up the axe, measuring its familiar weight in his hand. He knew Emma was eager to know her father had given his blessing. When he looked up from the axe, both girls were watching him.

Preston cleared his throat and spoke in his most proper voice, "I spoke with Mr. England this morning. He would like to know there's a house for you to live in."

Emma smiled at his antics, appreciating his attempt to find humor in what she knew was a hurtful situation. She nodded and tried to convey her understanding as she looked into his eyes. Searching for a new subject that would ease Preston's discomfort she looked at the big trees laid on the ground. "Will you start building with these?"

"Well, I guess I thought so when I started chopping, but the fact is that it will take a little money to build even the kind of simple house that I can build myself. So now I'm thinking I'll hew out the ties and sell them. At ten cents a tie, I can make close to a dollar from these."

"But where will you sell them?"

"Hmm, well I ain't got that part worked out just yet. Guess I'm still use to the loggin' camp where there's a wagon sitting ready to load 'em and haul 'em."

Emma laughed and tried to hide her eagerness. She resolved that she would not rush Preston as he worked to create a home for her. She searched for lighthearted things to talk about but there was an idea sprouting at the back of her mind and it was hard not to talk about it. It was easy enough to comment on the coolness beneath the trees and the sweet smell emanating from the sappy oaks. As the trio sat and talked, the birds renewed their singing and squirrels chattered overhead.

Emma had been quiet longer than usual when she caught the question in Lena's eyes. "Oh, I let my mind wander off, didn't I?"

Lena nodded at her sister, "No, I don't think you were here with us."

"Preston, I've been thinking how I might be able to help you."

"With what Em?"

"Well you're doing all this work to get us a house built and of course I have my hope chest that I've been working on with quilts and such to make that house into a real home."

"Uh huh," Preston tried to sound like he understood but he had to admit to himself that he really had no idea what went into a girl's hope chest.

"But we need some cash, right?"

"You don't need to worry about that Em. I'll work out what we need."

"Oh Preston, if I'm to be your wife that means God made me a help meet for you. So let me."

He cocked his head not understanding, "Let you?"

"Let me help you."

"Yes ma'am," Preston grinned, enjoying the bit of challenge in her words.

"Mama has taught all of us about the herbs we need for medicine. I know some of those can be sold. Between the big

Plans for Emma

creek down the hill and the marshy area on your land I can find a lot of those plants. So I will start gathering them and that should bring in a few cents for us. What do you think?"

"I think I'm proud of the way you are thinking."

Emma shook her head at him and turned to Lena, "Have you spotted any Lo-Billy since you've been living here? There was always plenty of it in the fence rows in Roslin and it sells real good."

"You know, I haven't even been watching for it. I had not thought of trying to sell any and since neither me nor Charlie have breathing trouble I wouldn't have looked for it to use myself." The Native Americans had taught the earliest Appalachians to dry the Lobelia plant and burn it to open air ways and the Englands had always known the value of the herb.

Emma was nodding as she mentally walked the Martha Washington roads she'd been using for the past few months. "I'll bet Mama's had her eyes open, Little Gip took a cough last summer and she burned some for him. She'll be planning to do the same this year when it gets so hot that he can't breathe."

"Well we can start watching for that."

Emma turned to Preston, "Do you know what Ginseng looks like? I'm sure you've been walkin' right over a patch coming and going from that bluff. It always grows on the hillside – north side right Lena?"

Lena nodded, remembering the lessons Mama had taught them in searching for the elements of the spring tonic. She always wanted Ginseng in it because she said it would give them a boost after the sicknesses of winter while helping them have enough energy to get the hard work of springtime accomplished.

Emma was still talking, explaining to Preston that he must begin looking for these valuable plants, "It's got a pointed leaf and there'll be a little berry on it sometimes like a blackberry before it's ripe. But of course there's no briars on 'seng and the plants aren't out in the sun like blackberry briars."

Preston was nodding and smiling. *This girl will make you rich if you give her half a chance. She can see money in the ground.*

Emma caught the humor in his eyes and stopped her plotting, "Preston, are you laughing at me? We can just take these herbs up to Peters' Store and they'll bring a little money. It might help us get the nails and hardware we need to build the house, or maybe a few cookin' pots. If you can't think of anything to spend it on, I'll buy yard goods and make red checkered curtains."

The quick nod of her head was all he needed to set him laughing aloud. "Emma, I wonder how long you're gonna' amaze me. We can spend the money, no trouble there. Do you think you can sell enough to buy a milk cow?"

Emma laughed with him, appreciating his humor. With the remaining cornbread crumbs, Preston wiped clean the tin plate she'd filled for him. Realizing he was a little out of breath he wondered how quickly he'd eaten. "Guess I was pretty hungry."

He unfolded his long legs and stretched his back. "If I don't get back to it, I'll be asleep after that good meal. And I'm not planning on wasting any time here."

The girls giggled at him and Lena picked up the basket to repack the dishes. Emma stood with eyes reaching up to his face, "Thank you Preston," she whispered.

"Em I'll be thankin' you for the rest of the life I'm planning to share with you."

He settled his hat firmly on his head and turned to his work.

Emma and Lena set off at the fast pace they always used. Emma veered off their usual path and made a circuit around Charlie's big field. She walked with her head down focusing on the many plants growing in the untilled corners. Lena watched her sister as she made her own way home and smiled, thanking God for the teachings of their mother that now seemed so valuable to Emma and Preston.

Plans for Emma

For weeks Emma had been finding time each day to work on filling her hope chest. She'd finished two more quilts and dish towels as well as embroidered several table runners and stitched thick pads for kitchen work. Now she divided that time with searching for marketable herbs. Donning her heavy farm skirt and almost always wearing her boots, she walked miles of creeks stooping every few steps to carefully pull the roots of the yellowroot plant. She combed fencerows for the low-growing Lo-Billy that Mama always kept in her kitchen.

After a day in the hot sun she wrapped them in scraps of muslin and kept them right beside her hope chest in a little wooden box Papa provided from the barn. Each day she'd lift the side of the box weighing it. Somehow it never felt any heavier to her yet she continued to work.

Beth Durham

Chapter 29

Preston settled himself into his bluff-home. He reported he'd made it quite livable and never offered a word of complaint. Despite his singular focus on clearing his little farm and preparing a home for Emma, he found many opportunities to help both Tom and Charlie. Both men were thankful for the extra hands and grew to appreciate Preston's proficiency on the farm. He would follow the plow in the cornfield without protest, effortlessly swung the scythe to cut hay and worked a team of mules as though they were an extension of the man.

Charlie wiped his brow as he looked across a field of thick grass as he and Preston worked to cut it. "Preston, I sure appreciate your help but I worry that I'm takin' too much of your time."

Preston swung the heavy blade and waited to speak until the return stroke, "Nah, I would'a starved this summer had it not been for Lena and Jane. I owe you and Tom more than the few hours I've spent in your fields."

Charlie shook his head as he leaned back into the work, "We couldn't stop the women if we wanted to. They're worried to death about you living under the hill there."

"Nothin' to worry 'bout. I'm as comfortable there as I've been in any home I've ever had."

"You get that house built over yonder and I'm bettin' Emma will make you a home like you can't even imagine."

Preston's blade paused at the thought. "I know that's the truth Charlie. Sometimes it seems like that's awful far down the road but I know it'll come to pass eventually."

He resumed the rhythmic swing of the blade and by day's end Charlie had a good patch of hay on the ground and

Plans for Emma

Preston felt he'd repaid a small amount of kindness to his friend.

He had a growing pile of five inch by seven inch logs which he explained to everyone he could either sell to the railroad when the opportunity presented itself or otherwise he could use it for the house.

With a few more trees down, Emma found a large flat rock and swept it clean of grass and leaves. "Preston, wouldn't it be wonderful if this was right out the back door? You'd never have to worry about mud tracking into the kitchen and it would make a great work space."

He didn't need to hear another word and he walked past her to step off the dimensions for a small house just six feet from that rock. *I'll want her to have a porch one day soon so we won't build over her rock,* he told himself.

Emma came with one of her sisters almost every day and she didn't even try to hide her excitement over the changing landscape. Still, as the summer days lengthened and he kept piling up the timbers, the excitement threatened to turn to exasperation.

She confided in Lena as they walked away one afternoon, "Why doesn't he start putting the house together? Papa won't even hear a word of planning until he sees a house."

"Preston was over at our place two days ago and Charlie was asking the same question. He says he's got to get some cash money. There's no crop, no stock, no way to setup housekeeping. He keeps thinking he'll get a chance to sell some of that pile to the railroad but I don't know how without a wagon to haul them. Charlie talked like he would try to find a way to help him haul them once he's got his corn laid by. And I guess I ought to get my hoe and help with that now. Sure did make a difference at home when there were so many hands reaching for the weeds."

Emma nodded, "Preston took the day out of the woods and helped us get the corn finished. He's sure impressed Papa with how hard he'll work around the farm."

Many family memories were shared from the corn field and both girls enjoyed a good laugh. "You'll have more hands in no time. Mama says it seems like yesterday that she and Papa were marryin' and plannin' for their own children. She's always talking about how time flies but this has been the longest summer of my life."

Lena peered at her sister from the corner of her eye, "Longer than the winter when you didn't know if you'd see him from one week to the next month?"

Emma elbowed her sister and looped her arm. "It didn't seem this hard with you and Charlie."

"Only because it didn't concern you."

True to his word, within a week, Charlie hitched his team and wagon and pulled up to Preston's stack of timbers. He announced they would haul a load to Isoline that day.

"Do you reckon I ought to go tell Emma where we'll be?" he wondered.

"Lena knows and you can bet she'll be spreading the word before dinner."

Both men loved the closeness they saw in the sisters and Preston was proud he could provide Emma a home near her people. He thanked God every day that he'd provided a way without the couple having to go way out west.

The trip to Isoline was a hard drive and it was well dark before they were halfway back to Martha Washington. Finding a spot by a cool spring Preston and Charlie propped themselves against a wagon wheel and pulled out the last of the food Lena had packed that morning. Taking an apple from the cotton sack, Charlie handed it to Preston who fished out a hunk of bread wrapped in a scrap of muslin and tore off a thick piece.

The katydids sang not far from them and a loud bullfrog announced his presence to anyone interested. Preston had already forgotten how hard it was to ride a wagon all day but his pocket bulged with three dollars and he hoped he would still have two and a half after settling Charlie's haul bill. And Charlie had introduced him to a man by the name of Hale

Plans for Emma

who'd worked in the Horsepound timber the past two winters when his farming duties were lighter. He certainly thought he could get Preston work there whenever he needed cash.

At first light they re-hitched the team and started toward home.

"Charlie, I been thinkin'. I'm going to start setting the logs for the house out of that stack I've got hewn. Might be able to sell a few more of them for cross-ties but if I start workin' on the house now I might could have it finished before I try to get work over in the Horsepounds."

Charlie stared past the point formed by the two horses' ears and took his time with answering for there was no rush to finish. "What are you planning to build?"

"Well, I was thinking I'd just build one room eight and a half feet square. I've cut the timbers that long so they would sell for ties and I don't see reason to chop them off, do you?"

"Nah. But that ain't much house for a family."

"I know that, but we can add to it as we need to and it will suit fine for me to winter in. Emma is worried about me spending the winter under that bluff."

"Women worry. It's what they do. Didn't your mother worry?"

"I guess she did, she sure had plenty to worry about."

Chapter 30

When they arrived home, Preston borrowed a hoe and mattock from Charlie and went to work preparing the land where his house would sit. He knew plenty of old cabins had never had anything but dirt floors, still he couldn't bear to bring Emma into that kind of place. He intended to lay a floor from the hewed timbers.

Despite his midday start, by dark he had the square cleared of leaves, twigs and any roots that protruded from the ground. Finding strong saplings, he built a sled small enough he could pull it himself and took it with him back to the bluff that night.

Emma arrived at Lena's house before she could even wash her breakfast dishes and there was worry in her voice. "I didn't hear from Preston last night."

"Rest easy honey. Charlie says he got all fired up about starting building and he lit out as soon as they got the horses stopped."

"Building? Oh I can hardly believe it. Let's go see."

"Now? I don't think it's a fit time to be callin', do you?"

"Oh Lena, I can hardly wait. I've worried all night that something might have happened to them and now to hear such a wonderful report. Oh, did he even manage to sell the cross ties?"

"Yes, yes. There's good market for cross ties. Seems the railroad can never get enough of them."

"Come on then."

Lena smiled as she dried her hands and smoothed her apron. As they stepped off the low back porch she called to Charlie in the barn, "Goin' with Em."

"No use tellin' him where we've gone, he can guess that quick enough," she said half under her breath.

Plans for Emma

Emma smiled at her sister's playful grumbling knowing she would always be at her side. Still she felt like Lena was dawdling this morning. When they arrived, the work Preston had accomplished yesterday was apparent, but he was nowhere to be found. Finally, Emma called for him.

He answered from the west and both ladies spun in surprise. After a few more minutes, Preston came into view leaning against a rope with the little sled gliding along behind him. It was loaded with flat rocks still wet from the creek.

"What are you doing? Where have you been?" Both Emma and Lena pelted him with questions.

"Went down to the creek first thing this morning to get rock for the pilings of the house."

"You pulled that up the hill? Oh my!" Emma exclaimed, trying to check herself for both Lena and her mother had warned her that she was being too protective of her fiancé.

"It'll get too hot to do this too many times today. I can maybe get one more good load, then I'll spend the afternoon trying to chisel 'em down and set them." As he answered their questions, he started piling the heavy stones near the flat rock.

"Well, it looks like there'll be a house here before long."

"I'm afraid it will take me a while since I've never done this kind of work before."

Emma stepped closer to him, lowering her voice. "Thank you Preston."

He smiled at her and the look in her eye gave him all the encouragement he needed. His eyes were still on her as he stepped around the little sled and caught his foot in the protruding runner. Trying to regain his balance, he stepped onto the pile of rocks he'd just unloaded and they gave way, some catching his ankle and others pounding against it. In a split second, the lanky man lay prone on the ground, his leg turned at a painful and unnatural angle.

Lena and Emma both rushed to his side. Lena reached to free his foot as Emma helped him pull his body into a straighter alignment with his trapped limb.

Preston bit hard into his lip, trying to mask the pain he felt. He almost flinched at Emma's touch and bared his shame in a pleading look. Big drops of sweat beaded on his brow and Emma reached into her apron pocket for a handkerchief.

Emma's soft hand was on his brow and her lips moved as though she was speaking. However, his mind blurred and he wasn't sure if she was talking to him. Soon he realized she was only saying comforting words, as she might have done with a child or an animal. It worked and he was able to give her a weak smile.

He took a deep breath and tried to swallow. His foot was free of the rock trap and with a gentle hand Lena laid it onto the ground. "I think we need to get that up higher. Let me see if I can find a short piece of log."

"Preston, can you sit up here? Let me get over to the water bucket and wet this cloth."

After a while he regained his voice and wondered how much time had passed while he was trapped. "Oh Em, I can sit. It's just a turn, I don't know what you and Lena are carryin' on about."

Emma's lips curved upward as she let out a long breath, "I thought you were going to black out on us."

He shook his head, still not sure how clear his head was. "Truth is, I thought I might too. But I can't sit here lettin' you girls nurse me. There's too much work to be done"

Lena returned with a piece of wood from his scrap pile, "No more work for you today I think. Let's get you as comfortable as possible and then we'll go get Papa and the mare. You're not going to be able to walk."

"Nonsense." He reached for a sturdy stick he'd used to lever logs into position for hewing and moved his good leg to stand.

Emma put a gentle hand on his shoulder, "Preston, you'll do yourself more harm. Please be still till we can get back. Mama won't hear of you going anywhere but to our house."

Plans for Emma

She left her hand in place, quelling any protest he could offer. They made him as comfortable as possible and hurried to get the help they'd need to move him.

His ankle doubled in size before Tom could get him back to the farm on the back of the farm sled. Jane took one look at it and shook her head.

"You're going to be down for a while with that son." Without another word she disappeared into the kitchen and soon returned with a basin of amber liquid and strips of brown paper. As she got closer to him his nose realized she had vinegar in the pan.

"It don't smell too good but we'll wrap it up and it will draw out the swelling. Best cure I know for a sprain. We'll have to pray the bone is in place in there or you'll be lame the rest of your life. That's all that's left to do."

Preston closed his eyes and bowed his head. "*Lord, don't let that be.*"

Jane realized she'd discouraged him and tried to change her tone. "Oh, Preston I'm just talkin' nonsense. I'm sure there ain't nothin' broke. Why, a strong young man like you has got bones of iron. The vinegar will fix you up. Vinegar and time. Now you're gonna' have to take it easy for a few weeks or it won't ever heal right and that's the truth."

"Weeks! I don't have weeks to sit on the porch." He dropped his head as tears swelled behind his eyes.

"What you have is no choice son. The good Lord has slowed you down a might for sure but he ain't completely stopped you." Jane's hands worked with obvious experience soaking the paper and wrapping it around his ankle.

As he watched Emma's mother working, Preston's heart cried out to God. *Why Lord? I was gettin' so close. Emma's worried sick about me wintering under that bluff and I've even managed to sell a few ties and have a little money in my pocket. Please don't let this thing be broken so's I'll have to spend these few dollars on a doctor's bill.*

Jane and Emma left him on the porch, insisting he should try to close his eyes but his mind refused to rest.

Emma followed her mother into the kitchen and looked around for something to busy her hands. She ended up just wringing them.

Jane watched her from the corner of her eyes as she peeled potatoes that would stew for the noonday meal, "Em why are you a'standin' there working your hands like kneading air? Your man out there is gonna' be as fine as ever in no time."

Somehow Emma couldn't still her hands. "I'm sorry Mama, I know how you hate to see us standin' around fretting. My mind seems to be darting from one corner to the other and I can't seem to light on anything to do."

Jane smiled and continued her work. "You can sit with him for a spell. We've got a house guest for a while so we'll have to make him comfortable in both body and spirit. I know his foot's painin' him right now but I'm thinking it's his spirit that needs more attention. He looks plumb broken."

Emma nodded, "Oh Mama, how can I comfort him when my heart is broken too? I've been longing and praying for a life with this man and right when things seemed to be working out for us, this goes and happens. Don't it just seem like every time we get a ray of sunshine a clap of thunder hits?"

Jane opened her mouth to answer but her chuckles escaped. Taking a quick breath she managed, "Honey, it's not all as bleak as that. This is a little setback. Thirty years down the road when you are sittin' round the table watching your grandkids play you won't even remember it."

Emma dabbed at her eyes, "I hope you're right Mama."

After a moment she had to smile, "You are often right you know. So you think it's alright for me to sit on the front porch with him alone? Or do you want me to get Metie?"

"No no. I can't have both my girls wastin' away the hours moonin' over that lop-legged boy. Let Metie go, she needs to churn and you know how slow she is at that. Anyhow, he's going to be with us for a while, it's okay for you to interact with him the way you do the rest of the family."

Plans for Emma

"I hope Papa agrees with you, otherwise the next few days and weeks may be pretty tough."

When Emma stepped out the door again, Preston had favors to ask of her. "Emma, I'll have to make me a crutch. Can you please go back over to our place and get my axe? I've got a big knife but I've left it down under the bluff so maybe I can rough out what I need with the axe. Then, if you'll see if you can find a thick branch that's about as long as I am tall and bring that to me maybe I can get back on my feet."

Emma smiled as she pulled the straight back chair near his. "Preston, later I will go get your axe because I know you don't want it left out in the weather. But you don't need to be tryin' to get back on your feet right now. Mama says if you don't take it easy then you'll be troubled with this injury the rest of your life. Now you know you don't want to carry that with you, do you?"

"No, of course not. But how can I sit here when I'm so close to getting a house started?"

She took a deep breath and prayed that she'd sound more sure than she felt, "You can because you must. We'll get that house built. It's just that the good Lord has other plans right now."

"How can this be in anybody's plans? I can't believe I've been so foolish and careless."

"It wasn't foolish, it was an accident. They happen." She stood up feeling like she could no longer hold back her tears, "I'll bring you some more cool water."

Rushing back into the kitchen Emma steadied herself on the doorframe and Jane looked up from her work with a wordless question.

"I was convinced when I walked in there but it's not going to be easy staying convinced that this is God's plan."

Jane chuckled as she returned to her potatoes and Emma filled the pewter cup from the water bucket. As the sun began its western descent, Tom returned from his field work and helped Preston move into the front room of the house. There he found a bed had been setup for him. When he was settled in it, Emma came with a plate of food and a welcoming smile.

"How can you wait on me and smile like that?"

"Because I... because... oh Preston, there isn't any because. It's just what I'm gonna' do." A pale pink crept into her cheeks as she settled the food on the side of his bed and hurried from the room.

Preston had to admit that he enjoyed the time and attention he received from Emma over the following days. Yet he became ever more anxious to return to his work in the woods. When everyone returned from Sunday's preaching service along with Charlie and Lena, Preston renewed his request for tools and wood to make a crutch.

"Charlie I can't lie in this bed any longer. If you'll get me a strong branch that I can whittle into a crutch, I can get back to work. I been asking Em but she won't do it."

"Well Preston, Emma is doing the best she can for you. I'd try to argue with you myself but I'm seeing that it's no use. If we don't get you a crutch, you're gonna' hobble out of here on your own, ain't ya'?"

Preston was nodding as Charlie answered him. "Thank you Charlie, I knew you'd understand."

"Well I heard Miz' Jane telling Em to be looking for wild strawberries. She'll feed them to you and that'll give more strength to your blood. My grandma always swore by wild strawberries."

Preston shook his head with a grin, "She's gonna' sell all them herbs she's collecting so we can't be wasting them on me. I think she's plannin' to buy all our stock with money from herbs."

"What will she sell them for if you're crippled up and can't farm or keep stock? Take the medicine they give you. These Englands have been on the mountain for a long time and they know what to do with all these green things you're always a'walkin' on." With a chuckle Charlie stepped out onto the front porch.

Plans for Emma

By noon Monday Preston was testing his rough prop on the England's front porch. When he heard Tom stepping through the back door for supper he shambled into the kitchen before Emma served him in the front room.

"Well looky there," Tom exclaimed. Jane, Emma and Metie turned together following his gaze.

Emma rushed to his side and helped him ease into the nearest chair, "Preston, you shouldn't be up."

Tom scowled at her, "Leave the man alone Em. He knows what he can and can't do. How's the leg feelin' Preston?"

"It's still tight but it's better. No doubt Miz Jane's vinegar is doin' the trick."

Jane smiled as she carried the remaining food to the table. "You still need to rest."

"I thank you ma'am, but I've got to get back to the woods tomorrow."

"What?" Emma's face blanched. "You can't stand and swing an axe."

"No, I guess you're right. But I can sit and chisel on that load of rock. I figure I can work on the pilings for the house. By the time my foot's all healed, I should have a solid foundation."

Emma breathed a sigh of relief.

Tom seemed to ignore her as he called his family to pray over their food. With an echoing 'amen' Tom reached for the pone of cornbread. "Sounds like a good plan Preston. Workin' on the rock is a good way to keep at it. I'll help you get over there in the morning and then I'll bring you another load up from the creek."

Preston swallowed hard, "Thank you Sir. I wouldn't ask you to do that."

"Glad to son, I'm glad to do it."

Preston's eyes shot toward Emma and caught the smile she tried to hide by lowering her head to study her empty plate.

For a week Tom delivered him each day to the little clearing in the woods. Emma and Metie came at noon with a basket of food and fresh water then Tom returned near sunset with the horse and sled to carry him back to the England's home. Saturday morning Preston announced he would no longer be needing their help.

"I think I can get over to my place on my own today. You have all been far too kind to me."

Jane waved away his thanks, "There's no such thing as bein' too kind to family Preston. Are you sure you can manage?"

"Yes ma'am, I'm sure. I'll put in a good day's work today and plan to see you all at preaching tomorrow morning."

When the meal was finished he took the crutch under his arm and with one slow step after another slow step he made his way over the hill. Just after noon Emma showed up as usual with the leftovers from Jane's lunch table. "You didn't think we'd let you starve today, did you?"

He looked up with a smiles, not even trying to stand when she approached. "Ya'll have fed me so much over the past two weeks I'm not in much danger of starvin' for a long time."

"Well I've brought you extra bread and a few boiled eggs for your supper since you didn't talk like you'd be back tonight."

Preston was sore when he woke Sunday morning. Walking on the crutch was painful and the downhill walk to his bluff-home had been slow and grueling. As the last rays of sun filtered down the deep hollow he dreaded the walk out in the morning.

He didn't bother building a fire that night for the August heat drove away any hint of dampness even beneath the overhanging rock. He was thankful for the constant drip of water on the western edge as it sang him to sleep; that drip had provided some of the best drinking water he'd ever tasted this summer.

In the morning, he piled a few dry twigs and built just enough fire to boil the single cup of coffee he allowed himself each day. He'd saved a couple of eggs from Emma's

Plans for Emma

basket yesterday and he began peeling them. Along with the bread he would have a fine breakfast before facing the walk to church.

The following week Preston traded the crutch for a long staff and managed without it while moving round his woodland clearing. The following Sunday morning he left the staff at the top of the hill above the bluff. He had not resumed the long confident stride he had always taken for granted but now he was determined to strengthen the joint and walk unaided into the Martha Washington church.

Chapter 31

The heat of the dog days had settled over the congregation and everyone seemed a little quieter than usual.

They noticed that Preston arrived at church on his own and they flocked around him to ask about his leg and comment on how well he'd healed. They asked who'd been doctoring him and he was happy to give Mrs. England the credit. He wasn't sure if the vinegar treatment was common knowledge so he stopped short of revealing her secret.

Preston noticed that Charlie was not among the well wishers. In fact, he had very little to say and Preston was concerned he may have offended his friend. In fact, it seemed Charlie was talking to every man in the church yard except for Preston. Preston grew uneasy with the feeling he was the subject of talk among the group. However, Tom England seemed jovial. He slapped Preston on the back asked, "You sleepin' good on that bed of rocks under the bluff?"

Preston managed a slight grin and answered without taking his eyes off Charlie's movements among the congregation. "Sleepin' good sir. With hard work and a clear conscience a fella' can sleep most anywhere, can't he?"

Tom nodded vigorously as Jane stepped close enough to speak.

"Preston, you'll be joining us for supper, won't you? We missed you at supper last night but Emma said she'd taken you some bread and eggs. I hope that was enough."

He turned to her genuine kindness and reflected it in his smile. "Oh yes ma'am. It was plenty. In fact, I had an egg saved for my breakfast this morning. Thank you very kindly for the lunch offer. Of course I'll appreciate your fine meal."

Tom started toward the wagon, "We'd best be loadin' up now. You'll ride instead of walkin' won't you boy?"

"Thank ya' Sir, my leg would sure appreciate the rest."

The family left amid chatter and laughter but Preston couldn't help a last look back to Charlie who was still talking with a few men in the yard. He was careful not to voice his concern and focussed instead on enjoying the special treat of Sunday dinner.

Emma seemed to notice something changing. "Preston, you look like you're relaxing a little and I'm sure glad to see it."

He held tightly to the wagon's sideboard as he tried not to use his leg for bracing against the constant bumps. "Do you know how much I enjoy these Sunday dinners? I can have a great meal and your company without feeling like I need to rush back to the woods."

"We're sure glad to have you." She ducked her head, always a little shy with him.

"I know you've worried about me staying under the bluff but the only thing I regret is the food. I'm a pitiful cook you know."

She looked directly into his face as she gently chastised, "Well I don't think you keep enough provisions down there for the best of cooks to make a decent meal."

He grinned and dismissed her concerns with a slight shrug.

Charlie and Lena did not join them today, even after the meal. It was the first Sunday Preston could remember when they had not shown up for some kind of a visit and Preston was getting worried about their friendship.

As the sun arched toward the western horizon, Preston voiced his concerns to the Englands. "I'm going to head out, I believe I need to go by Charlie's house before I turn in. He didn't say a word to me at church. In fact, I've not talked to him since I was laid up here. I'm wonderin' if I've said something to anger him."

Tom looked at Jane and she gave him a nod of her head as though urging him to act. "Now, I wouldn't be worryin' about Charlie Adams. I've never known him to wear his feelings on his sleeve. Could be they went to a neighbor's house today. You'll see him tomorrow or the next day I'm sure."

Preston stepped to the end of the porch with his arms stretched to the rafters for support. He studied the shoulder-high corn crop that Tom had worked all summer. "Well, I don't want any time passin' if I've said something wrong."

Jane stepped in now, "Emma, I'll bet one of the watermelons is ripe. Do you reckon it's daylight enough to find one? Sure seems like that would taste good about now, don't you think so?"

Emma and Preston walked toward the garden enclosure but he was very quiet, still wrapped in his own thoughts.

They all enjoyed the sweet summer fruit and kept Preston talking until he barely had enough light to descend the hill to the bluff with some degree of safety. There was no time left to stop at the Adams home.

At first light he was at the house site, hewing out the longer cross members that would span across the pilings. The loud, rhythmic report of iron on wood masked all other forest sounds and he did not hear the three wagons that arrived together before he'd half finished the first beam. He saw movement and let the axe fall into the tree and wedge there. Looking up, Charlie greeted him.

"How many of these beams have you got to hew today?"

Preston reached a hand toward him, "I'm glad to see you my friend..." before he could say more, he realized he was not alone with Charlie but was surrounded by faces he knew only from preaching services at the Martha Washington Church. A moment of near-panic flashed across his mind.

"What's this?"

"A house-raisin'," Charlie announced and a cheer rose among the men.

Preston let out his breath and stood amazed by the number of hands who'd come. "Is this what you were planning yesterday?"

Plans for Emma

Charlie grinned and bobbed his head, proud of his accomplishment. "A'course. What did you think?"

"I don't know. Church discipline or something."

Charlie rarely missed an opportunity to jest, "What have you done that needs discipline?"

Preston gave him a good-natured push. "Go on now, you had me worried is all."

"Well stop a'worryin' and get to workin'. That beam ain't gonna finish itself. Do you want to tell these men what needs doing?"

Each man had tools and experience so with little direction everyone was at work. By the time the sun stood at its zenith the floor was in place and the timbers were notched for walls. Another wagon arrived with half a dozen women and baskets in every arm. Food was spread across the wagon's bed and the men turned to their dinner with the same gusto they'd shown the timbers.

When the shadows reported the day's end was near, a small cabin stood among the stumps Preston's axe had left behind. Only part of the roof was shingled but Charlie, Tom and a couple of other neighbors promised to return tomorrow and complete that part of the project.

There had been little chance for Preston to speak to Emma all day. Now he saw her looking up at the new structure from the flat rock which she had declared was her favorite part of the whole property. He stepped to her side.

"Did you know they were planning this?"

She shook her head, still looking at the new house and seeming to find no words.

"I thought I'd lost my friend Charlie, he wouldn't even speak to me at church yesterday."

"Yeah, I thought it odd that they didn't come by for a visit. They always stop in on Sundays, you know. But to tell you the truth, I was too busy with you to realize it until I was in the bed last night."

He smiled down at her, amazed that he could fill her thoughts. "Well, what do you think about the little house

Em? Can you rest easier with me sleeping in this little house through the cold winter instead of under that bluff?"

She smiled and wrapped her arms around her waist in an attempt not to reach out to the man. She turned to look up at him and saw something in his deep brown eyes that she knew was love. Somehow in that moment she knew that God had given Preston Langford to her and that this little house would be home to a happy family for many years to come. It seemed that every plan had fallen into place and she could not remember a single disappointment. He was talking about the short term but she couldn't pull her mind away from the very long term. She heard children's laughter and saw clotheslines filled with diapers. She smelled fresh bread and imagined wild strawberry preserves. She'd spent years dreaming and spinning stories in her head of the life she would lead. It brought a small smile to her face now to realize that in the past months she'd stopped dreaming. Now, she could see her whole life in this place and it was a wonderful sight. Preston cocked his head and she knew he was waiting for an answer, knew that he was desperately trying to read her thoughts.

Before Emma could find any words, Tom England interrupted their revelry when he stepped between them with a hand on each back, "I guess we're gonna' have ourselves a wedding."

Epilogue

1935

"Charlie, it ain't right for a poor man to eat as much as I've had today." Preston Langford stretched his long torso and rubbed his stomach. Years ago, Preston had built a big wooden table for Emma to use on her flat rock and it had often served this growing family. He kept it in good repair and today it was filled with fried fish, boiled potatoes, sweet corn, fried apples and the last of the cantaloupe and watermelons.

Charlie chuckled and grasped his friend's shoulder, "Who's poor here Preston? Look around at all these young'uns and our wives cackling like two old hens as happy as can be. I can't see that we're wantin' for much."

Preston did look toward Emma and Lena sitting in straight back chairs in the shade of the house. He smiled as he admired his beautiful wife. With a final pat on Charlie's back he moved toward Emma just as Lena stepped away.

"It's a fine day, don't you think so Em?"

"Hmm, I'm tired after putting everything together, but you know I am always happiest when we're surrounded by our family. It's good to see Papa still able to be out with us."

Preston snorted as he looked at his father-in-law, "Able? He can work most of our boys into the ground. Can't nothin' get that old man down."

Emma smiled, watching Tom talking with her oldest son. "He has doted on Herman from the first time he saw him and now Herman's got his own daughter and Papa adores both of them."

Preston nodded as he leaned his chair back on two legs, "He's been good to all of our kids, and to us."

Beth Durham

His eye traveled over the little farm, remembering the years and sweat he'd poured into creating a home. "Do you ever think we could'a had a bigger place if we'd gone out west?"

She turned her head and locked her eyes with his, "No."

He couldn't quell the smile she always put on his face. "Well, you might have had a nicer house. Something really planned instead of a room added here or there whenever we needed one."

"Wouldn't be a bit happier in any other house."

Preston was half teasing her even as he reflected on the possibilities, "We could have had more land. Sure, we doubled the size of our farm a few years ago, but out west I think they measure by hundreds of acres instead of our twenty."

Emma was no longer looking at him. She'd turned her eyes to watch the children playing as she swung her crossed leg. "There's a dust bowl out west. Ain't you read them newspapers you bring home all the time? Could be that day you turned back from heading out west God was saving us from a whole lot of trouble."

"Could be. What them papers are telling me is that there's no shortage of trouble. We thought we'd never see another war like the Great War but there's a man in Germany right now that's itchin' for a fight. I don't much see how we can stay out of it."

"You don't think Mister Roosevelt would get us involved in other people's troubles, do you?"

Well, I don't know but I guess we've got troubles of our own here with this drought. Your Papa was just questioning the boys whether they'll have enough corn to see the cattle through the winter. Crops were mighty short this year."

She nodded and her hand automatically reached for the handkerchief she always kept in her apron pocket, "It's been a hard year, that's true."

"Ah Em, I know it's about killed you losing our Beulah this summer."

Plans for Emma

Unable to speak Em nodded.

Sixteen year-old Beulah had been a shining gem in the neighborhood. She was bright and caught on to sums and figures quicker than anybody else in the little Martha Washington school. So when she was asked to work for a few months at a roadside inn in Jamestown helping with housekeeping as well as bookwork, everyone thought it was a blessing straight from heaven. When word arrived she'd been hit by a car, it was a blow to every one of them. Em continued loving and caring for everyone around her as though nothing had changed but Preston often looked into reddened eyes and found her more often than ever sitting out on her flat rock finding comfort in the scriptures.

He wrapped her hand in his oversized calloused fingers. "God knew about that too. Knew when she found work in Jamestown and thought she'd be helpin' us out by earning a few dollars that she'd be hit by that car. Nothin' good will ever come of havin' all these automobiles zippin' from one place to another. I heard tell that some of them can run over sixty miles an hour. No good, you mark my words."

"Oh Preston, you're right that God knew. And he's been faithful to bring us through this. It wasn't that car that decided it was time for our angel to go home. It's a hard thing for a mother to bury her child once she's got her the same as raised."

They sat enjoying the melody of children's voices. Em watched ten-year-old Merita playing with Cletus and the baby of the bunch, four year-old Jannavee. Her pain melted in the love she felt for her family and the gratitude to her Lord.

"Yes Preston, it's been a hard year both for the Langfords and the crops. But we've put away a right smart of vegetables and there's a hog down there in the holler that's fattening up nicely. We won't starve this year." She smiled at him as she added, "And the way you've eaten today, it won't hurt you to eat a little less."

Patting his stomach, Preston nodded his agreement as he breathed a silent prayer of thanksgiving for this woman who could endure such hardship and still put a smile on her face.

"Preston, all those years ago everybody had a plan for you and me. God had a plan and I've learned again and again that his plan is the very best one. The trick for me is to remember to wait on him. The Lord has proven to me that if I'll just obey and trust him then he'll see me and my family through every trial. How dare I look at someone else's blessings and think God's plan in my life was somehow insufficient.

You take a look around and tell me, can you even count all of our blessings?"

**

"For I know the thoughts that I think toward you, saith the LORD, thoughts of peace, and not of evil, to give you an expected end." Jeremiah 29:11

The End

A Note from the Author

Preston Langford's childhood was not easy. But he learned early on that God loved him and would see him through any troubles. Years after accepting Jesus Christ as his savior, he allowed other things to take priority in his life. God used Emma's faith to draw Preston back to Himself.

If you asked Jesus to save you in the past but have drifted far away from him, I'd like to remind you of the parable Jesus taught in Luke 15. In that story, a son left his father and after a while he realized his mistake. All he had to do was turn and start back toward his father – the father ran to meet him. God is waiting to do just that if you have wandered away from him and I urge you to turn back to him right now.

Although she struggled, Emma's relationship with the Lord guided her through many confusing and difficult days. We all face those dilemmas and tough choices but if you do not have a personal relationship with Jesus Christ, you must face them alone. Jesus is eager to walk with you and to guide you; you need only accept him as your savior. It's as simple as ABC:

Accept that you are a sinner; repent and turn away from your sin. (Romans 3:23)

Believe that Jesus Christ is the Son of God and that He died to pay for your sins. (Romans 5:8)

Commit your life to God and ask Jesus to be your Lord and Savior. (Romans 10:9,10)

Neither I nor this book is affiliated with this site, but www. needhim.org is an excellent place to learn more about experiencing the peace of God through Jesus Christ our Lord.